WITHOUT APOLOGY

WITHOUT APOLOGY

Book Three in the Jane Smith Trilogy

CHARLOTTE TAFT

Cover Art & Design by ABCD Book Cover Art, Design & Marketing Support

EMPRESS
PUBLICATIONS

WWW.EMPRESSPUBLICATIONS.COM

"Women have always been the gatekeepers of life. It is not just our right, it is our *responsibility* to decide when to bring new life into the world through our bodies."

Said by an unknown woman at my
Beyond Roe V. Wade workshop held at
the Michigan Women's Music Festival, August 1989

This book—this trilogy—is dedicated to all who stand for kindness, decency, justice, opportunity, care for the planet, and a recognition of the power and value of the feminine. To those who, without permission, without authority, and without apology, seek to bring our world into balance.

CONTENTS

Although there are more than 50 indigenous peoples in Peru, none is called the T'ana, and the medicines attributed to the T'ana in this work are fictional.

PROLOGUE

Present day

I have never known anyone like Jane Smith.

Though her name is simple, her life was anything but. Jane was born in 1914. In 1939, at the age of 25, she sailed from Connecticut to Paris to be a teacher at her aunt's boarding school. She fell in love with her seven-year-old charges, especially my grandmother, Lucie, and Lucie's classmates and best friends, Socorro from Peru, and Paulette from Italy. When the Nazis occupied Paris, Jane smuggled Lucie to New York.

My grandmother and my mother didn't get along. Grand-mére Lucie lived in France, and I didn't meet her until I was twelve. After my grandmother died, I went to New Mexico to meet the fabled Jane Smith to learn about her life and get a better sense of my grandmother. When I understood the significance of Jane's work, I was determined that people needed to hear her amazing stories, especially now that access to abortion has been so restricted in the United States.

Jane was 102 years old when we gathered her letters, journals, and clippings and sat together with a tape recorder for hours at a time. I took on the job of writing a trilogy about her life's adventures. In the first book, *Without Permission*, I recount Jane's time risking her own life in Occupied Paris, helping to smuggle little girls out of France, and being initiated into the complex world of abortion. I share her experiences as a Navy nurse, learning more about providing abortion care in spite of men's laws, being jilted by an admiral's daughter, and nearly losing her beloved Lucie to an illegal abortion. The second book, *Without Authority*, follows Jane as she establishes an unlikely abortion practice in a convent outside of Paris. Jane struggles to find love and to establish an authentic life, finally daring to tell the truth to the person whose judgment she most fears. In *Without Apology*, I chronicle the last decades of Jane's life and her mission to transform abortion care and all health care to attend to the spiritual and emotional lives of patients.

Jane believed in women. She believed in our strength. She believed that if women experienced and acted on their fury, took charge, and stopped apologizing, it would be a better world.

Jane is gone now. I miss her indomitable self every day. I am privileged to bring the stories of this extraordinary woman and her extraordinary life to you.

Abbie Wilder

CHAPTER 1

A MYSTERIOUS LETTER

Our Lady of Perpetual Grace Convent
Countryside outside Paris, Winter 1959

The heavy oak door creaked open, and Sophie's footsteps echoed across the stone floor. She set a bag of groceries on the kitchen table, her breath still frosted from the cold, then peeled off her coat and mittens. I was at the sink, rinsing dishes, while Françoise carefully punched holes in the "recipe cards" we had collected from women. Each one was, in truth, a patient's record, disguised and alphabetized by first names in thick loose-leaf notebooks. We kept them on the kitchen shelves beside the cookbooks—trusting the gendarmes would never think to look for secrets between recipes for stews and cakes.

Sophie kissed my cheek, then slipped her hand into her pocket. "We have a letter from Peru. From Socorro."

I pulled a dish out of the water and dried it with a striped cloth. "How wonderful."

"Read it to us," Françoise said, without looking up, her brow furrowed as she tried to align the fragile papers.

Sophie unpacked the groceries—a baguette, a bottle of olive oil, rice, potatoes, eggs—small comforts against the winter chill. Only then did she sit down, draw a knife across the envelope, and unfold the letter.

Dear Mam'selle—Sophie, and Françoise,

> *I hope you are all well. I miss you and think about you every day as I go to my classes that, I'm afraid, have little to do with healing. I promised you I would finish my medical studies before starting the work you taught me at Our Lady, but sometimes it is hard. There are only two other women in my class. The men boast they will become rich and get pretty wives because they are becoming doctors. I have to remember I will soon be changing the world when I work with women as you do.*
>
> *There are so many things I want to talk with you about, but I can't*

*do it over the phone. Something is happening here that I cannot explain.
Peru is a country with many ancient peoples. The magic and the power
of the Grandmothers is strong. I feel it all around me. It reminds me of
my mother who was a princess of the T'ana people. I feel her energy
although she died when I was very young. When I was a child, she took
me to gatherings of the healing women. My memories are faint, but
now...now it feels as though those women are trying to reach me. I feel
watched. Followed. I don't know what they want from me, only that it
seems to be bound—somehow—to our work. My father always laughed
and called Mamma a curandera. At the time I didn't understand. Now
I feel like everything is going to be turned upside down by the time I see
you next.*

*There is no one else I can tell. If anything happens to me, at least
you will know.*

Love, Socorro

Françoise's hand stilled. "Is she warning us? Or asking for help?"

"I don't know." My apron suddenly felt heavy, and I untied it and took it
off. "It takes a lot to frighten Socorro." I pulled out a chair beside Sophie.

She touched my arm, frowning. "Her mother—a princess? I don't recall
her ever telling me that. Did you know, Jane?"

"I know her father was British—a diplomat. His family opposed his marriage to a Peruvian woman. But a princess? That part I never heard." I paused.
"And what's a *curandera*?"

Sophie understood a lot of Spanish. "It means healer. Among the tribes, it
would likely be a woman with a garden like ours, with knowledge of herbs
and plants we've never even heard of, passed down through the centuries."

"Should I go to Peru?" As the question left my mouth, I heard my fear.

Françoise looked up. "I don't think she's asking you to rescue her. Only
that we remain her witnesses—that she knows she is not alone. And she better
not think she is going to turn *this* world upside down, after all the work we've
done. Still…" She slid the finished notebook onto the shelf, its spine neatly
labeled, its secrets hidden in plain sight. "What disturbs me is her last line. 'If
anything happens to me.' That is not something Socorro would write lightly."

The wind rattled the convent windows. None of us spoke for a long while.

As we returned to our tasks, each of us carried the same unspoken thought:
somewhere across an ocean, in the high Andes, a mysterious energy had begun to stir around Socorro. Could it be that, somehow, it had already reached
us?

CHAPTER 2

YOUR LOVING MOTHER

The next day brought another letter—and a new worry. Françoise had gone to the village stationer's to buy more of the colored paper we used for recipe cards, and she stopped at the post office on the way. Once in the kitchen, shaking the cold from her boots, she handed me an envelope with the distinctive red-and-white stripes of Air Mail. I knew at once it was the weekly letter from my mother. Though we had parted on good terms when she flew home, I felt a wave of apprehension. I asked Sophie to read it aloud.

"Of course." She tucked her long blond hair behind her ear, slit open the thin envelope, and settled across from Françoise at the table.

Jane darling,

I already miss you and Sophie. She is a dear, and I can see how much you love each other. I can hardly believe it's been seven years since you wrote that you'd fallen in love with her. That wasn't easy for me to hear, but I was glad you'd found happiness. Now Sophie feels like another daughter.

All those years ago, I had hoped there would be no more secrets between us. Yet, for so long, I kept mine and you kept yours. Thank goodness we finally shared them when I visited. I never understood why you didn't want me to come to the convent, and now I know it was because you thought you had to keep your work providing abortions a secret from me. Thanks to my dreadful mother, we both learned to hide the most important parts of ourselves. Sharing my teenage experience of having an abortion lifted a shame I thought I'd carry to my grave.

I love the name you chose—Our Lady of Perpetual Grace. Using the convent as your clinic, caring for the daughters and wives of the local police—it's brilliant, if risky. You are so brave. Please be careful.

Isn't it strange that everything came to light because of that poor woman who was uncertain about her abortion—and Brigitte pounding on the door?

When you were twelve, you told a friend you wanted to be "as good as your mother, and as consequential as your father." Your papa and I laughed, but we also felt the weight of your admiration. My darling, you are as good as I shall ever be, and as consequential as your father. I am proud of your work, and even more of the tenderness with which you listen to women. I could never have spoken so honestly to a doctor. How do you make them trust you?

I hope you and Sophie will visit Connecticut. I confess I am lonely without your father. At seventy, I feel like a new person beginning a new life. Thank you for giving me courage.

Your loving mother

P.S. I worry about Lucie. She never calls, and when I visit, Oliver and his mother make me feel unwelcome. Lucie insists she's better since getting care in California, but she's thin as a rail.

By the time Sophie finished, all three of us were quiet, remembering the turmoil of that visit. The grandfather clock chimed two o'clock, ending our reverie.

Françoise sighed. "That was quite a letter."

"I never imagined receiving anything like that from my mother."

"Sharing your secrets took courage on both sides." Sophie dabbed her eyes.

"In forty-four years, I've never lived without shame and secrets," I admitted. "This is all so new."

Sophie managed a small smile. "It's ironic that your old nemesis, Brigitte, helped bring you and your mother closer."

"About Brigitte—" Françoise interjected. "I forgot to tell you. She called while you were out. Lydia's doing well."

"That's good. It must've been hard for her to bring her niece to us, since she is the head of an anti-abortion group." I remembered Brigitte boasting she had founded *The Voice for Those Who Have No Voice*.

Françoise said, "People opposed to abortion usually apply their rules only to others. Remember how she insisted her niece was 'different,' not like the other women we help?"

"I'd forgotten that. I was just relieved she didn't arrest you, Jane." Sophie said.

"Believe me, so was I. With her pounding on the door, it seemed inevitable."

"Do you think she actually changed her mind about abortion?" Sophie asked.

"I don't know. Perhaps her passionate opposition to abortion was more obedience to church teaching than conviction." I'd worked with many women who were obedient to the church.

"That teaching is powerful," Françoise murmured. "I still hear it in my head sometimes. But, you know, there are also some beautiful parts of the church. I have always loved the idea that there are angels watching over us."

Sophie nodded. "I know, Françoise. I don't regret being brought up Catholic. Although I can never accept the things they say about women and sin, I have always loved the story of Jesus washing his disciples' feet at the last supper. It was such an act of love and humility."

I weighed in. "I just wish the women who come to us in such desperation could find a way to appreciate the teachings that give them solace, like those, without being harmed by believing they are sinful and unworthy. Even though it was against abortion, Brigitte's organization was trying to show women they matter." I shook my head. "Now I am giving Brigitte credit, of all things. I can't even believe she is back in my life."

Sophie tilted her head. "After all those nightmares—and after what you told me—that she threatened to turn you in to the Nazis during the war—I expected a monster. But she was so kind to Lydia."

"Brigitte knows how to behave when she wants something. I don't trust her, but I couldn't refuse her niece. Not with my mother here." I sighed. "And now Mother's letter has me worried about Lucie. I thought her time at River Oaks would help, but it seems her struggles after Tildy's birth are continuing. Depression after childbirth is more common than most people realize. It is just well hidden."

"Does she feel close to her adoptive parents?" Françoise asked.

"She loves Sadie and Hymie, but she always missed her real mother. She was only five when her father enrolled her at Aunt Mathilde's school."

"I've never understood sending children away so young," Françoise said.

"Neither have I. Mathilde cared for her, but she was always busy. I tried too, but Lucie kept searching for a mother. Maybe that early loss is part of her unhappiness now."

Sophie quipped, "Having Oliver for a husband can't help."

I nudged her playfully. "Is that a critical remark from kind Sophie?"

She laughed. "Oliver Butterfield Hanover the Third deserves it."

"Lucie wanted that name, Hanover," I said. "Being Jewish at a Connecticut girls' school was brutal. She thought marriage would protect her. Anyway, the Goldfarbs love her, but they're in California now—and when they see Lucie, Oliver is hardly civil to them."

"Should we visit her again?" Sophie wondered.

"I don't know. There was so much conflict during our first trip. Anyway, even if Socorro won't talk on the phone, I'm certainly going to check on

Lucie."

My thoughts drifted back to my mother's letter. "Putting Lucie aside for a moment—do you two think we're right to ask women to speak so honestly with us?"

"Of course," Françoise replied firmly. "Remember Dr. Levy's patient, Suzanne?"

I nodded, recalling the heartbreak of her regret. "But what if women want to stay private, like my mother?"

"Then you put on your habit," Françoise said, "and make it safe for them."

I smiled at the memory of my old teaching robes, though unease lingered. "It matters to know how women feel before we help them. If it seems intrusive, we just have to face their disapproval."

Sophie took my hand. "You told your mother the truth about our work. If you can do that, you can do anything."

I put the letter in an inlaid box I'd kept since my years in Paris. It was filled with weekly notes from my mother and almost weekly notes from Lucie. My phone call with Lucie was frustrating. No matter how much I attempted to intrude, she insisted that everything was fine.

Fine is a very tricky word.

CHAPTER 3

HENRI HAS QUESTIONS

And so, we went on with our work. As the saying goes, 'we had our good days and our bad days.' One of the very worst was the day our beloved dog, Gracie, died. I couldn't bear to call Lucie. Since Gracie had adopted us, we didn't know how old she was. For a few weeks, she had abandoned her job of faithfully meeting our incoming guests at the bus and escorting those who were leaving. Lately, during the day, she mostly lay curled up in the kitchen on an old rag rug Françoise had scrounged for her. At night, her place was at the foot of our bed. She was slow and stiff, but never failed to greet me with her tail wagging madly, until one morning, she didn't. We buried her in her own special corner of consecrated ground—she is one of the most beautiful and loving souls ever to lie among the ancient remains of the sisters who lived in that secluded cloister, and the more recent remains of the water babies. I still dream about that wonderful dog.

It wasn't Our Lady without a pup, so before long we adopted a new stray— a black and white Sheltie. In many ways, we felt like strays ourselves—just outside polite society—so the dog fit right in. We let eight-year-old Henri name her. He said she ran as fast as a jet plane, and wanted me to tell him the word in English. We all agreed that *Jet* was a better name than *avion à réaction.*

I was feeding the pup one morning when the door flew open and Henri, disguised as a whirlwind, zoomed into the kitchen and buried his head against Sophie. Françoise followed, smiling, carrying milk and cheese from the dairy.

In those years, little Henri was our constant companion. He came into our lives when a woman brought her daughter for an abortion and she turned out to be in labor. Françoise's niece, Anne-Marie, had several miscarriages, so adopting Henri was a dream come true for her and her husband, Thomas. They worked hard at the dairy, so they were delighted that we loved having Françoise bring Henri with her.

"*Ça va,* Henri?" Sophie said, ruffling his hair.

He looked up with a dimpled smile. "*Ça va, tante* Sophie." With that he zoomed off in search of something to play with.

When he was an infant, Sophie and I loved our turns to babysit. Before we knew it, he was toddling into the grain cellar and getting covered in dust, and then at six, learning to spell by reading road signs as we picnicked in the countryside. Henri especially loved Sophie and followed her around like a little shadow. When Henri spent the night, Sophie and I would tuck him in, and I'd tell him some of the bedtime stories I told my seven-year-old girls many years before when I was a teacher in Occupied Paris. I always ended with 'They had their good days and their bad days and they took care of their problems the best they knew how.' My girls decided this ending was more honest than *they lived happily ever after*.

Some of the women who came for their special abortion retreats played with him and cuddled him. Others didn't want anything to do with him. We were fine either way. One day, when Henri was eight and it was just the two of us in the kitchen having cocoa, he asked me about the women.

"They are very quiet and sad when they first come. But when they leave, many of them are smiling and humming little tunes. Do you tell them lovely bedtime stories, with good days and bad days?"

"No."

"Do they get an extra slice of cake after dinner?"

"No." I had forgotten how curious children naturally are, but I didn't know what to say. "We help them with a problem that is worrying them, and that usually makes them feel better."

"Oh. Sometimes they cry when they are leaving."

"I know. Grown-ups can be strange. Some of them are happy when they leave us, and some of them feel sad, even though they are also relieved."

"I don't understand."

"That's all right. You don't have to understand everything."

That night, Sophie and I talked about what we could explain that Henri might understand. The next morning we enlisted Françoise's help. We didn't have guests, so Sophie, Françoise, Henri, and I sat around the kitchen table.

"Henri, you asked me yesterday how we help the women who come to see us." I began.

He nodded his head.

Françoise took the baton. "We wanted to explain it a little better."

"All right," he said.

Then it was Sophie's turn. "Do you know who Madame Lagrange is?"

Henri made a little face. "Yes. She is the baker's wife. She works at the patisserie. I don't like to go in there when she is behind the counter because she is always angry."

"Yes, she is," I said. "Do you know how many children she has?"

Henri thought for a moment and counted on his fingers. "She has six children. No, seven because there is a new baby."

"Have you ever noticed how tired she is?" Françoise asked.

"I don't know if she is tired, but she is always yelling at her girls to take care of their brothers."

Sophie said, "She might sound angry because she has so many children to take care of. The girls who come to us don't want to have a baby right now. We help them with that."

"That's why they are sometimes smiling when they leave?"

"Yes."

"But women like babies. They are very cute."

"They are cute to visit, but it is hard to take care of a baby," I said. "Women want to do it when they have the time and the energy to give the babies love and attention. For some, it's hard to do that when there are so many to feed and so little food."

"So when they come here, they can pick a different time to have a baby?"

"Yes," Françoise said.

"Oh."

Before we were even finished, Henri was out the door throwing a ball to Jet. We watched them out the window, relieved that an eight-year-old boy and a dog can play fetch forever.

Sophie, Françoise, and I looked at each other.

"That seemed to go well," I said.

"For now," Françoise added, rolling her eyes.

CHAPTER 4

ENCORE BRIGITTE

I was in the market buying leeks and potatoes for Sophie's Vichyssoise soup when I next saw Brigitte sitting on a stone wall at the edge of the park. Her hair was loose and unkempt. She was not wearing the specially tailored gendarme uniform created for her as the first woman on the force. I put my head down and turned my back, hoping I could avoid her seeing me. But to no avail.

"Jane! Jane, it's me. Over here," she waved.

My mind raced, searching for a way to release myself quickly from the conversation. But, as usual, she had her own agenda.

"Hi, Brigitte. Beautiful day. How is Lydia?" I asked.

"She's fine, fine. She says she's got her life back. And you gave me a gift, too. I've realized law enforcement isn't for me. I've quit the Gendarmerie. I'm switching to health care." She might as well have told me she was flying to the moon. It was impossible to imagine haughty Brigitte emptying a bedpan or wiping a fevered brow.

"You are going to nursing school?" I tried, without success, to keep the incredulity out of my voice.

"*No, no.* I want to make governmental policy. Why can't we let women decide about their own lives and still care about mothers and children? These are the same women, *non*? Just at different times of their lives. My niece wants to have a baby, just not right now. Not with the *bâtard* of a boyfriend she finally got rid of. So I got a new job as director of a regional health agency. Perhaps the name of my organization was correct, but it is women who have no voice."

It was as if King Henry VIII, dispatcher of wives, had turned into Simone de Beauvoir, internationally famous feminist.

"Uh, that's great." Time would tell if it was great or terrible.

"When I was at the convent, Sophie mentioned that her Uncle Matthieu was high in the Ministry of Health. Would you introduce me to him?"

Yikes. What was I supposed to do? Matthieu trusted me. He had gotten us out of a handful of legal scrapes, and he wanted me to help him make abortion legal in France. The last thing I wanted to do was to foist a loose cannon like Brigitte on him.

"He is awfully busy. I'll have to see if that is possible."

Brigitte responded, "'We'll see' usually means no. Maybe you don't trust me yet. I understand. You and I have traveled a rocky road. Despite our differences, I respect you, Jane. Even as a young woman in Paris, you stood up for what you believed. You might not be able to see it, but I did that, too. Now that we are on the same side, I could really help. Just consider it."

We parted with a civilized, if not cordial, nod.

I wanted to hold the meeting in the convent, where I felt most comfortable.

"You are sure about this, Jane?"

"As sure as I *can* be. Trusting Brigitte requires a leap of faith. But if she could really help Matthieu and the others trying to change this law, I don't want my fear to get in the way."

Sophie made canapés of toasted bread with mozzarella cheese and fresh tomatoes from our garden. We both welcomed Matthieu with *la bise*, the friendly kisses on both cheeks endemic to the French. Brigitte came to the door minutes after him. I shook her hand and led her inside.

"Matthieu, I'd like to introduce Brigitte Delacroix. As I mentioned, Brigitte is working in our regional health office."

Brigitte had her wiry hair pulled back into a neat bun. She was wearing a navy blue suit—attractive, but not showy. Her pale pink Hermés scarf gave her an air of elegance I had never seen in her before.

"So lovely to meet you, Minister Neuville," she said, extending her hand. "I have followed your career with some interest."

Matthieu shook her hand, and the two sat down.

"Let's not waste each other's time," Brigitte said. "I imagine Mademoiselle Jane has told you something about our tumultuous relationship."

"Yes," Matthieu said, hesitating. "I must inform you that my colleagues and I are *progressistes*. As much as we want abortion to be legal, we also want to create a general society where everyone is valued and respected."

"Of course. The Jewish question. I was once a supporter of the Nazis and, for a brief time, their prisoner. I got involved with a man who was Jewish and a Communist. They arrested us both. If Jane hadn't managed to intervene, I would have been sent to a camp. I learned the hard way. I, too, wish for a society where every citizen is respected."

"I am concerned about how you are putting that," Matthieu answered. "We demand respect and care for the immigrant, just as for the citizen."

Brigitte blushed, something I had never seen before.

"Forgive my misstatement, sir. That is what I meant. Exactly what I meant."

Matthieu looked only partly convinced, and I didn't know what to think.

Brigitte turned to me. "I mean it, Jane. I am one of those rare leopards who has changed his spots. I recently…well. About the time my niece came to me for help with her pregnancy, my brother revealed to me that our mother was Jewish. Under religious law, I am Jewish, too. My family fled from Poland to the south of France generations ago to escape a pogrom. They converted to Catholicism, though they retained a secret practice of Judaism. I've just learned Delacroix is not my family's original name. It is Dobrowlowski. But you must admit that naming themselves 'of the cross' was a clever ploy to be accepted as Christians. I was young when our parents died. I have a vague memory of my mother lighting candles and saying prayers I wasn't supposed to talk about.

"We were raised by strict Carmelite nuns who live a life of seclusion and contemplation, so it was a very lonely childhood. My brother sought to protect me from anti-Semitic prejudice by teaching me to hate other Jewish people. As you are aware, Jews have been expelled from many nations over the centuries, including France. So I find myself a *Convertie,* a Catholic in name only. As you can imagine, this is quite something to come to terms with."

Sophie, Françoise, and I sat with our mouths agape. 'Something to come to terms with' was quite an understatement.

"Mademoiselle Delacroix, this is quite a history," Matthieu said.

Brigitte hung her head for a moment, then sat up straight. "I am entirely ashamed of the way I acted. There is no excuse for it, and I feel I must apologize to you all as I embark on a new life. And now I want to help you."

We all made conciliatory noises.

Matthieu spoke first. "Mademoiselle Delacroix…"

"Please, call me Brigitte."

"*Bien sûr,* of course. Brigitte, how do you think you can help?"

"For a number of years, I have been running an agency that opposes abortion. I know the conservative ministers, and they know me. They trust me. I know how they think. I know how they talk about women and children and birth and, yes, even abortion. They don't use the same language as you do. They talk about duty, authority, purity, and loyalty. That has been my vocabulary. I can help you talk about abortion in a way that makes them see it through a different lens. It won't be this year, or even the next, but with some hard work, they can be converted to the cause of legal abortion. And if not converted, voted out."

Matthieu sat back in his chair. He ran his hand through his hair, then tapped his chin. "That is an intriguing idea. But I wonder…"

"What?" Brigitte asked.

"I have an idea that is not entirely fair to you. One of my colleagues has, like you, been re-considering his stance on abortion. He has agreed to stay silent about his views to maintain the trust of the conservatives and infiltrate them, if you will. He has an opening on his staff, but he hasn't been able to find anyone with whom we can share this strategy."

"You're imagining I could work for him? Be a double-agent?" Brigitte asked, considerably perked up.

My honesty-loving Sophie weighed in. "But Uncle Matthieu, as you say, that wouldn't be fair to Brigitte to ask her to dissemble when she can finally be honest about a secret she has carried all her life."

Matthieu looked abashed.

But Brigitte said, "It is brilliant. Mademoiselle Sophie, isn't this a cause worth almost anything if it can be won?"

CHAPTER 5

A RESTLESS WIND

It was a usual Wednesday afternoon when she appeared. We were expecting the patients who followed our long-haired black-and-white sheepdog, Jet, from the bus station. So when we heard the pounding of the large brass cross that served as our knocker, Sophie opened the door to welcome our patients, Annalise, Madrigal, and Natalie. She ushered them in and showed them to their rooms. Left standing on the steps was the dog, looking anxious, and a woman who easily matched my six-foot height. Porcelain skin, dark hair, dark brown eyes. The unmistakable scent of Joy perfume. It was *Betty*?! Or some impossible taller version of Betty. The resemblance shocked me to my core. I was transported a dozen years back to the Navy, where I met the admiral's daughter who broke my heart.

Grinning at me, the woman took a drag on her cigarette, threw the butt on the step, and ground it out with her foot. I bent to pick it up and slide it into the wide pocket of my robes. My relationship with her may have been determined by that fateful first moment.

When I stood up, she was still grinning, insouciantly.

"Jane," she sang, as if she had a claim on me. "I'm Addie." She proffered a letter.

I took a step back, shaking my head, my mouth dry. "You look exactly like her."

When I started to breathe again, I slid the pale blue envelope open. I knew the stationary well.

Dear Jane,

I hope you have forgiven me enough to read this letter. This is Addison, the half-sister I never knew about. Fifteen years younger. One of my father's extracurriculars. She showed up at my office last year after my father died with a bunch of pictures that revealed he had a secret family. She is an Ob-Gyn doctor. I didn't know what to do, so I gave her a job. But she couldn't stay here. She's just too...exuberant for private practice. The truth is, she seduced the wife of one of my partners, and the whole thing blew up. Discretion is 'not her thing,' as she puts it. I had to get her out of town before the situation exploded into violence.

She's had a rough time—expelled from several boarding schools for her escapades with other girls. And my father made her feel like a failure. She was top of her class at Columbia Medical School, but she had a hard time finding an internship program. I think it was my father's money that finally had her end up at a program in New York. By the time she found me, she had burned half a dozen bridges, but she knew her stuff. Poor Daddy. I wonder how he reconciled having two daughters who rivaled him in conquests of the fair sex? That bastard. Serves him right.

Anyway, I thought she'd be safe with you, and hoped you could use the help. She knows everything about us, of course. I have kept track of you after you left. It seems as though you are doing well. Sophie, isn't it? I hope she's making you happy.

I became a Nurse Practitioner when I left the Navy. Sandi and I broke up after years of bickering. I'm sorry I didn't realize what I had with you. Anyway, I'm single now. Until Addie (Rebecca Addison Marston) came to town, I was leading a boring life, if you can believe such a thing.

I always and only wish the best for you. And, I know! Subtract fifteen years and add eight inches to me, and we are twins. It's spooky.

All best,
Betty

There was so much going on inside me as I read that letter that I could hardly look at Rebecca Addison. I didn't even know where to begin, so I gestured and said, "Might as well come in."

She came in carrying a small satchel and an instrument case.

"Is that all you have?"

"I travel light." She smiled what I have always thought of as 'that Betty smile.' I was doomed.

I directed her to a bedroom suite, sure, at least, that she would need the bathroom as other mortals do.

When Sophie reappeared from taking our guests to their rooms, she looked at me quizzically.

"Who is our unexpected visitor?"

"She…she is…" I handed her Betty's letter.

"Oh, my," she said as she read it.

"Is…is it all right with you for her to stay?"

"Do we have a choice?"

"I think we have to let her stay the night. I can figure something else out tomorrow."

Sophie rolled her eyes. "Don't be silly. Of course she can stay. The girls loved her. They told me she talked non-stop on the bus, and even sang them a song. She entertained them all the way here on the walk, and they didn't understand a word she said."

"What? She doesn't speak French? What was Betty thinking sending her here?"

"I have a feeling Betty knew you were someone who could not say no to her."

Later on that evening, I learned more about Addie. While Sophie took the lead in answering questions from our patients, I turned to Addie, saying to myself over and over, *This is not Betty. This is not Betty.*

"Where are you from?" I asked.

"I was born in Texas, but I spent my growing-up years in a small Tennessee town called Fallon. There is a Naval base there. My father…Oh, I forgot. You already know my father is an admiral. Anyway, since I was otherwise an embarrassment to him, he invested in turning me into a valuable product. I love being a doctor, but my fatal flaws keep getting in the way. That's all there is to say."

"What are your plans?"

She made a face. "I don't like plans. I am more of a rolling stone. I'll stay here as long as it's working—as long as you'll have me."

When we were finished eating, the three patients went out into the garden with Addison, Sophie, and me. Addie pulled out her instrument—a ukulele. Against the *plink-plink* of the instrument, her voice was mesmerizing. Deep and even. Like warm honey. You could fall right into it.

Just as I knew that face, I knew that voice. When Betty betrayed me so thoroughly, I never wanted to hear that voice again. Yet I found myself leaning in and closing my eyes, remembering a harmony that it turned out was only in our voices.

Addie began with songs we all knew, and everyone joined in. She sang in English, and the rest of us sang along in French. When she began a plaintive cowboy song, the other voices fell away.

"Oh the wayward wind
Is a restless wind
A restless wind
That yearns to wander

And I was born the next of kin
The next of kin to the wayward wind."

Addie's voice faltered. "Sorry. I just can't get through that danged song."
She was crying. In four years of living with Betty, I had never seen her cry.

She smiled ruefully and began a jolly rendition of "She'll Be Coming
'Round the Mountain" that we all sang, our voices and languages blending.

It was too close to the bone for me. I excused myself and, unconscionably,
left Sophie to clean up, literally and figuratively.

When Sophie came to bed, all I had were apologies.

"My darling, it's all right. We all did the dishes together. Another bonding
experience for these guests who are now planning to rent a big house in Paris
and live together!" She laughed. "But what about you? Do you want to talk?"

"About what?"

Sophie gave me one of her Sophie looks.

"Oh. You mean about Addie?"

"About Addie, and the baggage she brings with her."

It crossed my mind to say that her suitcase was actually very small, but I
am not a glutton for punishment.

"What baggage?" Okay. Maybe I am a glutton.

Sophie didn't even bother with the look.

"You mean Betty?"

Sophie let out a sigh.

"What do you want me to say?" I asked.

"Oh, Jane. Haven't we gotten past the secrets? It's obvious that having
Addie here is upsetting you. I have lived with the ghost of Betty ever since I
met you."

"I don't have any secrets from you. You know all about Betty."

"Obviously I do not. I watched you this evening staring at Addie. I haven't
seen you so nervous since you decided to tell your mother about doing abortions. You don't even know this woman, do you? What is going on?"

I didn't want to tell her. I was embarrassed she had seen my obsession. I
finally whispered, as if that made it easier. "She looks exactly like Betty." I
wanted to swallow my voice entirely.

"Oh, honey." Sophie wrapped her arms around me. After a moment, I relaxed into her and cried. "Should I be worried?"

"No. No. It was such a long time ago. It just took me by surprise." I really
believed what I was saying.

"Just don't make me sorry I am so nice."

I kissed her goodnight and slept a fitful sleep with dreams of ghosts from
my shameful past.

CHAPTER 6

I'LL BE FINE

The next morning, I raised the question over coffee.

"Do you want me to make her leave?"

"I don't know," she said. "I don't want to spend my days being jealous of a memory. Can you handle it?"

"It was just a shock. I'll be fine." There was that damnable word again.

"As long as you are going to be all right with having her here, I guess it couldn't hurt to have a doctor now that Levy is working in Paris," Sophie said. "But are you concerned about what Betty wrote? About her *exuberance*?"

"We'll need to make sure Addie understands that we are vulnerable. The last thing we need is a loose cannon," I said. Then I changed the subject. "It's a good thing we're not letting Henri come over now that he is in school. There is only so much worrying we can do about our secrets being accidentally shared. Now that Henri has seen a goat give birth and wants to be a veterinarian, I'm more worried than ever about how to explain our work to him."

Sophie changed the conversation back to the one that was worrying her. "How did…How did Betty know where to find you?"

"I haven't been in touch with her, if that's what you're wondering."

I didn't mean to sound defensive, but I knew Betty was a sore spot with Sophie. She sometimes joked, "How am I to compete with the love of your life?" Only partly a joke.

"I think she may have asked Nick," I said. Betty and I had been friends with my colleague, Dr. Nick, and his boyfriend when we lived together in Kyoto after the war. Nick knew all about Betty's 'double life' with 'Sandi with an i,' the other girlfriend whose surprise appearance spilled the beans Betty had been guarding for four years. The girlfriend whose letter to the Navy resulted in my humiliating discharge. "That's the only thing I can imagine. He knew what she did to me, but he still might have told her how to find me. Betty is pretty good at getting what she wants."

Sophie was quiet. She understood there were layers of meaning in everything I was saying, and everything I was not saying.

The day was uneventful, though my mind was racing. I asked Françoise to orient Addie to Our Lady and I stayed out of her way. Our patients had their counseling and they took Addie with them into the village for supper. Sophie and I shared a quiet meal. Afterwards we read and then went to bed. Sophie noted that our guests were staying out very late, and I surmised that it was probably Addie's influence. We kissed goodnight and Sophie turned over and went to sleep. I did not. Addie's uncanny resemblance to Betty haunted me. It was like a jolt of caffeine.

I slept fitfully and was wide awake in the small hours of the night. I slipped out of bed, put on my robe, and went to the grape arbor. It was so dark that I sat down on a bench and admired the stars before I realized I was not alone.

Addie. I smelled her perfume before she spoke. She was sitting on my bench.

"You have trouble sleeping, too?"

I cleared my throat. "Sometimes. It's so beautiful and peaceful. I just love sitting out here."

"I'm sorry if I have taken your private spot."

In four years of living with Betty, I had never heard her apologize.

"No. It's fine."

We both leaned back into the bench and gazed at the vast expanse of sky.

"Addie...did Betty...did she ever talk about me?" I wanted to take the question back the moment it had left my lips, yet I hungered for the answer.

"Oh, yeah."

Her answer ricocheted in my head. I wanted to ask more, but I felt embarrassed for even broaching the subject. I was glad the darkness hid my red face. I sat with that answer that was such a non-answer until I could sit still no longer.

"I'm going to see if I can get some sleep."

"Aw, now I've run you off. I'll go..."

"No, no. It's fine."

I spent the rest of the night in my bed staring up at the ceiling—memories racing in my mind like pinballs ricocheting.

The next few weeks were a roller coaster. When you are doing something in a unique and unorthodox way, you can imagine that the first step in any training is 'untraining.' That is particularly challenging when the person you are training is confident she already knows it all.

"Training? No need, Jane. I am an Ob-Gyn. I could do a D&C in my sleep."

"We are doing something different here, Addie. Different from start to finish. For us, abortion is more than just a medical procedure. It involves the emotional and spiritual aspects of a woman's life."

"I am not on board with emotional and spiritual—that's your department.

But isn't the 'just a medical procedure' what they are coming to you for? Let them see Dr. Fraud for the rest."

"Addie, it is Dr. *Freud*."

"So you say."

"We don't separate the mind and heart from the body here. We believe all the parts need healing." I hated sounding like a Sunday School teacher.

"Well, you can count on me to fix up whatever is ailing with the body, but I guarantee you don't want me messing with the mind. And as for the heart, the best thing for that is a song. So if you want me to pull out my ukulele after each procedure, I'm on." She grinned at me, challenging me to disagree. I didn't. The last thing I wanted was a sparring match with another admiral's daughter.

"All right. But we are not doing a traditional D&C."

"Now you are just messing with me." Addie had a glint in her eye that told me she was back to speaking in layers.

"I assure you, that's not what I am doing."

I explained the Uterine Suction Apparatus invented by Dr. Nick, which he decided was so safe and easy that even I could use it. I demonstrated its use by emptying a bowl of water with the siphon. Addie acted skeptical. I told her how many thousands of abortions had been done safely and successfully using the gizmo, in California, Japan, and France. We agreed that she would observe the abortions we were doing the following day.

We began with Annalise. Sophie had already counseled her and determined she was at peace with having an abortion, so I covered the explanation of the medical procedure to identify and answer any questions. Annalise thanked me for explaining everything and said she was ready. We showed her to the procedure room and instructed her to use the bathroom and disrobe from the waist down, then closed the door and allowed her to get ready.

"I don't need a demonstration. I can do this one." Addie seemed ready to attack me. I had found it difficult to discuss anything with her without getting into the weeds. She disagreed with everything I said and wasn't above lording her physician status over my lowly status as a nurse.

"You may be a licensed physician, but I have experience that you will never have. Addie, if you want to be here, you have to do this our way." That was the closest I could come to the word "no."

I never said no to Betty either.

Addie was a quick study, and meticulous in her sterile technique. Dr. Nick's siphon abortion apparatus intrigued her. Within days, she performed abortions as if she had been doing them forever. At Our Lady, we had a team approach to nearly everything. We took turns answering the phone and making appointments, explaining the procedure, performing pregnancy tests, doing pelvic examinations to ascertain the length of pregnancy, cleaning up, stocking rooms, and managing our patient records that were hidden in plain sight in the form of Françoise's brainchild—the cookbooks. But the teamwork ended there. Neither Françoise nor Sophie was confident enough to do the abortion procedure, so I had been the only one to do it. Now we had two clinicians, and I had someone on premises with whom to consult. It was much better than having to call Dr. Levy and pull him away from his patients at the Paris hospital, where he had started working when he got married and left us.

But I worried. Would the price be too high?

CHAPTER 7

AGREE TO DISAGREE

At the end of a busy day, after our patients had left to walk to the bus stop, Addie and I sat together in the backyard sipping tall glasses of lemonade.

We were still feeling each other out.

I began. "I'm glad you agree with our policy of explaining the procedure."

"That's just good medical practice," Addie said flatly. Like her sister Betty, she viewed all *her* opinions as fact. "The only snag is this emotional exploration hogwash. I can't do that, Jane. I don't agree with poking your noses into these women's business. Why they want to do something is their affair, not yours."

Her self-righteousness made me want to strangle her. Did *I* sound like that? "We are not asking them to justify themselves. We just want to make sure they have resolved anything that could get in the way of them having peace afterward." I felt so defensive that my stomach hurt.

"Life isn't about having peace. I hate to say it, but I am afraid that is really something *you* need. Something to assuage your conscience and assure you that you are doing the right thing. I don't want to be insulting, but I'm not going to be anything less than honest with you. Impersonating a nun? That would get you kicked out of any hospital in the States. Why is it all right to trick them into thinking their church forgives them when you know it doesn't?"

I didn't have an answer to that one. Although I knew in my heart that my donning the habit had saved so many women so much grief, my heart was pounding. My dear friend and colleague, Dr. Nick, held a similar opinion. Years ago in California, when patients were struggling with their decision, he acted like it was so simple. He had said, "Yes or no, Janie. It's just a medical procedure." I argued with Nick, but I didn't want to argue with Addie. I gave in, but it felt like a terrible compromise of women's souls.

"Can we agree to disagree?"

"You mean can I live with it? I can live with almost anything as long as you don't ask me to do it," she said.

But her judgment still rankled.

The next morning, Françoise arrived early with a basket of freshly-baked croissants from the village *boulangerie*. I cornered her before Sophie and Addie came into the kitchen.

"Françoise, you know that Addie hasn't been shy about her disdain for us putting on the habit for the patients who are struggling emotionally. Her criticisms have been bothering me. The whole thing started with your abortion back in Occupied Paris. How do you see it?"

"The nineteen-year-old girl I was then still lives in my heart. Finding out I was pregnant when I was supposed to marry a German commandant was the worst thing that ever happened to me. If the Nazis had found out, they might have killed my whole family. Because of that abortion, my parents were able to stall for time, claiming I was too young to be married. I remember how sad, and scared, and innocent I was. I'd known Dr. Levy my whole life, so I trusted him. But meeting you in your robes and having you hold my hand meant everything to me. I still see you as my angel."

I put my arms around her and we laughed, fondly remembering the young women we were.

"That prayer you made up for me—I have said it over and over to myself all these years—as if it were the words to its own new kind of rosary.

Hail, holy Queen
Mother of Mercy—
Our Lady of Perpetual Grace—
Honor our love and courage—
Remember our goodness.
Show unto us
Thy forgiveness
And thy mercy.

"You spoke of my love and courage—of my goodness—things I couldn't imagine the church saw in me. You gave me permission to have the life I yearned for. We are not *impersonating* anyone. We are speaking with the voice of love and grace that *should* be the church's voice. I just don't think Addie understands. Trust yourself, Jane."

That night, I brought the question up with Sophie as she massaged my neck, trying to work out a knot that I'm pretty certain originated with Addie.

Sophie took a moment to think about it. "When I came here with my sister, there was so much troubling her that she didn't want to talk about. I was afraid she would have her abortion but not find any healing. Then Lucie put on the robes and spoke with her as Our Lady. Her conversation with Gertrude was like a miracle."

"I'll never forget that morning. Even though I had been teaching Lucie, I was amazed. It's like she invented the heart of what this work was meant to be," I said.

"It made every difference in Gertrude's life. Jane, one of the many things I love about you is that you are always willing to reconsider—to change your mind if you need to. But I believe in our work and I believe in the way we do it. Do you remember Suzanne, Dr. Levy's patient? She was so adamant about our doing an abortion for her, but she refused to talk about her feelings, so we told her we wouldn't do it."

"And Levy was so angry with us that he did it himself."

"And when she was distraught afterward, he apologized to you and begged you to help her. He had to admit you were right."

"I wonder why this seems like such a point of contention for Addie?" I mused.

"Do you remember what your Aunt Mathilde told you about the rule not to go into the dormitory?"

"She told me Madame Rochand didn't want to be disturbed."

"I'm wondering if what we do is disturbing to Addie. It might scare her. She's great—but I'm afraid she is not very comfortable with emotions."

"That is an understatement."

I did the best I could with Addie, but no one could teach her to sit still and listen to a woman's feelings. Each of us made a go of it.

Françoise encouraged her to pretend the patient was her little sister. "Wouldn't you want to know if she was scared? Or if she wasn't sure about her decision?" she asked.

Addie shrugged and said, "Sure. Those questions should appear on the intake form."

"Mademoiselle Addie, we don't *have* an intake form."

Addie smirked. "Just one more deficiency that any self-respecting health inspector would note."

"We want our interactions with the women to be more personal than just filling out a form."

"Whatever it is you want, it is not medicine. The whole point of medicine is to quantify things. I can measure a tumor. I can give an exact amount of medicine. I can determine a patient's temperature and blood pressure. You are describing what happens between women over the back fence. Gossip. It is not science, and I don't want anything to do with it."

Sophie took the philosophy that you can catch more flies with honey than with vinegar. "Addison, I realize our approach may seem unorthodox to you. But if you would just sit in on a few sessions, I believe you would see it differently. After all, there was a time when the use of Penicillin, or inoculation, wasn't accepted as science. A time when the earth was flat and orbited by the sun."

"Now I have heard everything," Addie laughed. "You are trying to convince me that the weeping and wailing that goes on in those rooms can be compared to the discovery of penicillin? Or Galileo's assertion that the earth orbits the sun? I am speechless."

I told her it was protocol.

"I have no intention of interfering with your protocol. Just don't ask me to make a fool of myself by asking these patients to make fools of themselves."

After a month, we gave up, and I made the compromise I said I would not make. Addie was the doctor in the white coat. Despite all my speeches about empowerment and women wanting to be equal, our guests seemed to like it. At dinner and on walks, they crowded around her with questions.

Addie loved it, too.

She charmed us all and put our patients at ease. As she picked up French words and phrases, the women who came to us were delighted to hear their language spoken with a Tennessee accent. Addie made every woman laugh, and that was more than most doctors did.

Françoise, Sophie, and I prepared our guests for their abortions. Then Addie came into the room, said hello, said something funny, and emptied their uteri. She did it quickly and virtually painlessly, with a skill that surpassed Dr. Levy's, Dr. Nick's, and my own. She didn't complain or make any suggestions. She was perfect. Even though we didn't want a hierarchy at Our Lady, our patients were used to doctors who were in charge, and who didn't care much. The fact that Addie was a doctor carried extra weight and made her their favorite.

In the evenings, we sat in front of the fire. Addie cried as she told me and Sophie about the doctor's wife she swore had seduced *her*, and made us laugh as she recounted tales of her raunchy exploits among the nurses at her last hospital. She had a guidebook about Paris with multiple pages dog-eared. From time to time, she borrowed the car to do what she smilingly called her 'due diligence' of sightseeing. Each time she visited one of the sites, she unfolded its page. I wondered if it served as a sort of advent calendar counting down the days she would be satisfied being part of our quiet, orderly country life.

I realized later that Addie made Sophie feel displaced when she insisted on managing the care of the Xenopus clawed toads we used for pregnancy testing.

"I was trained to care for these frogs at my old lab. I can do it with my eyes closed. Thank goodness you are using the Hogben test so you can inject the same toads with women's urine over and over again. I hated working in places where they had to kill the rabbit to determine changes in its ovaries.

This is so much more humane."

"I'm glad you think so," Sophie said. "I have been taking good care of the toads up until now. I know where to find the minnows and worms they prefer. There is no reason to change."

"But Sophie," it came out almost as a whine—unusual for Addie—"this will give me something useful to do."

Sophie looked at me, pointedly, and folded her arms across her chest. When I didn't say anything else, she left the room. If I hadn't been in the heady rush of adrenaline, I would have taken note.

Françoise narrowed her eyes. "Jane, be careful."

When I still didn't say anything, Françoise shrugged her shoulders and gave in. We all gave in to Addie. But I knew I would hear more about it.

That evening, Sophie confronted me as we were getting ready for bed.

"Jane, I understand you feel some kind of responsibility for this woman, but it seems you don't care very much about how I feel."

"Oh, Soph. Of course I do. It's just temporary. It has been really useful to have Addie here, but I'm sure she won't stay much longer." I hoped I was right. I felt an uncomfortable pull between loyalty and expediency, but it was a lot easier to reassure Sophie than to deal with pressure from Addie. Or so I thought.

"I don't like it. We don't need her here. We were doing fine before she came. You are treating her differently from everyone else. I don't feel part of a team anymore."

I had no answer to that, so I just hugged her and we went to bed.

Addison flirted with Françoise mercilessly, and Françoise seemed to love it.

"Is your patient ready, beautiful Françoise?"

"My patient is called a guest, as you know perfectly well, Dr. Addie. And she'll be ready when I say she is ready."

"Oh Françoise, you are such a demon."

By this point, Françoise was blushing and beaming and the rest of us were laughing. But it didn't go beyond the harmless, and it kept us all entertained.

We forbade Addie to find a girlfriend in our neighboring village, so she agreed to take her enthusiasm at least two towns over.

If only I'd realized the danger was much closer to home.

CHAPTER 8

MADAME TRÉDIVIC

The sun was out and I was in a wonderful mood. Sophie and I were sitting outside enjoying breakfast. Françoise came with chocolate croissants.

"My favorites. Thank you, Françoise."

She didn't sit down. She was wringing her hands as if in the midst of a disaster.

"What is it? Sit down and have breakfast with us."

She still didn't sit down.

"Jane, I have someone who wants to talk with you and you are not going to like it." Françoise had one of those 'up to something' looks on her face.

"What do you mean I am not going to like it?"

"You know I have a lot of friends."

"Françoise, of course I am aware you have many friends. I know you want something. Just tell me."

"Well," she hesitated, biting her lip. "This particular friend lives in Paris. She has gotten herself in a bit of trouble and she needs help."

"What's the problem? Is she too far in the pregnancy?"

"She is not the one who is pregnant. She was sort of trying to help a woman and now it seems there is an infection."

Sophie's mouth fell open. "Françoise, is your friend an abortionist? One of those we are always warning women about?"

"She has been doing it for years. This is the first time she has had a problem. I'm pretty sure."

"Oh, Françoise. This puts us in a terrible place—trying to take care of someone who has been harmed! I can't believe you expect me to do that. That you would put the convent at risk that way. What are you thinking? Don't you remember your friend Mimi?" I didn't mean to stand up and raise my voice, but I did. "You'll have to tell your friend to take the woman to the hospital."

I had never seen Françoise looking so nervous.

"I, er. I can't tell her that. They are here. Out in the wagon."

I'm pretty sure her friends could hear me bellow, "No!"

Sophie was already on her way out the door. Françoise followed her. I followed Françoise. Against my will, a wizened older woman with long white hair wearing layer upon layer of black clothes came into the kitchen with a young girl who was crying, wiping her face on a none-too-clean sleeve.

"Don't tell the priest," the girl said, over and over.

The stooped old woman said, "No one is going to tell the priest. We are just here to make sure you are all right."

"Take her into the procedure room," I said. But not before I scowled at the woman to let her know I disapproved of her. She scowled back.

"Françoise, get Addie." Sophie and I helped the girl up onto the examining table. Per our protocol, Sophie took her blood pressure and temperature. I was relieved to hear both were normal.

Addie rushed into the room. "What's the problem?" she asked, putting on surgical gloves.

"It's a rash," the old woman said. "She's got a rash I never saw before." She had a strong accent that I didn't recognize.

"Let's take a look. *Comment vous appelez-vous?*" It had taken Addie weeks to learn how to ask a patient's name, and she was proud of herself.

The girl whimpered and said, "*Je m'appelle Kiki.*"

Addie and Sophie helped move the girl's legs onto the rests. Addie sat down on the stool to examine the girl. Sophie told her that the girl's temperature and blood pressure were normal. The old woman pressed in next to Addie and spoke urgently to Françoise. She said, "Tell her Kiki has a thick white fluid coming from down there."

Francoise translated for Addie, whose shoulders relaxed as she examined Kiki. "This is Candida. You can smell it."

I declined to smell it. But my shoulders also relaxed. In French I said, "This is called a yeast infection, but it is more an imbalance than an actual infection. It is not serious and is not associated with the abortion. It's probably because of your nylon underwear. It doesn't let your sensitive areas breathe."

Addie turned to me. "I have samples of Mycostatin, a new treatment for this." Then she turned to Françoise as the designated translator. "Tell Kiki we will have her cleaned up and treated in no time, but she should stick to cotton underwear." Addie took off her gloves and tossed them into the basin on the floor. She instructed Sophie to clean the woman's vaginal area with soap and water and went to get the samples she had in her room. Addie returned with a tube of ointment and had Sophie apply it to the woman's vagina. The relief in the room was palpable.

I broke the silence. "Let's let Kiki relax in the recovery room. We need to have a serious discussion."

I was glad there were no other guests that day because I could not contain my anger. We sat around the kitchen table. The old woman was named Madame Trévidic.

"I know about people like you. Françoise's friend Mimi died at the hands of a practitioner like you."

Sophie said, "Jane, lower your voice. Kiki will hear you. This is not her fault."

Madame Trévidic gave as good as she got. "I do the best I can to help girls who don't have the luxury of spending three days with a pack of women pretending to be nuns."

Françoise tried to shush her.

I turned my anger on Françoise. "Have we no secrets here? Is there anything you don't tell the world?"

Addie tried to intervene and play umpire, but her French wasn't good enough, so she listened to the argument, her eyes wide.

The woman and I traded insults until Sophie stood up and slammed her hand on the table.

"Stop it, both of you!" she shouted. Anger had turned her neck red and she was shaking. "You are acting like children. We all want women to have choices and we want them to be safe." She turned to the woman. "Madame Trévidic, we are always worried about the women who can't come to us. We worry that the practitioners in Paris don't care about safety and don't know how to provide abortion in the best way. You are here—can we teach you what we know? Perhaps you will pass the knowledge along to others in Paris."

Madame Trévidic pursed her lips, considering the offer. "I would like to learn a better way. I was taught by my aunt. She was taught by her mother. None of us had any schooling. We did what women needed and hoped they would be all right."

I was ashamed to have been so blaming. "Years ago, a patient died in my arms from a massive infection. I have blamed the person who did her abortion, but it is really my fear you are hearing. I know that no matter how careful we are, or how much we learn, it could happen here."

Françoise was translating under her breath for Addie.

We agreed that Madame Trévidic could come back for the 'schooling' she needed on the condition that she share what she learned with other Parisian practitioners. By then, I had figured out how to put together the Uterine Siphon Apparatus, so she wouldn't have to wait for one from Japan.

Several weeks later, Madame Trévidic arrived one afternoon with our patients. She didn't seem to have talked much with the guests either on the bus ride from Paris, or the walk to Our Lady. She had reluctantly agreed to spend three days with us, as our patients did, so she could see the whole process.

Sophie welcomed them all at the door and showed the guests to their rooms. I decided to begin her schooling with the technical aspects of abortion. I collected Madame Trévidic and, after offering the ladies' room where she could freshen up, as they put it, took her into a procedure room to explain our process and the equipment we used. She wasn't the friendliest of creatures. She made disdainful sniffing noises when I explained the leg rests. She examined the instruments as if they were from another planet. I finally realized that the fault was mine. I was trying to teach her what we did without ever learning how she went about terminating a pregnancy.

I asked if she would like something to drink. Finally, an idea she liked. We adjourned to the kitchen with glasses of tea.

"Madame. I feel as though we got off on the wrong foot. We have been doing the same work—perhaps for the same amount of time. Won't you tell me a bit about how you learned to do this?"

She looked at me suspiciously. "I know you believe you are superior. How will it help me to expose my ignorance?"

"Please forgive my arrogance. It was only by good fortune that I had the chance to learn from doctors. And no matter what I have learned, there is always more to learn." I shrugged my shoulders as if to acknowledge my imperfection.

"And the woman I saw when I was here—the one who does not speak French—she is a doctor? She is not going to teach me?"

"But she doesn't like to be a teacher. Like the rest of us, she practices in the shadows. We must each have our own story about how we came to do this work. I would love to know yours."

Madame Trévidic looked at me to see if I could hold her gaze. I did, and that seemed to break the tension. Her eyes were green, like a cat's. She took off one of her layers of black clothes, then put her hands behind her neck and lifted her long white hair and tied it with a ribbon. That made her look younger, though I still couldn't have guessed whether she was fifty or one hundred.

"I'll start, then, eh?" She looked at me quizzically, and I nodded.

"I was born in Bretagne as the century turned. You call it Brittany. My grandparents owned a farm. We were good Catholics. My mother had seven children. My aunt had six before she died. Thirteen of us. Other children went to school, but we worked all day. I don't like to talk about it. When I grew up, I went to Paris to be near my father's family, and worked in a factory. I have never had an education. My aunt told me she had learned a trade that would always be needed. She taught me to use a long wire to break the amniotic sac."

"Oh, my. That sounds scary."

"As you can guess, it doesn't require any of the equipment you have shown me."

"Does it work?"

"Usually. But if the woman moves while I'm doing it, bad things can happen."

"Like a perforation."

"I don't know what that is."

"It's when an instrument you are using, like a piece of wire, pokes through or makes a hole in the woman's uterus."

"Is that her womb?"

"Yes."

"Why not just say that, then?"

"Have you ever spoken a language other than French?"

"Of course. Breton. And I spent my life being punished for speaking it."

"I'm sorry to hear it. My point is that different languages use different words to mean the same thing, right?"

"Yes, of course."

"So if we think about medicine as a separate language, it makes sense it has its own words for things."

"Oh."

"I can teach you how to end a woman's pregnancy the way I have been taught. I learned different words from the ones you use. You don't have to use my words to do it."

"Good."

"But I'll be using the words I know when I teach you, so you'll have to tell me when you don't know what I mean."

"I will do that." Madame Trévidic folded her arms across her chest. "What is it that makes you think your way is so much better?"

"From what I have learned about a woman's body and how it is shaped and how it works, I think this is a very safe way. You and I both know there are girls and women who die every day in Paris from abortion. They die from bleeding or from infection."

"And here they do not."

"That's right."

That seemed enough to convince her. We proceeded to the class—interestingly, the same class I gave to Oliver and Lucie after she nearly died from the abortion he performed on her in 1950. I talked a little about the history of abortion—that abortion had been part of the human experience since the beginning of time. I reviewed various methods of abortion that had been used, including the use of herbs, insertion of a foreign object—here I had to explain the meaning of 'foreign,' since Madame Trévidic asserted that the wire she used was manufactured in France. I went on to explain curettage—the use of an instrument to remove tissue from the walls of the uterus—
and finally attempted to describe the siphon, or suction method, devised by my nursing school mentor, Dr. Nick.

Unlike my patients in Japan, she seemed to understand the concept of a siphon, but couldn't quite picture how it was used. I wasn't surprised. I had to see it to understand. I showed her the mechanism, explained she would be able to make one for her own use, and assured her that a demonstration would be coming soon. In closing, I used a papaya to simulate the uterus so she could practice with a curette. I kept swearing under my breath. This woman had been doing abortions for twenty years and had never seen a diagram of a woman's anatomy. She had never done a pelvic examination to determine the length of pregnancy. She had been taught to dip her wire into whiskey before she inserted it—the only measure taken to prevent infection. I could not even imagine the death and destruction she must have left in her wake. I felt sick, but I kept reminding myself to think of the women who could be saved in the future.

Madame Trévidic was quite sharp, and her questions showed me that she was listening intently. With a break for an afternoon snack, we were done with the instructional aspect of her education at Our Lady. After all those hours together, she didn't seem an iota less prickly. I could not imagine being a woman forced to seek help from such a foreboding source.

Françoise was staying for dinner. As we ate Sophie's delicious *coq au vin*, Madame Trévidic remained quiet. Sophie and Francoise had spent the afternoon doing their counseling assessments, so the three women who had come for abortions laughed and chatted as if they had known each other forever. Addie laughed and joked as she always did. I sat at the end of the table watching the outsider—a woman who practiced in a way I had so often criticized. Françoise hardly spoke to her. I wondered what kind of friendship they actually had.

After dinner, as the others gathered by the fire to sing along with Addie and her ukulele, Madame Trévidic excused herself and went to bed. I pulled Françoise to the side.

"Do you know *how* she has been doing abortions?" I hissed.

"Jane, of course I don't. And I am guessing I don't want to know. I should have warned you that Enora is difficult. She has had a very hard life."

"She is nothing like you. How is she even your friend?"

"Maybe friend is too strong a word. One of her brothers was in the camp with Claude. I met her when they were released. It was a lifetime ago."

"How did she know to seek you out when she had a sick patient?"

Françoise had the good sense to look embarrassed. "I don't know. Really, Jane, I have tried to be careful only to tell people I thought I could trust. I was shocked when she showed up at my dairy farm with her patient."

I shook my head. "You are going to have to be more careful."

The next morning, Madame Trévidic watched Addie perform an abortion. From the pelvic examination to the tissue examination, the whole thing took seven minutes. I thought that would be enough to impress her. She was especially interested in looking at the tissue. She sent her patients home to pass their pregnancies, so she had never seen it before. In a rare fit of pedagogy, Addie explained what was the lining of the uterus, what was the placenta, and what was the embryo. And she added how important it was to examine the tissue after every abortion to be sure it was complete.

We left the patient sleeping comfortably and had some lunch. Enora, as she had finally told me to call her, took hers outdoors. She ate alone in the garden. I knew what it was like to feel like you don't belong. After the dishes were done, I was surprised to see her with her small suitcase and hat on, seeming ready to say goodbye.

"I thank you all. I feel ashamed that I did not know these things," she said.

"Madame, we are not finished," I said, holding her arm. "We have so much more to share about how to assist women with the spiritual and emotional aspects of ending a pregnancy."

She looked at me as though I were speaking Russian.

"I have no need for that. I have to see these women very quickly. I don't have time for gabbing with them. They don't have time. We are all just trying to survive."

Addie gave me a 'told you so' look, which I dismissed.

"You don't understand, Madame. This is one of the most important things we do here. This is what makes us more than, how did you put it, 'a pack of women pretending to be nuns.'"

She snorted. "Well, good for you. You can play psychiatrist and priest all you want, but it is not for me."

"Will you at least send any women who are unsure to us? We'll reimburse your fee."

"That is a ridiculous way to run a business. You must have more money than you know what to do with. But if I see a woman like that who can spare the time, I might send her to you."

She turned and strode out the door. I started to go after her, but Françoise said, "Jane, there is only so much you can expect from her. I know Enora well enough to know she will make a real go of what you have taught her. But you can't imagine she will establish Our Lady in the slums of Paris."

I protested, but Sophie stood behind me and rubbed my back in a movement I recognized as 'take care of Jane when she has gone too far.' I shrugged my shoulders and turned back to the work in front of us, hoping my work with Madame Trévidic meant some women would be safe. Once again, I was going to have to make do with not nearly enough.

CHAPTER 9

THE KISS

The months passed by and Addie and I fell into an easy routine, avoiding issues where we disagreed. One morning, Sophie and Françoise left early to catch the train to visit Françoise's cousins in Alençon. Addie planned to go to some hot springs several hours' drive away. I said I'd stay behind with Jet because someone had to be at the convent.

Addie said, "Come with me. There are no patients scheduled—why sit home alone for two days? Look at the picture in the book. It's as pretty as the Garden of Eden."

She held out the guidebook, showing a photograph of a quarry surrounded by a high rock wall, with deep green trees and aquamarine water.

"Come on, Jane. All you do is work. Have some fun for a change."

I didn't have any resistance to a challenge. So I packed a bag with a bathing suit and the other things I'd need to spend the night in a hotel, took Jet to the dairy, to Henri's delight, and we set off. Addie drove, and I navigated and related places of interest that we passed on our route.

After a while, I fell asleep, relieved not to be responsible for a change.

We arrived at the spring in the late afternoon. It was as inviting as in the photographs, and totally deserted. Addie hopped out of the car and, to my chagrin, peeled off her clothes and got in the water.

I didn't avert my eyes, though I should have. Like her sister, Addie was even more beautiful with her clothes off than with them on. You can't say that about many people.

"Addie. Put on a bathing suit. What if someone comes?"

"Don't be such a prude. The water is like silk on my skin. I don't want to miss an inch of it. Come on. There's no one here. Take your clothes off and join me."

"Now you're calling me a prude?" I took my outer garments off, but left my knickers and camisole on. I dipped my foot into the heavenly warm water and, in a moment, stood up to my neck behind Addie. I turned my back to her to gaze at the sunset, spilling gold and vermilion across the sky.

"Close your eyes and turn toward me." Addie's voice sounded heavy with an energy I hadn't heard in…well, a long time.

I obeyed her, already complicit in something that seemed out of bounds. I didn't anticipate the waxy, perfumy smell and the sensation of something soft and moist being applied to my lips.

"There. See, with a bit of lipstick, you look like Veronica Lake."

I glanced down and saw my reflection in the still water. Addie had painted my lips scarlet—the color of fire. I looked dangerous. I felt dangerous.

When I was seven, there was a picture window on one side of our house. I sometimes perched on a large rock and basked in my reflection, imagining myself a ballet dancer or a movie star. I'd put my hair up or borrow a pair of earrings from my mother's jewelry box. I loved to put on an old gown of my mother's and imagine I was a princess. Mother found me there once and laughed out loud. "Oh, darling," she said, "that's just not your style, is it? I'll get you some old spectacles and you can play at being a teacher." But now, the lipstick, and the proprietary way it was applied, hurtled me back into the fantasy that I was alluring.

Addie smiled, and I pulled her close and kissed her.

I *kissed her.*

Maybe I did it because I yearned to kiss Betty again. Maybe I fell for that image of myself as a femme fatale. Maybe I was just a fool.

Addie's eyes widened. She placed her hand behind my neck and started to kiss me back. I pulled away.

"I'm sorry. No," I mumbled, ashamed of giving confusing signals.

"What's wrong?"

"This. Everything. I never should have come with you."

"Jane, you're taking this too seriously. It was just a kiss. There's nothing wrong with a little fun."

"There is something wrong with breaking a vow. A promise."

"I shy away from those," she said.

"Well, I don't."

"It was only a kiss. Don't go overboard. You are making too much of it."

"Perhaps you're not making enough of it. How am I ever going to confess to Sophie?"

"Why tell her anything? It will only make her unhappy."

"Honesty is very important to Sophie. To both of us. We have worked very hard to trust each other."

"What's the fun of something that takes so much damn work?"

Addie leaned toward me again, but I pushed her away and got out of the spring, shivering, as I wrapped a towel around me. "I'm sorry. I made a terrible mistake. Let's just go."

We drove back to Our Lady in silence. Addie came inside just long enough to pack her bag.

"I was hoping I'd finally found a place I could fit in. Guess not. Say good-bye to Françoise for me." She wasn't foolhardy enough to give her regards to Sophie.

Sophie. What was I going to say to Sophie?

As I watched Addie leave, I had to admit to myself that this was not her fault. I was overcome with shame that, with all my talk of resolving feelings, I had not resolved my feelings for Betty. And it was going to cost me everything.

That evening I didn't eat. I took the nearly full bottle of scotch down from the high pantry shelf and sat in front of it. The pull into the dark place was strong. After what seemed like a lifetime, I decided it was too cowardly to seek oblivion. Sophie was going to be hurt, and I deserved to hurt too. I had to find the courage to tell her.

Sophie got back from visiting Françoise's family full of stories about the beauty of the town and Françoise's funny cousin. We had dinner, she unpacked, and we went to bed. I didn't tell her Addie was gone. I didn't tell her anything.

The next morning, we drank coffee at the kitchen table.

I said, "I need to talk about Addie."

We spoke over each other.

"I don't trust Addie," Sophie said.

"I kissed Addie," I said.

"You did *what*?"

I don't even want to describe the expression on Sophie's face, or the pain of knowing that I put it there. I wanted to say I had been addled by sunspots. Or that I was hypnotized by Joy, a perfume that should have been illegal. Or that I got confused about where I was. Or who I was. Or that there was something about that red lipstick. Or anything that would absolve me. I didn't want to admit that my unresolved feeling for Betty was like a dry sponge. Just add water and it softened and bloomed again.

"It was a mistake."

"This is the last straw. You kissed her by mistake? I'm sorry, Jane. You are going to have to do better than that."

I wanted to explain, but all I could do was cry.

Apparently, I couldn't do better than that. Sophie packed a bag and left to go to her sister's, saying I should contact her when I was ready to be in a true relationship—all she had ever asked of me.

I couldn't work. I couldn't think. I couldn't believe Sophie had left, not just me, but our patients. Losing Sophie meant losing everything. The woman I loved. The woman who created instant rapport with guests. The woman who maintained our records. The woman who knew where everything was kept.

The woman who fed us. And the woman, usually, who kept me in line. So at a time when my misery was so heavy that I could hardly get out of bed, I had to fill in the gaps. I gave Françoise a garbled account of what had happened. Then I couldn't bear the way she was looking at me. Or at least the way I thought she was looking at me. My shame was as heavy as my sadness. As I listened to the heartbreaking stories of the heartbroken women who came to us for abortions, it was safe for me to mingle my tears with theirs.

I took the scotch back out of the pantry. I sat alone in front of the fire for a long time before I decided not to drink it. I tried to lock my feelings away in a drawer. What I had always done before Sophie. But after a decade of being honest, I had lost the key.

I felt so ashamed. I didn't know what to do to persuade Sophie to come back. Finally I telephoned Lucie to ask for help. I told her the whole story in one sentence.

"Oh, Jane. I am so sorry. You must be in terrible pain."

"I am, but I can't complain about something that is my own fault."

"You still deserve comfort and support, even if the situation came from your behavior. Can I ask you some questions?"

"I guess so."

"What happened when you found out that Betty had another girlfriend?"

"I left our apartment and got drunk."

"That's it?"

"Pretty much. I stayed drunk for a few months until Levy called and told me you had lapsed into a coma after an abortion. Then I left the Navy and flew from Japan to Connecticut. So I guess I have you to thank for my sobriety." I gave a pitiful laugh.

"Have you ever talked with anyone about your experience? The shock of it? The humiliation? Losing—no, being betrayed by—the one person you believed you could trust?"

"Mostly I kept it secret, like so many other things in my life. Dr. Nick knew. He tried to be kind to me, but I wouldn't let him. It was *humiliating*. That's why I was scared even to try with Sophie. And now I have hurt her like Betty hurt me."

"You *did* hurt Sophie. But I don't think you can compare one kiss to four years of deception."

"She felt betrayed. The only thing Sophie ever asked of me was honesty. That includes fidelity, doesn't it?"

"These are hard questions. You know what you need, don't you?"

"You are going to say I need therapy. Ever since you got back from that residential place, it is your solution to everything."

"Not everything." I sensed that sweet Lucie smile. "I think what happened is that seeing Addie activated an old wound. You never got to resolve anything about the situation with Betty. You were thrown from being numb from drinking, directly into the traumatic experience of thinking I was going to die. Frankly, I'm surprised it has taken so long for that sleeping dog to wake and growl."

"Perhaps you're right. Do you think Sophie would come back if I promised to go to therapy?"

"It works the other way. You go to therapy, and then when you reach out to her, she sees for herself that you have worked on healing."

I sent a card to Sophie in care of her sister.

Dearest Sophie,

> *I am more sorry than I can express. I am going to find a therapist to help me heal whatever had me make such a terrible mistake. I will reach out to you when I can hope to be the woman you want to spend your life with. I don't know if you will ever come back to me. I don't know if you will ever trust me again, or if you should. But I will spend the rest of my days doing everything possible to be worthy of your love.*

> *Forever yours, if you'll have me,*
> *Jane*

My therapist, Céleste, was in her 60s. She was crusty and wise and funny, and I wish I had known her when I was 25. To my surprise, she didn't want to start by talking about my relationship with Betty. She wanted to start with my mother, my fear of not belonging, and my fierce need to be accepted. It was painful, but I could see that Lucie was right.

Every week, I sent a note to Sophie telling her about my therapy sessions.

- *Today I was in such a terrible state that Céleste opened her arms and invited me in. She held me as I wept, thinking about all the mistakes I have made in my life. She didn't give me a tissue or tell me to stop. She just let me cry, making a mess of her blouse and my own.*
- *Today Céleste asked me to remember as far back as I could the times I thought my reality had to be a secret. I wrote down all I could think of. There were dozens.*
- *Today I wrote a letter to my seven-year-old self and told her how much I loved her. I told her it is not her job to keep my secrets. That I would be here for her now, as much as I could.*

- *Today we explored how I had both gratitude and grief at some of the most important and pivotal moments in my life.*
- *Today we talked more about the dance of grief and gratitude. When I was very young, I thought there was only room for one of them. I denied my grief and locked it with my other secrets in a deep drawer. Céleste is helping me honor my grief. I wrote this poem:*

Grief and Gratitude.
Gratitude and Grief.
Such strange dance partners.
They step on each other's toes
And argue about who should lead.
Yet, when the music's over,
They sit together on the porch
Hands entwined,
And marvel at the splendor
Of the night sky.

Two months later, when I got up the nerve to call Sophie, we spoke over each other again.

"I want to come home," Sophie said.

"Please come home," I said.

She laughed, a sound I had been aching for—then we both laughed and cried at the same time.

I racked my brain to find a way to show Sophie that I had found some humility. I wanted her to experience the tenderness and reverence I felt for her. Writing a poem was too cliché. Singing a song had the same aura of theater. The answer came to me in a dream.

When Sophie finally returned, I took her by the hand to our bedroom, sat her down in the comfy chintz chair, and motioned for her to wait, with a finger to my lips. I brought a basin of warm, soapy water and a towel, removed her shoes, and gently began to wash her feet. Sophie bent down to stop me, but I insisted. She leaned back and let me share my love.

Would it be enough?

CHAPTER 10

A WONDERFUL SURPRISE

I continued my therapy, and Sophie and I trusted each other more. We didn't talk much about Addie. Lucie wrote, not hesitating to say 'I told you so' about the value of therapy.

Our old friend and protector, Inspector Chastain, visited occasionally, even when there was no disaster at hand. We were heartened when he told us there had been a reduction in the number of deaths attributed to abortion. Could the improvement be attributed to our work with Madame Trévidic?

Even though it had been years since Paris was occupied by the Nazis, there were still reminders of the war. Around the corner from a new hotel you might see an old building still with barricades put up by the Germans. One such reminder came on an evening when Sophie, Levy, Claude, Françoise, and I decided to break from the usual and have dinner in Paris. We sat down at our table at a restaurant that had been recommended. The waiter came over and handed out menus. Claude sprang to his feet, knocking over his chair. He pulled up his shirt sleeve, held out his arm, then embraced the waiter with an ebullience I had never seen in him. A moment later, he left the building. Without a word to us, the waiter disappeared into the kitchen.

Françoise said, "Don't mind Claude. He just needed to have a cigarette and clear his head. He'll be back."

Sophie, Levy, and I looked at each other with bewilderment. Françoise shook her head. "This happens occasionally. When Claude was in the prison camp during the war, he experienced things he will never talk to me about. I used to push him, but now I don't. The prisoners tattooed circles on their forearms so they would be able to identify others who had the same experience. When he sees one, it brings too much back."

I thought about how lonely it is to be the only one to understand something. I wondered what it would be like for women who have had an abortion to recognize each other by some external sign. Claude came back to the table, calm as usual. In the ensuing conversation about a leak in a pipe in the convent, I forgot about the whole thing.

When Lucie got married at the convent, before she and Oliver moved back to the United States, her dear friends Socorro, from Peru, and Paulette, from Italy, came to the wedding. All three of them had been seven-year-old students at my Aunt Mathilde's boarding school in Occupied Paris. I was appalled that Lucie told them about the illegal work we were doing at Our Lady, and astonished that both girls told me they wanted to complete their medical training and set up similar practices in their own countries. Though they kept us apprised of their adventures through regular letters, we hadn't seen Socorro and Paulette since they came to Our Lady to learn how to give the very special care we provided to women. They were both working hard to complete their studies, and also keeping an eye out for an opportunity to begin offering abortion care. Abortion was still illegal in both Peru and Italy. Thankfully, Socorro wasn't scaring us with any more mumbo jumbo about magic.

Socorro rarely telephoned, so when Sophie called out to me that she was on the line, I hurried to the phone. I was out of breath when I answered.

"It's Jane. Is everything all right?"

Socorro laughed. "I am very well, but have you run a marathon to get to the phone?"

"I was worried. Are you having any problems?" I asked, still huffing a bit.

"No, everything is going better than I could have dreamed. But I need to tell you about something—not on the phone. It's a wonderful surprise."

"Are you pregnant?" I asked, not knowing whether that would be at all wonderful.

"My goodness Jane, even you? Is that the only thing anyone thinks can be a great surprise for a woman? No, I am not pregnant. This is a surprise about my work—about *our* work. It has changed everything. Are you still seeing patients on a regular basis?"

"Of course."

"I want to come visit. Paulette is going to come too."

"That is wonderful," I said tentatively.

"But that's not the surprise. You'll have to wait. Can we come in October?"

"Yes, but Socorro…"

"I need you to have a few urine samples we can look at."

"Why?"

"I just do. And we'll need some time to talk."

"Okay. If you come on a Friday we'll have urine samples from the patients who have just left, and we'll have the whole weekend to talk," I said, still having no idea why she wanted urine samples.

"No one else can know about this," she said.

"Socorro, you are being very mysterious."

We set a date, then she said, "I have to go. I can't wait to see your faces.

You're going to love it," she said, and then the phone went dead.

I returned to the kitchen, where Sophie was making a pie.

"What was that all about?" she asked, taking off her apron and pushing a loose strand of hair behind her ear.

"Damned if I know," I answered. I had taken to more colorful language than when I was an innocent girl. "Socorro is coming to visit and says she has some wonderful surprise that she didn't want to tell me over the phone."

"Is she pre…?"

I interrupted. "No. That's what I asked, and she was insulted. She said it is something about work, and she wanted to be sure we wouldn't have patients here."

"I wonder if she has fabricated some new instrument," Sophie mused. "Ever since she became a physician, she has seemed so interested in finding better ways to do abortions."

"Maybe. Especially since Paulette is coming too. They will be staying for a week. We can put them in the bedroom next to your old one."

"A whole week? They have never visited for that long since they were here for their medical training. This must be something very special indeed."

We were busy that month, but I couldn't stop wondering about the promised 'surprise.' The girls finally pulled into the driveway in a rented car, toting an unexpected number of large suitcases. We exchanged big hugs. Sophie and Françoise started to take the luggage into the bedroom, but Socorro motioned them to stop.

"Leave this one out here," she said. "Is there anybody visiting right now?"

"No," Françoise answered. "Our guests left a little while ago for their bus. There's no one coming over the weekend."

"Good. Let's bring this bag into the kitchen so I can show you my surprise."

"Have you two eaten?" asked Sophie, always the quintessential hostess.

Paulette answered, "We met last night in Paris and stayed at our favorite hotel, then had breakfast on our balcony."

Our little band traipsed into the kitchen following Socorro, who carried the smallest of her several cases. She plopped the valise up on the kitchen table and began to open it, calling, "Wine for everyone—or better yet, champagne!"

Sophie and I looked at each other. "My dear, it is a bit early for champagne," Sophie said, laughing. "We can't wait to see the show."

Socorro smiled as she set a few things out. "Let's get started. As you'll learn, this isn't just a great show, it is a momentous change for all of us." She sounded very official, very much like the doctor and researcher that she was becoming.

I could hardly believe these two sophisticated women had been just seven years old when I was their teacher.

"There are two parts to this. The first part requires urine samples from pregnant women."

Sophie nodded that she would fetch the vials of urine we had kept at her request.

"And Sophie," Socorro said shyly, "Will you also bring a sample of your own urine?"

Sophie shrugged as if to say, 'Why not?' and left the room.

"Now I need some small bowls," she instructed. I opened a cabinet in the pantry and brought several over.

Françoise made a face. "Mademoiselle Socorro, these bowls are used for eating!" she said sharply.

Socorro laughed. "Françoise, I promise we will clean them so well—so well you could eat off them!" She was obviously enjoying herself.

Sophie came back from the lab carrying five stoppered vials on a rack. Each had the date collected, the woman's initials, and the length of pregnancy written on the glass in black grease pencil. Socorro instructed Sophie to pour a sample from each vial, keeping track of which urine sample went into which bowl. Socorro pulled a small box out of the suitcase and opened it. There was a coarse white powder inside. She dropped a pinch into each bowl, then swirled it around a little bit. Almost instantly, the urine turned various shades of blue. Paulette let out a little cry of excitement. It seemed she already had an idea of what Socorro was conjuring.

Next, our young scientist pulled out a piece of paper with graduated shades of blue. She set one of the bowls to the side and said, "Sophie, I am going to put these in order by shade of blue. Will you put the correct vials behind each bowl, and we will see what we have got?"

Socorro put the bowls in order according to the intensity of the color, and Sophie placed a vial behind its corresponding bowl.

"Now I'll start with the palest one and tell you the number of weeks of pregnancy for each sample. I think you'll find that the first one is six weeks," Socorro said, smiling. "Then seven, nine, and ten."

Sophie looked perplexed, but picked up the vials and read, "Six, seven, nine, then ten." She looked up and gasped. "You're exactly right. What is this magic?"

"It *is* magic—just like you told me!" Paulette said, smiling broadly.

Sophie pointed to the bowl Socorro had put aside. "But what about that one? It didn't work."

"That one, my dear Sophie, is yours. When there is no pregnancy, the urine doesn't change color," Socorro said triumphantly.

When I finally found my voice, I asked, "Are you telling me that a speck of this stuff makes the urine change into a color that matches a specific length of pregnancy?" I asked, motioning to the paper with the varying shades of blue.

"Exactly," Socorro said. "Isn't it amazing? Let's just sit down and I'll tell you the story behind it. Let me toss these out and rinse the bowls." She gathered the bowls and started toward the sink.

"Wait a minute," I said. "I have about a hundred questions. Did you invent this, or is it a natural substance? Is it accurate—does it work every time? Are you using it *instead* of pelvic examinations? And where did you find it?"

Socorro and Paulette washed the bowls out with hot water and soap, with Françoise supervising. Socorro looked over her shoulder and said, "Jane, as usual, you have all the right questions. Let's sit down with a cup of coffee, and you will know everything."

So we sat around the table. Françoise brewed a new pot of coffee and poured us each a cup, and Socorro began her fascinating and mysterious story.

CHAPTER 11

I UNDERSTOOD IT ALL

Peru, 1960

"While I lived in France, and during my years of school in Switzerland, I didn't think much about the T'ana—the indigenous people who were my mother's tribe. Even when I was about to graduate from medical school in Peru, I was so busy juggling classes and my part-time job in the laboratory that I couldn't think about anything else. When I finally met them, I could hardly believe both how different and how similar their work is to ours."

"Wait a minute," I interrupted. "How did you meet them? How is it different and similar? You have tantalized us with the promise of mystery. We need the details."

"It's a really long story," Socorro said.

"I don't care. We have as long as it takes," I answered, and Sophie, Françoise, and Paulette nodded their agreement.

"All right," she said, shrugging her shoulders. "A few months ago, I was assigned to assist one of my professors who had a practice caring for women at high risk for miscarriage. I had the rather unglamorous job of performing the Hogben pregnancy test—the one that you use. And I cared for the frogs. Women in Peru rely on their own knowledge of their bodies, and don't usually even have a pregnancy test or see a doctor until many months into pregnancy, if at all. But our high-risk patients often have irregular periods, and the doctor wants to be alerted to a pregnancy as soon as possible.

"I went into the lab first thing in the morning on Wednesdays and Fridays to inject urine under the skin of the African Xenopus frogs. As you are aware, if the woman is pregnant, the hormones in her urine stimulate the frog to lay eggs by the following day. It is a great method—much better than the old-fashioned A-Z test which requires dissecting a mouse or rabbit to determine how their ovaries responded to the urine."

Françoise interrupted. "How big is your laboratory?"

"No interruptions!" I said.

But Socorro answered. "We have nine of the clawed frogs. Each of them lives for many years. I must have been a bit lonesome, because I found myself naming them and even taking my homework into the lab in the afternoons to visit them. And there the mystery begins. One Tuesday morning, I took three urine samples out of the refrigerator and gathered the syringe and towels I needed. I keep careful records of the name of the patient, the date and time, and which of my girls was injected. Each frog swims in her own small tank, marked with a number. When the frog releases eggs, the tank is cleaned out and refilled with clean water.

"Although it may sound strange, I love them all—Lucia, Mayra, Rosa, Chacha, Sheyla, Ana, Tatiana, Luz, and Maribel. I began with number four— Chacha. I had already drawn the urine up in the syringe. I reached into the water for her, wrapping her in a towel so she wasn't too slippery, when I noticed a brightly colored feather floating in the tank. It was about four inches long and seemed to be from some kind of tropical species, although I didn't recognize it. It didn't make any sense. There were no birds of any kind nearby. I put the feather in the breast pocket of my lab coat, completed the quick subcutaneous injection, and returned the frog to her tank. Then Luz and Maribel had the same treatment.

"I do the paperwork as I go along so that I don't get confused, noting the number of the urine sample and the number of the frog. Then I had to get to my classes and didn't think about the lab again. The following morning, there were eggs in Chacha and Maribel's tanks, so those urine samples indicated a pregnancy, but no sign of eggs in Luz's tank. I noted the results on my paperwork. As I started to clean the containers, I found a small rose-colored crystal at the bottom of each tank. I had never seen them before. There weren't supposed to be any foreign objects in with our ladies, so I fished the pieces of quartz out, dried them off, and put them in my pocket along with the feather. After I cleaned the tanks, I fed the frogs the tiny bites of dried shrimp that we buy in bulk, and then went to talk with my supervisor.

"Dr. Ramirez was always busy with phone calls and patients and students filing in and out of his office, but I told his secretary that I needed an immediate appointment. Within twenty minutes, I sat across from him. He was tall and skinny, with a shiny bald head, a fierce black mustache, and a permanent scowl. Even when he was seated, I found him intimidating.

"He looked down at me through his bifocals and asked if everything was all right. I told him yes. I thought so. He asked if the toads were healthy, and I told him they were. Then he looked at his wristwatch and said, 'Socorro, I don't mean to hurry you, but I'm scheduled for a patient in just a few minutes. What do you need?'

"I sighed, not wanting to feel stupid. 'It's just,' I began, and then pulled the crystals and feather out of my pocket and put them on his desk. 'I found these in the frogs' tanks,' I said.

"He looked at me in confusion. 'I appreciate it that you are fond of the frogs, Socorro, but you must not put things in the tanks,' he said, obviously not understanding what I had told him.

"'No—these were already *in* the tanks,' I said. 'In Chacha's, Luz's, and Maribel's—I'm sorry—number four, five, and six. Someone must have put them in there, but I didn't do it. I don't think they affected the results, but I can't imagine how these things got in there.'

"'Well, that is very strange. Does anyone but you have the keys to the lab?'

"'No one but the cleaners.'

"'Well, let's keep an eye out. But as long as it is not interfering with our test results, I have nothing else to say. I don't have time for frivolities,' he added brusquely. He stood up to signal that it was time for me to leave his office, so I did.

"My crazy schedule didn't leave me much time for wondering, but when I lay down that night, I felt worried. Finally, sleep overtook me, and I found myself dreaming of strange conversations with the frogs, as if Chacha or Mayra would tell me who had been disturbing our little world. On Thursday morning, I had four urine samples to inject. When I gathered my clipboard and records, I found a rattle made of bone on the desk. It had bright red yarn wrapped around it, and leather cords with silver bells at the ends. Next to it was a small pot of white powder. Beneath the rattle, there was a piece of paper—or something that looked like paper, although rougher and more textured. At the bottom of the page was a band of blue ranging from very pale to very dark with numbers beneath it. And there was writing. *Mix one pinch of Abra with urine. If it turns blue, the woman is with child. Compare the shade of blue to learn the age of the pregnancy. Only for you to see, daughter of Azucena.* I felt chills on my neck. Azucena was my mother's secret ceremonial name in the language of the T'ana.

"At first, I thought someone was playing a trick on me. I looked over my shoulder to see if I could discover someone laughing. Then I remembered the feather and the crystals, and I realized that something else was happening. I gathered some bowls and performed the same steps with the urine that we just did, with the same results. I could hardly believe that the color of the urine in the bowls matched the length of pregnancy exactly as we had estimated it by examination. I didn't know what to think, but I was certainly not going to tell Dr. Ramirez about it.

"Over the next few weeks, I began to find unusual items on my doorstep at home—rare feathers, brightly colored stones wrapped in vines, large pieces of bark with carvings and writing I couldn't decipher, and animal bones that were painted and inscribed. It had to be the T'ana. I still don't have any idea how they learned where I was living. But find me they did."

While Socorro talked, Sophie gathered a baguette that she tore into pieces, and some cheese and small plates that she passed around. We were all grateful.

Socorro continued. "T'ana Wise Women were communicating with me, but I didn't know what they wanted, or how to get in touch with them. So I waited. Sure enough, one afternoon I was accosted in my garden by a young boy, about seven or eight, barefoot and covered in dirt from head to foot. When I say accosted, I am not exaggerating. He grabbed my elbow and started tugging and said, 'They say you must come to them. You must come now. I must bring you.'

"He told me his name was Alejandro. He was an unlikely messenger, but by then my curiosity was piqued. I resolved to follow him. He had left his burro, Pedro, tied up behind a shed. I didn't want to get on that thing. My only experience in riding a horse ended in disaster, and this smelly creature seemed even less approachable. But Alejandro insisted I get on behind him. It wasn't too difficult to mount the beast because it wasn't very tall—so I did, and I held on to Alejandro's waist for dear life. I cannot tell you where we traveled that day because we were in and out of clearings, up and down hills, and around thickets and brambles. As much as I was scared and uncomfortable and jostled around on that donkey, I was thrilled at the prospect of finally meeting the Wise Women.

"After more than an hour of riding, we stopped abruptly in sight of a small stone building. By then, my legs felt numb. Alejandro helped me get off, and he tied the burro to a gnarled tree. He sat down at the base of the tree and gestured for me to go into the building.

"'You must go. I am not allowed,' he said emphatically. 'I will wait for you.'

"I admit I was frightened, but I hobbled to the building. Everything in the landscape looked gray—the sky was gray, the stones of the building were gray, the ground was gray, so when I walked into the entrance, I was almost knocked down by the dazzling colors. There were paper cutouts every-where—the dirt floor was covered with weavings in hues only found in trop-ical birds—and there was a smell of something that jogged my memory, some kind of incense. Six women sat in the middle of the floor around a fire. I couldn't tell you if they were fifty years old or one hundred and fifty. They were wearing traditional Peruvian clothes—multi-layered skirts with stiff crinolines of impossibly bright pinks and blues and—well, every color."

"Like the women on the postcard you sent us," Françoise said.

"Yes—exactly," Socorro answered. "On the shelves all around them were more 'totems' like the ones I had received. Feathers and rocks and bones and flowering branches. One of the women looked at me with her dark, weathered face and smiled broadly. In her deep voice, she said, 'Welcome, Socorro. We have been anticipating your arrival.' Their daily language was Spanish, but in their sacred meetings they spoke T'ana, which I only understood a bit. I still don't know what town we were in that first time. Maybe Q'enko, or Saqsayhuman—they had many meeting places so that they wouldn't be compromised. When I knew them better, I even got to participate in packing up the space to move all their glorious paraphernalia. Like nomads, they had a system, and in just minutes they could pack everything up and get it on a little wagon that was grudgingly pulled by the burro, Pedro. That first day, I just sat around the fire with them and listened. I didn't understand anything, but in a way, I understood it all."

When Socorro paused, I stood up to stretch. "This is all so mysterious. Were you scared?"

"At first I was. But after a little while, I felt at home. In fact, I felt like you were there with me, Mam'selle."

Hearing the nickname my students gave me all those years ago was heartwarming.

Socorro yawned. "I was so excited about telling all of you that I didn't get much sleep last night," she said.

"And you never remember about the time difference," Paulette said, giving her a playful shove. "Lima is six hours behind Paris, so you'll never get yourself settled."

I thought how remarkable it was that these two had remained such close friends after more than two decades. The memories of that time made me miss Lucie, who was having her own troubles in America. The three of them had kept in touch since they were children.

By then, we were all standing to stretch our backs.

"Are you too tired to finish?" I asked. "Do you need to take a nap?"

Socorro and Paulette laughed. I imagined they were thinking of the little pink blankets I covered them with during naptime when I was their teacher.

"No. There is plenty of time to sleep. I want to finish if you can stand a bit more."

We all nodded our heads.

CHAPTER 12

THEY COULD NOT TOUCH OUR SPIRITS

As we sat back down at the kitchen table, I said "I wish Lucie were here."

Socorro agreed. "Me too. She is the only other person I'd want to tell. But I can't put anything in writing, or talk about this over the phone. When is she going to visit?"

Sophie and I exchanged a glance, recalling my mother's concerns about Lucie. "Soon, I hope," I said. "But let's get back to your story."

Socorro took a deep breath. "Alejandro came to fetch me four or five more times. Each time he took me to a different location—once a cave, once a clearing in a grove of trees, once a barn, once someone's home. When I was lucky and the road was passable, Alejandro brought me in the wagon. Even though it jostled as Pedro pulled it over the stones and ditches, it was a lot more comfortable than the burro's bony back. Each time, the meeting place was decorated with the same extraordinary textiles and colors. At least one time they were using *moscocero*, a sacred herb that creates a sort of intoxication and amnesia. They offered it to me, but I had the good sense to decline. I had a hard enough time getting back and forth on Pedro without being drunk."

Françoise was getting impatient. "Why did they want you to come to them? And what has this got to do with that Abra powder?"

"I'm sorry. Their world is so different that even talking about it sometimes makes me get lost," Socorro said.

Uncharacteristically, Sophie glared at Françoise. "Take your time, Socorro. We can all hear that this was very intense for you," she said. "Let's not interrupt the story. We can ask questions when it is finished."

Françoise looked chastened and mumbled, "Sorry."

Socorro continued.

"I believe they summoned me to their circle all those times to get a sense of me—and to let me get a sense of them. Even though I didn't speak T'ana, I recognized that their rituals were powerful healing. Once there was a young woman lying prone next to their fire who I feared was dead. When they finished their incantations, they poured some liquid into her mouth, and each of them touched her. Suddenly, she sat up and took a place in the circle, looking perfectly normal. I was fascinated, both as a doctor and as a woman.

"In one of the meetings, Alessa, the woman who had originally spoken to me in T'ana, addressed me again in Spanish. I thought she was the leader, if a circle has a leader.

"'You are the daughter of Azucena. You are a healer. You hold powers beyond those that men have taught you. We invite you here to learn and to meld your education with your innate gift. We can share with you ancient secrets, *los misterios de sangre*, that will empower you to attend to women as they bring in new life or return life to the One.'

"'I would like to know those secrets, Grandmother—mysteries of the blood,' I answered her. 'These are the secrets my mother wished me to have. How can I become worthy of this magic?'

"It turned out that I was required to experience a session with the *moscocero*. In the ceremony, as I prepared to drink it, I felt a connection to my mother, knowing this is a ritual she must have experienced. I can't describe what it was like, but they were kind enough to have one of the women accompany me home in the wagon and put me to bed afterward. I missed my classes the next day—and possibly the next—I lost track. When I finally woke up, I felt wonderful, even though I didn't remember anything that had happened. It was so strange—as if those elders had inhabited me—as if I had become one of them. I could hardly wait for the next gathering. I felt as though I would understand everything.

"A few weeks after my experience with the intoxicant, Alejandro came to get me again. This time, he was unusually talkative. As we rode, he pointed out his favorite birds and waxed on about the full moon the night before. He told me he had two older brothers and that his great-grandmother was one of the women in the circle. Alejandro accepted me in a new way after the initiation into *moscocero*.

"'Do you use *moscocero*?' I asked him.

"He laughed. 'Of course not,' he said. 'It is forbidden until the eighteenth birthday celebration for a man, and the sixteenth year for a woman. These are the rites of becoming an adult. I have many years to wait before my first taste.'

"It seemed as though we rode in circles. We finally stopped at an isolated compound. As usual, when I got off the mule, Alejandro stayed behind. In the entryway of the building, there were faded frescoes on the walls, and a beautiful wooden altar with a huge crucifix hanging above it. As I passed through the atrium, I found myself in an open space that must once have been a garden. It was so overgrown that 'meadow' would have been a kind description. I followed the sound of music and the smell of incense down the walkway and down the steps. Alessa smiled broadly at me and gestured to the circle. There was a space left for me around the fire, so I sat down next to her on a brilliant fuchsia and red rug. She wore a tall, black hat. Her voice was so powerful that she didn't have to speak loudly to command my attention.

"'Today, my daughter, we begin a new chapter. Today, we welcome you, not as a visitor, or even as your mother's child. Today, we welcome you as a T'ana healer. Today, we share with you the legacy of the many circles of women who have sat around the fire before us.'

"The other women started shaking rattles and drumming. One played a wooden instrument with two strings, and one had some kind of wooden flute carved with a bird's eyes and a beak. The music was strange—and yet compelling. After a few moments, the cacophony stopped as abruptly as it began, as if these women were a flock of birds that signaled to each other in magic, silent ways. Then, one by one, the women around the circle spoke to me in Spanish.

"'I am Katia, which means pure. I knew your beautiful mother, and I welcome her beautiful daughter.' Her soft, sweet voice matched her name.

"'Welcome. I am named Roseangela—the rose and the angel.' She looked at me with a knowing smile. I realized I had seen her before. She was one of the women who cleaned the laboratory. I thought of all the little surprises left for me there. One mystery solved. She continued. 'I am wise in the ways of welcoming new life and returning life to the One. I will teach you all I know.' Her smile was like an embrace.

"'My name is Veronica—she who brings victory. We are so glad you have decided to join our circle as the prophecy foretold. I am wise in the use of all the ancient herbs. My wisdom encircles everything. I will teach you all I know.' Veronica's face was painted with startling geometric lines.

"'I am Zoila—life. You have shown us that you have strength and courage. These are the key ingredients in T'ana healing. Because of your courage, we are sharing secrets that have been held in our circle for hundreds of years. You must not betray the circle.' Zoila's hair was like white cotton. Her face was a spiderweb of wrinkles. She scared me.

"'I am called Laka, which means gentle. You live and work in the world of men, yet your heart aches for women. That is why we have brought you here. There is great risk to us—and risk to you—yet the signs tell us that it is time to share our knowledge. There will be consequences if we have misjudged you.' I almost had to lean forward to hear her, but I took her message as seriously as if she had shouted.

"The leader smiled broadly again at me. 'I am Alessa, the defender. Don't let our words of apprehension be of concern. We have had many discussions about you, Socorro, even before you returned to Peru. You were fated to come here, destined to learn some of these secrets and to use them in your medicine. It is time now for us to teach you. We will meet here again. This building has been, and still is, sacred. The Spanish built this cloister many years ago on the site of the most holy T'ana grounds. They stole everything from us—they made it illegal to speak our language—they turned our ways of dress into a costume for tourists to photograph. They even used the stones from our holy temples to build their churches on our sacred land. They forced us to adopt their religion in exchange for food for our families. They changed everything about our external world—but they could not touch our spirits. We practice our healing as the Grandmothers have done for generations, in honor of the Mother of the World, the God of the sun, and the Goddess of the moon. As you have seen, we move our meeting places to keep ourselves safe from those who wish to destroy us. As you shall see, we use *moscocero* to protect our secrets. We play our role in the turning of the planet, as we always have. Our next meeting will be at the full moon and will last for three days. Alejandro will come to get you on the eighteenth of the month. Bring your sleeping garments and a change of clothes. We will provide you with robes for our sacred rituals. Remember, it will be cold at night.'

"This was an instruction, not a request. When Alejandro dropped me off back at my apartment, I pulled out my calendar and was relieved to see that I wouldn't be missing any tests. I wondered if the Wise Women knew that before I did. Magic."

CHAPTER 13

IT IS DONE

"How wonderful. They knew your mother—and they also welcomed you as a healer in your own right." I shook my head, breaking the spell of Socorro's story.

"This is astonishing," Paulette said. "You haven't just been in another country—you have been in a whole other world."

"Did you take that stuff that makes you hallucinate?" Françoise sounded as fascinated as she was worried.

"You have to let me finish the story," Socorro laughed. "I'm afraid there is a lot more to tell, but you will recognize the work they are doing. It is your work, Jane."

We all indicated we would be quiet, and Socorro continued.

"Every encounter with the Grandmothers was fraught with mystery, a vague sense of danger, and unknowable possibilities. I waited impatiently for the weeks to pass before I would see them again. Just as Alessa had said, Alejandro stood outside my gate on the morning of the eighteenth. This time I knew where we were going, and the ride on the smelly burro seemed more comfortable than usual, although I confess that I might just have been getting used to it. The sun was warm as we made our way down the narrow path through the thickets to the clearing where the abandoned cloister sat in its crumbling majesty. For the first time, I looked at the once-magnificent building. The stone of the façade was weathered and stained, and ancient vines covered much of it. The huge wooden doors were intricately carved. As I approached the entry, I recognized the incised scene of Adam and Eve being cast out of Eden. The serpent in the design was center stage and had a distinctly female appearance. I smiled as I remembered an art history teacher saying that local artisans depicted Christian scenes through the lenses of their own culture. *There are many ways to exercise power*, I thought. *Some are more subtle than others.*

"Some of the colorful décor usually reserved for the central meeting space had found its way to the walls, as if creating a welcome or pathway into the center chamber. Inside, I was as astounded by the riot of color as always, but

I had walked in on something serious already in progress. The six women, by now familiar to me, were dressed in scarlet robes with flowered headdresses. They were kneeling, clustered around a young girl who was lying on a bed of tapestries. I couldn't tell if she was sleeping, unconscious, or dead. Seeing her raised a terrible dread in me. After a moment, Alessa noticed me and came over.

"'Good. You are here,' she said. She saw the expression of fear on my face. Her deep voice soothed and centered me. 'Don't be alarmed. She is fine. This is a situation for the Grandmothers. We will explain.' She motioned to the other women, and they assumed their usual places in a circle around the fire. The girl didn't move.

"Alessa extended her hands as if holding an offering, and the other women sounded the instruments I had heard before—the bells, drums, strings, and flute. As suddenly as the music started, it stopped, and Alessa stood up.

"'Grandmothers,' she began, 'This day Aiki is here. She is thirteen years old and her father has got her with child. Her mother brought her to us. Since no consent was given for the creation of this new life, no consent is required for the decision of its dispensation. It is up to us to decide whether this life shall be brought onto the earth or returned to the One.'

"From my previous visits, I realized there wasn't going to be a question-and-answer period, so I just held my peace. Alessa sat down, and Roseangela stood up. She wasn't smiling, but there was a warmth about her.

"'I know this girl. Though she has the body of a woman, she has the mind of a little child. When her mother, Yessica, suspected that the father was molesting Aiki, she came to me. I used the Abra powder to confirm the pregnancy, and I have brought the girl before you. She has held life in her body for three moons. In my prayers, I have been shown by the Mother of the World that bringing this new life into the community will destroy the life of Aiki. I have been counseled to honor all life by sending this fetus back to the One— by giving it to the sky.' She sat down.

"The woman named Veronica, who had already taught me so much about the plants these Wise Women harvested from the hills, stood next.

"'I brewed herbs to read the leaves this morning. I have that same message from the Mother of the World. Nothing good would come from this girl having a baby.'

"One by one, the women stood and gave their perspectives on the matter. It appeared that they all agreed. Although I understood their assessment of the situation, I was growing increasingly agitated about the idea that they were going to do some kind of abortion on this unconscious girl. Even though I didn't speak, Alessa sensed my consternation.

"'Socorro, you are here as witness to this work of the Grandmothers. We have brought you into our circle because we trust you. Your fear disturbs the balance here. Speak it, so that we may regain harmony.'

"I wasn't sure what I was permitted to say, but I screwed up my courage. It was the first time I had addressed this formidable group, yet they looked at me with open faces, so I proceeded.

"'I have worked with women in the process of bringing life in, and also sending life back to the One.' I thought it was right to try to use their words. 'You spoke of consent,' I turned to Alessa, 'yet this girl is unconscious. I don't understand how you agree to do an abortion when she is not awake. Doesn't that violate her just as much as her father has?' I sat down and let my shoulders relax, realizing how tightly I had been holding my body.

"Alessa said, 'Roseangela, will you answer?'

"Roseangela stood up again and looked at me kindly. 'It is because of your love and care for women that you are here. We share that love, and we share your wish for women to be fully present to decide the fate of their lives. But this one doesn't have the capacity to understand what has happened to her. Her mental understanding is that of a six-year-old. In the tradition of the Grandmothers, we take on the burden and responsibility of this choice. And we will give her *moscocero* so that when this is over, it will all be just a gentle dream for her.'

"Zoila stood. 'When she returns home, I will come to her and help mend the split that her father's actions have created in her spirit. I will help her return to wholeness and joy.'

"Laka stood. 'And I will bring the fury of the Grandmothers upon her father. He will understand that if he ever again violates his daughter or any woman, we will inform the community and he will face the wrath of all.' Her gentle voice took on a tone of iron. The look on her face told me that this was a fate no man would dare invite upon himself.

"I risked one more question. 'And her mother?'

"Alessa stood. 'This mother has four other children—sons. She has no family to take her in and depends on her husband to feed them. I myself will make sure that she has enough work to support her children, and that there are good men to teach her boys how to honor women.'

"I couldn't think that it would help for me to express any more concerns about just how they were going to go about doing an abortion without gloves or instruments or sterilizing equipment. Obviously, Roseangela had already done a pregnancy test with the Abra powder, so I had to assume they knew what they were doing. I closed my mouth and resolved to watch and learn. These women had never failed to amaze me.

"Even I could sense how the energy around the fire had shifted. There was a sense of peace. Zoila began to sing a heart-rending melody. The other women gathered around Aiki. One knelt behind her and held her shoulders. Others moved to either side of her and held her legs open. Roseangela sat in front of her, holding what looked like a long, slender white bone. She dipped the rounded end of the bone into a bowl and then slid it gently into the girl's vagina. I was sitting behind Rose, and I got up onto my knees so that I could see what she was doing. But she didn't do anything. As soon as she slid the bone in, she removed it with a look of satisfaction.

"'It is done,' Alessa said."

CHAPTER 14

TO THE SKY

I'm afraid my mouth was hanging open. "I don't mean to interrupt you, but I don't really understand what is happening."

"I don't either," Sophie said, shaking her head. "It all seems like a dream."

"It seemed like that to me, too," Socorro said. "It is impossible to understand magic."

"Jane, remember what your mother said about our work? She called that magic, too," Sophie said.

"She was talking about the power of transformation. I think that's the magic in your stories. But what did Alessa mean by 'it is done'? What happened next?" I asked.

Socorro continued. "After we had a simple meal, Alessa announced that it was time to sleep. We all curled up to sleep on pallets made of soft alpaca wool. Mine was quite near Aiki. I was both afraid and curious about how she would fare over the night. I slept deeply and woke, as the others did, with the sun. Alessa came to Aiki and bent over her, giving her instructions to lie back and open her legs to change the cotton pad. That accomplished, Aiki rolled over and went back to sleep.

"Alessa handed the used pad to me and quietly said, 'Look at this and you will understand.'

"Wrapped inside the cotton pad, there was a fully formed twelve-week fetus with a small bit of blood, and the placental and decidual tissue I recognized from my training at Our Lady. I was sleeping right next to her, and she didn't even whimper. The embryo came out intact on the pad.

"Then one of the Grandmothers cried out, 'To the sky or to the land?' In unison, the other women said, 'To the sky.' They laid the pad on the fire and within a moment it had turned to char.

"'Do you see?' Alessa asked me. I saw a lot of things, some that I could hardly believe. I saw how the T'ana herb had worked—I saw that the Grandmothers were willing to take responsibility for a decision Aiki could not make for herself—I saw that this miraculous medicine could change everything about women's experience of abortion. I also saw what I didn't know—

whether it was safe, if the results were always that easy, what it was made of, and if I could get any. But I looked at Alessa and nodded my head.

"'Will you show me more?' I asked.

"'Oh yes,' she answered. 'Alejandro will take Aiki back to her home now. Three more women will come to be with us for this ceremony, and you shall witness how the Grandmothers do our work.'

"Aiki woke up a bit, and they fed her a thick, dark, foul-smelling liquid. It took a bit of prodding, but the girl finally swallowed all of it. I recognized it as *moscocero*. Her eyes lit up, and for the first time, I saw her spirit. We all said goodbye to her, with many kisses and hugs, and a couple of the women helped her back up the path to Alejandro and Pedro because she was already getting sleepy again.

"A few hours later, after we had enjoyed a breakfast of beans and tortillas, Pedro's loud bray signaled that Alejandro had deposited someone at the entry. In a moment, a short, heavyset woman picked her way hesitantly down the walkway, as though she were expecting rattlesnakes.

"'Welcome,' Alessa said, beckoning her down the path. 'You must be Gaby.'

"'Yes,' the woman said, looking frightened. 'I am Gaby.' In spite of her fear, she continued down the walkway. 'My husband said I must come to this place.'

"Concern flashed across Alessa's face, but she composed herself quickly.

"There was food left in some of the pots, and it still smelled delicious.

"'Are you hungry?' Roseangela asked.

"'No. I couldn't eat anything,' Gaby said. 'I am so sick every day. Maybe you can't tell because I am plump, but I have lost weight, I am exhausted, and I cannot work. My husband says I must rid myself of this unwelcome parasite.' Her face scrunched up, and she started to cry.

"'My dear,' Alessa said, putting her arm around the woman's heaving shoulders. 'Do you wish to be here?' she asked.

"'I wish to be anywhere in the universe besides here, but I have no choice,' Gaby whimpered, almost unintelligibly.

"Just then, Pedro brayed again, and two women emerged from the entry and made their way down the path. One was dressed in widow's black. The gray strands in her dark hair made me think she was in her late forties. She said, 'I am Amalia. I have come for your help.'

"The other woman seemed a bit younger, but the deep lines on her face signaled that she had a hard life. She was wearing trousers and a poncho and looked very strong. She said, 'My name is Daniela.'

"Laka walked out to welcome them and drew the three women to sit by her. I was glad the newcomers were sitting with the woman whose very name meant 'gentle.'

"'Come to the fire,' Alessa called out to the Grandmothers. They each stopped whatever they were doing and came to sit around the warm, glowing flames.

"Once we had formed a circle, Alessa began to chant in an otherworldly voice to call in the spirits. The other T'ana women joined in, creating a discordant harmony. They added their drums, rattles, stringed instruments, and whistles, and the result was unlike anything I had heard. As before, the music and singing stopped abruptly, as if the singers obeyed a gesture from an invisible conductor.

"'Welcome to you all.' Alessa was speaking in Spanish again. 'Before we begin, I must be sure that you each understand that the work of the Grandmothers is determined by our ancient commitment to eliciting and strengthening the power and peace that is at the core of each woman we serve. These are the elements that connect us to Mother Earth. As we strengthen them in each individual woman, we strengthen and honor the earth. The process by which we do this is sometimes painful, and always intrusive.' She looked at the three women who had joined us. 'Although you do not know each other now, your lives will soon be inextricably linked, and you will be asked to tap into your own knowing to listen for that core wisdom inside you. If you do not wish to be part of this process, there is no shame, but tell us now, and you will be given the elixir of forgetting and taken back to your home.'

"Gaby was squirming, but she didn't say anything. Daniela looked stoic and said, 'It is my choice to enter into this process.' Amalia just nodded in agreement.

"Alessa took note of the responses and said, 'Very well. It is time to hear your stories. Daniela, will you begin?'

"'Yes. Thank you, Grandmothers, for being here to help us.' Daniela spoke in a strong and steady voice. 'My husband and I have very little, but we are happy. We have four children, whom I love more than my own life. Our youngest is just three years old. He has what they tell me is called Mongolism. I know that he will need me for all the rest of his life, and I am committed to being there for him—for all of them. My husband and I stayed apart for a long time so that we would not risk another child, but we love each other dearly, and we were very sad not to be together. So here I am. I already love this child growing within me, and beg its forgiveness, but I cannot welcome it. I have come here to ask you to send it back to the sky.'

"Roseangela was sitting next to her. She clasped Daniela's hand, and said, 'Daniela, you have told us that you love this life within you. How will you be at peace with ending this life?'

"Daniela smiled at her. 'I believe that the spirit of this child who will not be born will always be a part of me—part of my family. I am sacrificing the opportunity to know this child because of my loyalty to the children I already have. I am sorry to have to make this decision, but I have a deep sense of peace about it.' She held her head high. 'I ask you to help me end this life within me.'

"Roseangela squeezed Daniela's hand again and nodded at Alessa.

"Alessa reached out and threw something on the fire, which caused it to grow and blaze a deep blue. Then she cried out, 'Grandmothers! Consider this story.' The circle grew tighter with each woman's arms encircling the shoulders of the woman next to her. They swayed back and forth rhythmically, murmuring something unintelligible. Just as with the music, they stopped at the same moment. Daniela, Gaby, Amalia, and I were part of the circle, and we continued to move for a moment after they stopped.

"'Grandmothers, I ask for your answers,' Alessa said. One by one, the T'ana women threw something on the fire that changed its color. And one by one they said 'yes.' It was strange, but I felt a strong 'yes' voice inside me, although I was silent.

"Alessa passed something to Veronica. It was a petal from a purple flower—perhaps an orchid. Veronica dropped a grain of something on the petal and offered it to Daniela like the Eucharist. Daniela opened her mouth and swallowed it solemnly."

CHAPTER 15

THERE IS NO EVIL

"Even though this is another country—another culture—I feel as though I know these women. They are the same women who come to us every week," Françoise said.

"What we have in common is more powerful than language or custom," Paulette agreed.

"I want to hear how they worked with the woman who wanted to have a baby. Gaby, was it?" I said. "I've always thought these are the most poignant situations—when a woman wants to have a baby, but something or someone is making it seem impossible."

Socorro smiled. "Alessa worked with Gaby next. She turned to Gaby and said, 'Will you tell us your story?'

"The young woman looked stricken. She hunched up her shoulders and released them. Then she began.

"'I am here because my husband told me I must be here. All my life, I have wanted to be a mother. I have lost three babies late in term, and each time I lost a part of my soul. The doctors cannot tell me why I have lost these babies. They say I might die if I try another time. My mother says there is an evil spirit in my marriage. Against my husband's wishes, I am pregnant again. He is angry with me and has demanded that I come here. He is my husband and I cannot oppose him. But I am devastated to think of doing what he has asked.'

"The painted woman named Zoila shook a feathered rattle to get Gaby's attention.

"'You say your husband is angry? Is there another emotion beneath the anger? A kinder one?' she asked.

"Gaby sighed a long sigh.

"'My husband loves me so much. He is afraid—afraid I will not live through another loss, either physically or spiritually.'

"'And you? What do you think?'

"Gaby began to cry. 'I am confused.'

"In her gentle voice, Luz said, 'Sometimes when we are confused, it is because we know something we do not wish to know.'

"'But I *don't* know.' Gaby said in a small, pitiful voice. She hung her head. 'I don't want to live without a child, but I don't want to die. You have to take this life from me.'

"Alessa said, 'This time as we ponder, I ask that each of you women,' she turned toward Daniela, Amalia, and me, 'summon what is in your heart about this question. Each one will answer.'

"The circle tightened again, and the low thrumming began and ended abruptly, as before. Alessa spoke first. She threw her concoction again, deepening the blue flames, and firmly said 'no.' One by one, the women went around, changing the color of the fire, and each one said 'no.' When they had all spoken, Daniela looked around, as if unsure, and said 'no' in a quiet voice. I became aware of the 'no' in me and spoke it. And Amalia added a soft 'no.' Only Gaby said a plaintive 'yes.'

"Gaby looked frustrated. She stood up and spoke directly to Alessa. 'I was told to come here, and I did as I was told. You can't say no. You *must* do this!' she said, stamping her foot. 'I cannot have a baby, and I cannot end a life. I want to be good. I want to do the right thing.'

"Katia motioned for her to sit down and took Gaby's hands. Even though we were all listening, the softness of her voice made it seem to be an intimate conversation. 'Right and wrong, good and bad, black and white, dark and light. These are the way children see the world—simple, like the two ends of a stick. The choices you need to make now are deeper and older. These choices are like the circle of life itself. Within them are all the layers of contradictions that lie within our most significant life experiences—the grieving and also the sense of relief—the joy and the sorrow, the ending and the beginning, life and death. Some of life's sorrows choose us, and we must simply do our best with them. Sometimes we choose our sorrows—choose with which of them we can stand tall and straight, even though our hearts are aching. This is one of those times. The Grandmothers do not judge what choice you make, we only ask you to make your choice from the heart of a woman, not a little girl who is scared about what is good and bad.'

"'But I don't know *how* to be a woman,' Gaby wailed.

"Katia asked, 'Gaby, how old are you?'

"'I'm twenty-six,' Gaby answered in a petulant voice.

"'How old is that little one who stamped her foot?' Katia asked.

"Gaby looked puzzled for a moment, and said, 'She doesn't seem very grown-up, does she?'

"Katia smiled at her. 'Are there any little girls in your family?'

"Gaby thought for a moment and said, 'My husband's niece is six.'

"'Have you ever seen her have a tantrum?' Katia asked.

"Gaby smiled broadly—recalling a memory. 'Oh yes. Chio is a strong little girl. I have seen her control all the adults with her anger.'

"'Picture her and compare that angry little part of you. Are they alike?'

"'Yes—I think they are the same. Six. That part of me is six years old.'

"'Tell me about yourself at six. How did you wear your hair? What kind of clothes did you wear?'

"'I have a picture of myself at that age. I was a tomboy, so I always had on dungarees and wore my hair in pigtails. I loved to climb trees and play with the boys, and I was just as tough as they were.'

"'Were you a happy child?' Katia asked.

"'Oh yes. I was very happy and always laughing, and I loved to sing.' A shadow passed over Gaby's face. 'But something bad happened.'

"'What happened, love?' Katia asked.

"'My mommy got sick,' Gaby whispered. 'My father said all of us children had to be very quiet or else…or else…'

"'What did he tell you?'

"'My papa said that if we made noise, my mommy would die. It was my job to keep the other children quiet. I took them outside to play every day, even when it was too cold. I did my best, I promise, but sometimes the baby cried loud no matter what I did.'

"'So the baby cried, and that scared you because you didn't want your mommy to die?' Katia asked softly.

"'I didn't want to hurt my mommy, and I wanted to be good. But I was so scared, and I had to be so careful, and my sisters wouldn't listen.'

"'And what happened?' Katia asked.

"'Mommy died,' Gaby said, in a voice so quiet I could almost not hear it.

"'And did little Gaby think it was her fault?'

"'It *was* my fault. My daddy was so mad that he wouldn't even look at me. And I still had to take care of the little girls. There was no one else to do it.'

"'That must have been very hard,' Katia said.

"'Yes. It was very hard.'

"Katia took Gaby's face in her hand and looked deeply into her eyes. She said, 'I must tell you that your mother's death was not Little Gaby's fault—not *your* fault at all. Your father didn't mean to, but he made a mistake when he said that. You were just a little girl, and nothing you did harmed your mommy, and there was nothing you could do to save her. I need you to say that back to me.'

"'My father made a mistake. I didn't harm her, and I couldn't save her.'

"Katia held her gaze for a moment.

"'Grown-up Gaby, what does that little six-year-old girl need?'

"'I don't know.'

"'What if you did know?' Katia asked.

"Gaby paused, then she sighed. 'She needs a hug?' As much a question as an answer.

"'Who could give that to her?' Katia asked.

"'My father?' she asked, hesitantly.

"'Would that comfort her?'

"'No. He is too angry.'

"'Who knows every sorrow she has experienced? Who could love and comfort her?'

"'Hmm. I could? I could.' Gaby said, sounding more certain.

"'Wonderful. Go ahead and do that.' Katia took a very deep breath and waited. 'What does that feel like to you, grown-up Gaby?' she asked.

"At first Gaby didn't say anything. She closed her eyes, and a very sweet smile appeared on her face. 'It feels like a hole inside me is filled.'

"'And how does it feel to the little one?' Katia asked.

"'She feels warm and safe,' Gaby said. 'Safer than she has felt in a very long time.'

"'Good,' Katia said. 'Now, is there anything else this little girl needs?'

"'She needs to be forgiven,' Gaby answered quietly.

"'Who could forgive her?'

"'God?' Gaby said.

"'Wonderful. Which aspect of God? Jesus, or Mary, or one of the T'ana gods?'

"'Could Jesus forgive her?' Gaby asked.

"'Has she ever asked for his forgiveness?' Katia asked.

"'I don't remember.'

"'Gaby, look at me. Now come back to your full adult self. You mentioned Jesus. Tell me about Jesus.'

"'Jesus is the most kind, most understanding, most forgiving of the gods.'

"'Does Jesus know what is in your heart?'

"'Yes. He is always with me.'

"'Was he with you when your momma was sick? Was he with that little Gaby? Does he know how hard you tried to keep your little sisters quiet?'

"Gaby looked perplexed for a moment. Then she said, 'Ye...yes. He knows. But I forgot that he was there.'

"'Ah, I see. A little girl who is working so hard to be good can easily forget. What do you need to know from Jesus?'

"'I need to know if he forgives me.'

"'Good. Go ahead and ask Jesus.'

"'Je...Jesus, do you forgive me for...for letting my baby sister be so loud?'

"'Now, Gaby, take a very deep breath, and lend your voice to Jesus, so that he can answer you. What does Jesus say when you have asked for forgiveness?'

"Gaby took a deep breath as instructed and looked upward as if she were listening to someone. She said, 'He told me that it was not my fault. He said that my mommy was very sick, and it was her time to leave the world. Jesus said she is very happy in Heaven with my grandmother, and that I will see her one day, along with the three babies I have lost.'

"'Does Jesus forgive you?' Katia asked.

"'Yes,' Gaby said, turning a brightened face up toward Katia. 'He does. He says that he forgives me, and that I am good, and losing the babies was not a punishment. They just weren't meant to be in this world. Losing my babies was not my fault.' I was amazed to hear how her voice changed. How it became deeper, strong, and clear.

"'Hmm,' Katia said. 'Grown-up Gaby, how does that feel in your body to hear that from Jesus?'

"Gaby put her arms around herself and started to cry. 'I feel much lighter. The band around my chest is looser. The ache in my stomach is gone.'

"'And what about little Gaby?' How does she feel?'

"Gaby looked surprised. 'She is happy!' she said. 'She is playing with her dolls.'

"'Wonderful. Good work, Gaby. Now that you remember Jesus is always with you, and now that your little girl is happy playing with her dolls, what do you, grown-up Gaby, want to do about being pregnant?'

"Gaby sighed. 'I feel bonded with the life within me. I value my life and my love for my husband, but I will do anything I can to protect this life and to help my husband understand what it means to me.'

"It was clear that something important had shifted. It was the voice of a woman, not a child.

"Katia said, 'You are taking on this risk with your full heart?'

"Gaby answered, 'Yes. With my full heart.'

"Alessa stood up and spoke to the group. 'Grandmothers, we do not need another vote. Gaby, you have spoken as a woman. You have found the courage to say how much you want this new life. There is no evil spirit in your marriage, just a small muscle that needs some help. We can help you have your baby safely if that is your wish. We will use a loop of fine silk thread to close the mouth of your womb until this baby is ready to be born, and give you medicine to ease your sickness. One of us will be with you at birthing time to protect you in every way we know how. If the Mother of the World wills it, you will be safe. And you will give birth to this baby, not as a little girl, but as the strong woman that every child deserves to have as its mother.'

"Gaby was sobbing, but we could see the joy in her eyes. She could hardly speak for her tears, but she was saying, 'Thank you, thank you, thank you.'"

CHAPTER 16

TO THE HEAVENS WITH LOVE

Back in the kitchen at Our Lady, Paulette interrupted. "But that's a McDonald's Cerclage procedure! I read about it in a medical journal. An Australian doctor devised it a few years ago. I am surprised that they even know about it, but did they know how to do it?"

Socorro smiled. "The more I learn about these women, the more I am amazed. I was also aware of this procedure to put a temporary stitch in the cervix, but I had never seen one until Alessa showed me. According to her, the procedure goes back in their customs hundreds of years."

Françoise stood up. "I am overwhelmed. Can we take a break?" she asked. "I need to stretch my legs, and I'm going to want lunch soon."

Socorro stood up, too. "This is as good a place to pause as any."

Sophie asked, "But how can we stop before we discover what happens to the other women?"

Socorro smiled and said, "I promise you will learn what happens after we have eaten. I realize this story is too long. Are you all falling asleep?"

"Falling asleep? No! I am right there with them, throwing dried herbs onto the fire!" Françoise said, chuckling at her own little joke.

I nodded. "I am completely fascinated, but also hungry. Let's keep these wonderful women in our hearts until after lunch."

Paulette and Socorro asked if they could help prepare the food, but Sophie and Françoise shooed them outdoors. As the younger women put on their coats, they were already deep in a heated discussion about modern versus traditional medicine.

We had a lovely Niçoise salad for lunch, with creamy éclairs for dessert, and small talk, which we all needed as a reprieve from the intensity of Socorro's tale. After we ate, I took a short nap, while Françoise, Sophie, and the girls went outside into the garden. At about 2:00 p.m., we were ready to start again.

"All fortified?" Socorro asked, smiling.

"As long as we have wine when the sun goes down," Sophie said.

Socorro continued the story.

"The next to speak was Amalia. She said, 'I am ashamed after hearing Gaby, but as much as she wants a baby, I do not. My husband worked in a mine. He was killed two months ago when a shaft caved in. I didn't realize I was pregnant when he died. My children are already grown, with children of their own, and I do not want to start a new family by myself. I have worried about this and prayed about it, and I am certain it is best to say goodbye to this spirit and return it to the gods. I have no bad intent, only the knowledge that this is right for me. But I am sad to lose what is left of my dear husband, and I sometimes doubt myself.'

"Laka was sitting beside her and asked, 'Have you prayed to miscarry?'

"Amalia looked embarrassed. 'Yes.'

"'How would this be different if you had a miscarriage?' Laka asked.

"Amalia reddened again. 'I would not be the one at fault for taking life,' she said, her head down.

"'Ah, yes. Fault. Who would, then, be at fault?'

"'If it were a miscarriage, no one would be at fault. It would be God, or the Fates,' Amalia said.

"Laka smiled. 'Throughout our history, women have been the gatekeepers of life. Women have decided who will eat when there is not enough food—how to mete out shelter, and medical care. *Women*, not the Fates. It is our responsibility to decide when and whether to bring a new life into the world through our bodies. Men are rewarded for taking life when they put on their official uniforms, but women are not permitted to end even an incompletely formed life—even in the most responsible way. After all, abortion *is* taking life, isn't it?'

"'Yes. That is what makes it so hard. I'm not sure I can do that.'

"'You are the only one who can decide. What does it mean to you to end this life? You mentioned saying goodbye to the spirit…if you have an abortion, where will that spirit go?' Laka asked.

"Amalia looked up, as if the answer were in the clouds. 'I don't know for certain. In my Catholic faith, I was taught that an innocent spirit would go to Limbo if it was not baptized. My T'ana faith says that such an innocent soul would go back to the gods—perhaps to be born at another time,' Amalia said.

"Laka asked, 'What do *you* believe?'

"'I can't imagine an innocent one would be punished or kept away from the gods.' Amalia sighed.

"'So how would you feel if that spirit returned to the gods? Can you harm a spirit?' Laka asked next.

"Amalia was quiet for a moment. 'I don't think so. Our spirits are eternal—they are like water. They never disappear, but change form—like rain, ocean, fog, or ice.'

"Laka allowed Amalia to take some breaths. She asked, 'Do you need forgiveness from anyone before you take this action?'

"'I didn't think so,' Amalia said. 'But now I wonder if I should ask forgiveness from my husband for not having this child.'

"'Let's speak to his spirit and see.'

"Amalia hesitated. Her face paled with fear.

"Laka smiled gently and said, 'You can do it. Take your time.'

"'Cisco, I miss you every day. My life is not the same without you. I had the shock of losing you, and then the shock of learning that I am pregnant. I do not want to have a baby now—without you—at my age. I need to be certain you can forgive me,' Amalia said. There was a catch in her voice.

"Laka took her hands. 'Now, allow Cisco to use your voice. What does he want to say to you?'

"Amalia took a deep breath and closed her eyes. 'He says, "I miss you every day, too. I am safe and without any worries. I love you beyond measure, and I understand your choice. You do not need my forgiveness—there is no sin here, only love."'

"Laka smiled at her. 'How do you feel?' she asked.

"'I am so glad. That was weighing on my heart. I feared he would blame me,' Amalia said.

"'Blame is a very difficult thing, isn't it?' Laka asked. 'It leaves you a helpless victim.'

"'I'm not blaming anyone else,' Amalia said defensively. 'It was my doing. I lay with my husband. I thought I was past the age I could become pregnant.'

"'You become a victim whether you are blaming someone else or blaming yourself,' Laka said, gently, but firmly.

"Amalia was silent for a moment. 'You are right. I *have* been blaming myself. The words repeat over and over in my head: *Stupid woman, stupid woman.*'

"'I realize it sounds like your own voice,' Laka said. 'But you are not cruel. If it were not yours, whose voice could it be?'

"Amalia raised her head as if startled. 'It is my father's voice!' she said. 'He berated my mother over and over when I was a child. *Stupid woman, stupid woman*—he said it just like that!'

"'Do you want to give a seat in your mind to your angry father? A throne, in fact?'

"Amalia laughed, 'No. I don't want him to be there at all. He died many years ago, and I hoped I was done with him.'

"'It is simple to begin to remove the power of the old voices you carry within you. First—you must notice the voices are there. When we give someone a place of honor in our head, we often listen to their words without even realizing it,' Laka said. 'We listen, but we don't recognize it is not our own voice.'

"'You are right. I had no idea that I was treating myself the way my father treated my mother.'

"'The second thing to do is to remove the venom from the pit viper—in other words, to become impervious to the power of the words. Each time you notice the phrase *stupid woman,* try saying, "Thank you, Father, for sharing your opinion." Don't argue with him or agree with him—just thank him in a detached way. That allows you to listen for your own voice.'

"Amalia looked determined and repeated, 'Thank you, Father, for sharing your opinion.'

"Laka smiled. 'Exactly. And when he is saying *stupid woman*, what would you prefer to hear?'

"At first, Amalia shook her head, unsure what to answer. Then she smiled and said, 'I would like to hear, "Brave woman. Smart woman. Strong woman. Good woman."'

"'And who would say that?'

"'I would say it *myself*,' Amalia beamed. 'It would be my own true voice.'

"'My dear, can you tell me again what you want?'

"'I want to send the spirit of this baby to the heavens with love.'"

CHAPTER 17

EARTH OR SKY

"Do you see what I mean, Jane? They are doing your work. The work of Our Lady," Socorro said.

I nodded. "Of course, it is not *my* work. Or even *our* work. It is the ancient, sacred work of marrying the head and the heart. In some cultures, it would be seen as marrying the masculine and the feminine—the *hieros gamos*—the joining of power and conscience that humans have depicted for centuries. At Our Lady, we recognize that each person has both active and receptive features. We are helping women honor both parts of themselves in these sacred choices. It is really stunning to hear how these Wise Women interpret that ancient knowledge. What did they do next?"

Socorro continued, "Laka turned to Alessa and nodded. 'We are ready to hear from the Grandmothers.'

"Alessa cried out again, 'Grandmothers! Consider this story!' and the circle grew tighter with each woman once again encircling the shoulders of the woman next to her. They swayed back and forth again, whispering incantations. As with the music, they stopped at the same moment. Daniela, Gaby, Amalia, and I somehow stopped with them this time, as if we had become part of the tribe.

"'Grandmothers, I ask for your answers,' Alessa said. She threw her herb on the fire. One by one, the T'ana women each threw their herbs on the fire, changing its color. And one by one they said 'yes.' And this time, Daniela, Gaby, Amalia, and I each added our 'yes' without hesitation. Alessa passed the same kind of beautiful orchid petal that Daniela had received to Veronica. She added one grain of the sacred herb and proffered it to Amalia. Amalia nodded and swallowed it.

"The whistles, rattles, drums, and stringed instruments the women played started up again, as if to signal the end of our ceremony. When it was quiet, the women started getting up and bustled about, putting things away and starting to prepare dinner. Gaby, Daniela, Amalia, and I still sat by the fire with our arms around each other's shoulders. It seemed that we were not able to move. Laka knelt next to us. 'What you have experienced today will bind the

four of you throughout your lives,' she said. 'You will find each other when
you need help, as the Wise Women depend on each other.' She looked directly
at Gaby. 'Alejandro is here if you would like to go back to your village now,'
she said, gently.

"'No!' Gaby said, in a voice more powerful than I thought she could mus-
ter. 'I want to stay while my sisters complete their journeys here.' She looked
defiant.

"'Good,' Laka said, smiling. 'Good. Now you must find a way to release
each other's bodies, while still being connected to each other's spirits.' She
laughed in a loving way and stepped away to work on supper.

"Gaby took the lead. 'You all saw what they did with their instruments.
The music made everything begin and end. What if we use our voices?' She
began to hum a sweet melody that we all knew, *La palomita*—the little dove.
We blended our voices together—and made our own little circle, holding
hands. After a few moments, we stopped all together, just as the Wise Women
had. We laughed and hugged each other, and broke our connection, each going
off to seek out the Wise Woman we needed to talk with.

"I found Alessa setting the table. It was a most mundane, female thing to
be doing, yet I could feel her power.

"'My dear, I know you have many questions,' she said, handing me some
spoons to set out. 'But please, be with all of this until we are complete tomorrow. The other women will leave in the afternoon and you will have another
full day of training, as I promised. I will answer all your questions.' She
hugged me like a proud mother and went off to get more napkins.

"We feasted that night. Veronica must have given Gaby some medicine for
her stomach, because she was voracious. She, Daniela, Amalia, and I all ate
as though we had climbed a mountain. After dinner, we were exhausted. I
wondered if the hallucinogen, *moscocero,* would be used, but realized that
there was more to our story that needed to be completed.

"We bedded down early—Laka, Veronica, and Katia slept near us, but *we
four*, as I had come to think of us, cocooned together. We slept deeply and
woke with the sun. In the morning, Laka came to Daniela to change her pad,
and as with Aiki, there was a fully formed embryo on the pad—the size of a
raspberry. Laka asked Daniela if she wanted to say goodbye. Daniela took the
pad in her hand and mouthed some words. Laka got the attention of all the
other women, who, in one powerful voice, asked of Daniela, 'Earth or sky?'
In a firm voice, Daniela answered, 'Sky.' Laka beckoned Daniela to come
close to the fire and gestured to her to place the pad on the blaze, where it
burned quickly. With a pair of tongs, Laka swiftly reached into the fire and
brought out a coal. She instructed Daniela to open her robe, and touched her
with the ember above her heart, leaving a small burn. Daniela looked shocked,
but put her hand to her chest and closed her eyes.

"'As long as you have this scar, you will honor the life returned to the One. Because of the *moscocero*, you will not remember all that has happened here. But each time you see the scar, you will remember your love and courage and goodness. When the scar has faded, you will turn your face toward the future, but this life will always look down upon you and protect you.'

"Next, Katia approached Amalia to change her pad. The almost translucent ten-week embryo was about the size of a shrimp. Katia asked her, 'Earth or sky?'

"Amalia hesitated, then answered, 'Earth,' and held the pad with the embryo against her heart. Katia produced a spade and instructed Amalia to put her left hand out. Katia drew the sharp edge of the spade across Amalia's palm, and a brilliant red line appeared. Amalia gasped but didn't cry out. Katia clasped the hand that was bleeding and held it very tight. 'As long as you have this scar, you will honor the life returned to the One. Because of the *moscocero*, which we will give you, you will not remember all that has happened here. But each time you see the scar, you will feel your love and courage and goodness. When the scar has faded, you will turn your face toward the future, but this nascent life will always look down upon you and protect you.'

"Katia wound a clean cloth around her hand and beckoned to Amalia to follow. Amalia turned and looked at us, resolute, but with tears in her eyes. I got up to go with them, but Laka touched my arm and shook her head. Amalia told us later that she had buried the embryo—her baby that was not to be—in the consecrated ground of the cloister built atop ground sacred to the T'ana.

"Amalia seemed at peace.

"Gaby was the happiest of all of us. Relief shone on her face. Alessa turned to her and said, 'Now it is time to give you a circle of hope.'

"Gaby looked alarmed and almost pulled away.

"'Don't worry, child. We will give you medicine to block any pain as we put a tiny stitch in your cervix.'

"Gaby stepped forward as bravely as she could. Privacy wasn't a part of these proceedings—in fact, the opposite. It was as if we were all connected like an enormous Spanish cedar. In the Andean cloud forest, the Cedrela appears to be individual trees, but underground they are connected by an intricate network. We all gathered around as Veronica gave Gaby a drink of something that must have been bitter, because she made a face after she swallowed it. Alessa had Gaby lie down on a pallet, and Gaby asked if Daniela and Amalia and I could be with her.

"Alessa said, 'Yes, you two sit by her. But I need Socorro to be here with me.' She nodded to her shoulder. I gave Gaby an "I'm sorry, good luck" glance and knelt behind Alessa. Gaby already seemed to have fallen asleep. Daniela held her hand. She didn't seem worried, so I decided not to be. Alessa laid out instruments like none I had ever seen before. I don't know how they were fabricated, but I would guess some kind of alloy of gold and silver. The instruments glistened in the sun like jewelry. Next to them sat a spool of thread—perhaps from the Peruvian silkworm, Saturniidae, that we had studied in one of my classes. The thread was a brilliant red, no doubt dyed with carmine from the cochineal bug.

"In place of a speculum, Alessa inserted a cone that held the vagina open. It looked like the one the veterinarian put around my dog's neck one time. With the lantern, I could see well enough to tell that she had threaded the silk onto a needle. In a few deft movements, she encircled the cervical os and removed the cone.

"'She will sleep through breakfast, but wake in time to say goodbye.'

"We left Gaby sleeping on the pallet, a peaceful look on her face. Amalia kissed her on the forehead.

"I thought about what Laka had said about us being bound together—and wondered if we would remember each other...after...if *I* would recognize *them,* but they wouldn't know each other. It seemed that it would be unspeakably sad.

"We had breakfast of avocado, sausage, and eggs. Some of the Wise Women told stories and made jokes that I would never have imagined would come from their somber and august group. The energy was like that of any group of human beings who has finished a piece of daunting work together—raising a barn, bringing in a crop, birthing a baby, burying the dead. After breakfast, we had to say goodbye. My heart was breaking, and I already missed these women who had been strangers to me only two days ago.

"Laka said, 'Don't worry, dear one. You will see them again. You will be in each other's lives forever.'

"'Will you remind them of that too?' I asked. 'They are afraid that they will lose each other just when we have all found each other.'

"'Of course. Trust us,' Laka answered.

"I was skeptical, but I did my best to believe her. Amalia, Daniela, and Gaby had hugs and kisses and funny little taunts from women who had been formidable and a bit scary the day before. They laughed and cried and clung to each other. Then it was time for the *moscocero.*

"'My dears,' Alessa began. 'We have been on the most powerful of human journeys together—the journey of life and death—the journey to the heart. I want to assure you,' she looked pointedly at me, 'that you will never truly lose each other, even with the forgetfulness of the draught you are about to take. We honor your courage and love, and we thank you for trusting us. This elixir of peace and forgetfulness is as ancient as the hills behind us. It allows us to heal women without fearing the laws of men, and it will strengthen the internal connection between your heart and your head.' Alessa motioned to one of the other women to bring a small pitcher and tiny cups, which she handed to

Amalia, Gaby, and Daniela. She filled the cups with the thick greenish-brown liquid—the *moscocero*. With her right hand, she made a motion that I interpreted as some kind of blessing, and instructed them to drink. It was as thick as mud, with an unpleasant taste like tobacco and old coffee, but each of the women drank it down without hesitation. Well, it took Gaby two tries and another bad face, but she drank it all. They each turned their cups upside down to show that they had finished it, and an uncharacteristic whoop rose up from the Wise Women. It was a morning full of surprises. The whole group helped Amalia, Daniela, and Gaby carry their belongings through the cloister to Alejandro, who was asleep under a tree. Alessa woke him, and he scurried around, bringing Pedro and the wagon to the front of the building. I confess that I couldn't imagine how he was going to manage to get them all home, but he was able to pile the belongings on the back of the burro and load all three women into the buggy. The women waved to us as they started down the road. Before they were out of sight, they were folding in on each other for the sleep that was coming.

"And then my education began."

CHAPTER 18

WHAT IS THE POINT?

"I had even more questions than you do, Jane," Socorro laughed. "But now that all the women in the story are safe, I need to use the bathroom."

"Thank goodness," Françoise said, laughing herself. "I was going to plead age and infirmity for the same need!"

I silently thanked Claude for giving us enough plumbing for a building full of women. We scattered to the various bathrooms. By the time we got back to the table, Françoise had cleared off the dishes, and Sophie poured our favorite Bordeaux and put a chicken in the oven for dinner.

I sat across from Socorro, ready to begin my cross-examination.

She said, "Jane, I realize I have talked non-stop since this morning. You can ask me your questions if you must, but I think you'll find that my training with Alessa will cover everything. Are you willing to listen a bit longer?"

As frustrated as I was, I was also delighted that the little girl I had known had grown up. I nodded in silent acquiescence, so Socorro continued.

"Alessa and I sat together with our backs against large stones warmed by the sun in what was once the garden. I began by asking, 'If they take *moscocero*, what is the point of all the talking? What is the point of the scar?'

"Alessa got comfortable by putting a cushion behind her back and wrapping a shawl around her shoulders. 'The *moscocero* makes them forget most of what has happened, but there are some memories that are deeper than even it can touch. When we are asking questions, the entire group is casting their intention for the lessons to go deep and for the process to be remembered. We give them a scar to have something tangible to connect with their memories—to ground them. It is a badge—a symbol of a time when they were courageous and good. A time when they loved enough to risk. *Moscocero* doesn't entirely erase their memory of each other. This closeness is the historical bond of woman to woman. It can never truly be lost, only temporarily forgotten. So when they encounter each other in the future—and we will make sure they do—they will experience an immediate sense of kinship and trust.'

"I thought about the events of the morning. 'Shouldn't you prepare them to see the embryo? I have seen this before, but they haven't. Aren't they sometimes…?'

"Alessa interrupted me. 'Aren't they afraid? Dear one, this is what has been growing inside them. It is blood of their blood. Most of these women have had children. They work with animals; they help their sisters who miscarry; they bury the dead. They know of the blood mysteries. They know what an embryo looks like. They know the smells of birth and death, and they are not afraid. They understand that they are asking us to take life. If we have done our work well, we only do that when they have come to terms with what that means for them.'

"I felt chastened, but I continued with my questions. 'Is the medicine you give safe? And why was it put inside Aiki, but given to Amalia and Daniela to swallow?'

"Alessa pulled out a small box she had carried with her. Inside was what looked like coarse salt. 'This is the *Corazon de Gracia*. We create it from plants that grow in the mountains—and it is a recipe unknown outside our healing circle.'"

I couldn't stop myself from interrupting. "*What* do they call it?"

Socorro laughed. "I know. It is too much of a coincidence to believe. They call it *Corazon de Gracia*—Heart of Grace."

I must have looked perplexed. "How can that be?" I said, more of a statement than a question.

"All of this is somehow connected to the work we are doing, Jane," Socorro said. "I don't understand it, but, as you'll hear, it is as if they know about Our Lady of Perpetual Grace—as though we are all part of a family. I'm almost finished with the story, then you can ask all your questions."

I reluctantly agreed to let her continue, but my mind was racing.

Socorro resumed her story. "Alessa explained, 'Where there is no consent to intercourse, the medicine must be inserted, as you saw. But when there is consent, *Corazon* is taken by mouth. We use just one or two grains. I have never seen any medical problem with an abortion in the twenty years I have been giving this care. Once, a woman was brought to us when she was already very sick with a cancer. When the pregnancy was removed, she was strengthened. Perhaps the *Corazon de Gracia* made her better, or just the fact that her body no longer had to fight the cancer and also do the monumental job of supporting a new life. When a plant is failing, we often cut off the top leaves so that it can put all its energy into strengthening its roots—it may be that her improvement was like that.'

"'What about Gaby?' I asked.

"'I'm glad you got to see that,' Alessa answered. 'I am friends with her grandmother, so I had learned about her sorrows. As she shared, Gaby's mother died when she was young—seven or eight years old. She had to become a mother to her two younger sisters, so part of her grew up too soon, and another part never grew up at all.'

"'Will it last? Will she continue to feel like a woman and not a little girl?'

"Alessa sighed. 'The answer is complicated. It can last, but only as a possibility. Gaby will need to continue to choose it—or not. Intentionality and awareness are key to all healing.'

"'But you agreed to help her keep the baby.'

"'We do our best to allow the woman to choose what she most deeply wants. This talking magic is not the same as our drinks or spells. It is an imperfect magic of relationship—a magic of risking—a magic of trust, a magic of the mystery of the blood.'

"'I have seen this kind of magic before, at a place called Our Lady of Perpetual Grace, in France.'

"'You may be surprised, but we are aware of this place—and your friend Miss Smith,' Alessa said."

Françoise gasped, and Sophie and I both said, "That's impossible." She said it in French and I said it in English.

I followed up. "Really, Socorro. That can't be. There has to be some logical explanation."

Socorro shook her head. "Honestly I don't know, Jane. The best I can say is that there is no logic in magic. I didn't even ask Alessa to explain, because I knew she would just give me an inscrutable answer. But it did make me think about our work in a different way. That it is not just you here at Our Lady, or me and Paulette wanting to provide something in our countries. Our work is as old as time. Women have always needed people like us, and maybe we have always been here, speaking different languages and wearing different clothes, but somehow part of an ancient sisterhood."

Sophie smiled. "Socorro, when did you become so wise?"

Paulette rolled her eyes at the thought of her old friend as wise.

Françoise said, "Socorro is wise, and Jane, apparently you have become internationally famous." We all laughed.

"Wise or not, I did get to ask her more questions," Socorro continued. "I thought about some of the women I met during our training at Our Lady and asked, 'Do any women refuse to answer your questions? Do you ever say no?'

"Alessa replied, 'Not often. The talking magic usually leads the woman to her most honest choice. We stay true to our values. We do not wish to trick anyone, so we share our mission. Each woman chooses whether to go on this journey with us. It is very painful to be with a woman who is too frightened or too wounded or too angry to do the work of finding her own resolution and wholeness. When we are skillful, we intuit whether a woman needs us to bring tenderness, boundaries, fire, or intrusion in order to open her heart. Sometimes we fail. The most challenging ones for me are the women who are so angry. Even when I am aware it stems from a wound, I am not good with hostility. I turn to Zoila to work with those women,' she said. 'She is not afraid of anger. When we fail, we give them *moscocero*, and they return to their lives.'

"'They give birth? Even though they are not resolved?'

"'My dear, I am sorry to remind you that most babies are born to women who are not fully resolved about having them. Only the alternative of having an abortion creates a true choice.' I was surprised to see tears in her eyes. 'I do this work because it is my belief that each of us longs to be whole. Did I remember to say that to you? *This* is our work. Not abortion, or birth—wholeness.'

"'You have spoken many times about the mystery of the blood. What does that mean?'

"'In English you would say blood mysteries—the experiences of women's daily lives in which they bleed, but do not die. This phenomenon makes women either magic or dangerous in the eyes of men, depending on the culture and time in history. Abortion is one of those mysteries, which is another reason it is so hidden and is made illegal in so many places. Women, in our natural state, appear to threaten men. We are sadly aware of the witch burnings in America. There have been many such massacres of women all over the planet. Sometimes I wonder how it can be that they do not see our love?'

"Then I asked her about the McDonald's Cerclage.

"'That's what the men are calling it? I'm surprised. We call it a circle of hope.'

"'Why are you surprised?' I asked.

"'I'm surprised they called it a circle of any kind, since men don't like circles. They prefer straight lines. I'm not at all surprised that they named it for a man. After all, they have named some of the parts of our *bodies* after themselves—so why not their little techniques? As you are aware from your study of medicine, the tubes that extend from our ovaries are named after Gabrielis Falloppius, the glands that lubricate our vaginas are named for Caspar Bartholin the Younger, our hymens are named after the Greek God of marriage, and the space between our uterus and rectum is called the pouch of Douglas! It is no different from Columbus, who acted as though he had discovered something that was already there and well known to its many inhabitants.'

"I was surprised to hear such acrimony from the usually serene Alessa. So, that brings me to the end of my story. And you are still bursting with questions," Socorro laughed.

"Do you know what it is? How this stuff—this *Corazon de Gracia*—works?" I asked.

"My classmates who are in chemistry analyzed it, but they couldn't figure out how to synthesize it. When progesterone is present, as it is in pregnancy, the herb acts as," she glanced down at a piece of paper she had removed from her case, "a competitive progesterone receptor agonist. That means it blocks the receptors for progesterone, so the pregnancy—the embryo or fetus—dies. It also contains some chemical that causes uterine contractions that expel the tissue and makes the cervix soft and slightly dilated. Because of the dilation, the expulsion of tissue is very quick and easy and virtually painless. The embryo is passed overnight without the woman even knowing. And there is very little bleeding at the time, although the woman continues to have bleeding like a period for the following week or two as her hormones go back to normal—just as in a regular abortion."

"I'm not sure I understand the implications of how to use this," I said, shaking my head. "If we were to have this, we'd give the medication to women, then monitor the tissue that is expelled to be sure it matches the estimated length of pregnancy. But heck—if the powder—this Abra works so accurately, there isn't any reason to be uncertain about the length of pregnancy, is there? We could donate our toads to a laboratory in Paris." Sophie's face told me she would miss her little froggie pals. "I guess if we are concerned that the abortion is not complete, then and only then do we do a siphon or a D&C? It is abortion without the need for instruments—abortion by medication."

"But does it work? I mean, is it guaranteed to work?" Françoise asked.

"They only use it up to fourteen weeks, and for those pregnancies, it appears to work every time," Socorro answered. "I have watched the Wise Women use it on about two dozen women, and I have used it in my own practice on about another dozen. I have seen no pain, no unusual bleeding, no retained tissue, and no complications. I haven't used the siphon, let alone a curette, since my introduction to their medication. Obviously, I need to remain off the radar of the authorities. I know Alessa will give me *moscocero* if I want to give it to my patients to keep me safe from the law by making them forget me. But I haven't decided if I am going to."

We were all quiet. In my career, I had experienced one great leap forward more than a dozen years before, when my colleague in the Navy, Dr. Nick, crafted a siphon apparatus that made abortion much simpler, safer, and faster. But this seemed to be altogether another kind of advancement. From where I sat, it just seemed like magic. Even so, it was difficult to imagine that it could replace our time-tested methods.

"Do you think you'll see any of them again?" Paulette asked. "The other women?"

"This whole thing happened just a couple of months ago, and I have already seen Gaby. She has registered with me for her obstetric care."

"That's wonderful," Sophie said.

"I think it was probably Alessa's way of being sure there were no questions about the cerclage," Socorro answered.

I asked the obvious question. "Did she know who you were?"

"She didn't seem to remember me, but we had a very nice rapport," Socorro answered, smiling. "She lives in Cusco, so we are neighbors. I don't know where Amalia and Daniela live, but I feel confident that I will see them again."

"Would you ever tell them about how you first met?" Sophie asked.

"I don't think they'd believe me," Socorro said, laughing lightly. "But Alessa told me that it was my decision."

"So, is there some kind of catch with this magic?" Paulette asked.

"The first and most difficult 'catch,' as you put it, is that I am not in control of the supply. The T'ana healing women formulate it from some combination of mountain herbs. I don't know where they get it, or how they make it, and they are not interested in telling me. They are very guarded about all their work. The only reason they even talked with me is because of my mother. For years, people have come trying to exploit them. But they trust me, so they have helped me acquire the old convent I told you about in Cusco, where I watched them work with Gaby, Amalia, and Daniela. Of course, it is called *Convento de Nuestra Señora de la Gracia Perpetua*," she said with a smile.

"That is wonderful," I said, amazed at the whole story. "I can hardly believe it. And how can the name of this magic herb be so similar to the name of our convent?"

"How indeed," Socorro answered. "This magic was obviously destined to come to you, Jane." She looked triumphant and then said, "The T'ana have asked me to bring these herbs to you. There will be enough of all these magic medicines to provide abortions in France and in Italy for years to come. That is what is in the suitcases you were teasing me about."

"You brought us *suitcases full*?" Françoise asked.

"They have been making this for decades. Alessa told me that there was a foretelling—an omen—that a priestess would come who would need it. Don't laugh, Paulette," she said, pushing her good friend's shoulder, "Yes, they think of me as a priestess. But now it's your turn."

We refilled our drinks and got comfortable to listen to Paulette's stories.

CHAPTER 19

TITO *GARDINO?*

"Oh, Socorro. This is so exciting. I have nothing magical to compare," Paulette said.

Socorro smiled. "None of this magic is from me. I am just the messenger. Now we want to know what *you* are up to."

Paulette blushed and said, "Well, first, I am engaged." She held out her hand so we could admire the beautiful pear-shaped diamond. We all gave her joyful congratulations.

"You never wrote about anyone special," Socorro protested. "Is it the Greek boy you liked last year?"

"No. Gilberto is one hundred percent Italian. It is because of him that I found a convent. And because of him that I think we can make it all work."

"All right," I said. "Tell us the story, Paulette, and don't leave anything out."

She began. "When I got home after we were here for our medical training, I looked for opportunities to help with miscarriages and any other gynecological procedures scheduled in the hospital where I worked. No one considered that a woman might need an opportunity to talk about a hysterectomy, or breast cancer, or even birth. I tried coming to work early and staying late, but even the patients found it strange for a nurse to be asking about anything more than their bowel movements. At first, I was very discouraged. Then, by chance, I worked with a young woman who was sitting under a tree outside the hospital, weeping inconsolably. Her name was Camilla. She was a Palermo University student who contracted syphilis as a result of rape. After some prodding, she told me what had happened and said she was going to be damned to hell. Although her issue wasn't abortion, she suffered from so much of the same kind of self-doubt and shame we talked about in our abortion training. Thankfully, penicillin cured her illness. I helped her see that the shame belonged to the rapist, not to her. We met under that tree and talked several times, until she really seemed to believe that none of it was her fault, and that she had committed no sin. We became friends, and when one of her classmates was emotionally distraught over a breakup, Camilla brought her to me to talk.

"Within six months, there were eight of us meeting every month under that tree to talk about our lives. One of the girls had a copy of *Le Deuxième Sexe*— *The Second Sex*. We held a study group to translate it into Italian, and we passed it around until the pages fell out. Within a year, Camilla had formed an organization available to give help to any girl at the University. We called it *Le Donne*—the women. But it was Camilla's brother, Gilberto, who changed everything.

"When I first met him I didn't pay much attention. He was just Camilla's older brother—dropping off extra food or sweets for her. He had graduated and had already opened his own engineering company. He and I found ourselves sitting outside Camilla's dorm room a few times waiting for her, and we got to talking about our lives and our dreams. After a few months, I felt I could tell him everything."

Socorro began to protest.

"Don't worry. I didn't say a thing about any of you. But I told him about my dream of a place where women could come and be safe from the centuries of judgment against them for daring to want their own lives. He agreed with me completely. His dream was of a place where he could use his engineering skills to care for the world instead of exploiting it. He had some ideas I had never heard of—using old technology like windmills to create power—creating a kind of Garden of Eden without smoke and noise. Then he mentioned a place he had heard about. It was a *'paese fantasma'*—a ghost town. The only way to get there was to hike up a steep mountain. There are many places like this in Italy—towns that were deserted after earthquakes or other natural disasters made them uninhabitable. This one, *Città dei Miracoli*—City of Miracles—was completely intact. The inhabitants left when the nearby mine was depleted. The houses, shops, and convent were in perfect order. The minute I heard the word 'convent,' I had to go. We made the hike into a picnic and had a perfect day. It took three hours to hike up to the town. I felt as though I were in a film. I kept expecting to see you, Jane, or Françoise or Sophie coming out the door of the beautiful stone cloister.

"Gilberto showed me the broken tracks that once sent ore down from the mine to the railway station and explained that it was largely run by gravity— like a huge dumbwaiter. It was hard to picture our guests going up and down in ore-cars, but I had the basic idea.

"Halfway back down, we stopped for some water and I talked honestly about my vision for the convent. Without giving your names or locations, I told him the basics of what you were doing. He was very excited and wanted to help.

"My relationship with him was serious. When he proposed, I said yes." She turned to Socorro. "That's why I didn't write to you about it. I wanted to tell you in person."

"Oh, my dear, I am so glad you did." Socorro hugged her. "Gilberto will be your husband and Camilla will be your sister. I have the Wise Women. I am so glad you don't have to do this work alone."

"Once we got back to town, we started making plans. Of course, abortion is illegal in Italy, as it is in Peru. There is the added anti-abortion authority of the Holy See. So Gilberto had the idea of harnessing the power of the only organization that inspires more fear and awe than the Catholic Church—the Cosa Nostra—you know, the name for the Sicilian Mafia. Our brass sign reads:

Convento di Nostra Signora della Grazia Perpetua
Proprietà privata di Tito Gardino
Solo ospiti invitati
Omertà

This translates to:

Convent of Our Lady of Perpetual Grace
Private Property of Tito Gardino
Open Only by Invitation
Under the Protection of Omertà

Françoise sputtered, "Tito *Gardino*?"
Sophie looked confused. "The American gangster?"
"I wish you wouldn't use that word. But, yes. He went to America when he was just a teenager. Palermo and all around Sicily is where the Cosa Nostra was founded. Tito is a local boy who made good—or bad, depending on how you see it."

"What exactly does the word *omertà* mean?" Socorro interrupted.

"It signifies that the place is protected by a code of silence." Paulette said. "No one with half a brain would talk about it, especially not to the authorities."

"Well, that might be a clever way to keep people out, but who actually owns the town?" I asked.

"*Tito* owns the town. Hence, he owns the convent."

"Don't you see that as a bit of a problem?" Sophie asked.

"Tito's favorite sister died of an illegal abortion just after he left for America. He has never forgiven himself for not being there to protect her. He is 100% in favor of what we are doing, and he is proud of being more powerful than the Pope."

"But..." Françoise began.

"If you are asking whether I have a problem with the convent that will provide illegal abortions being owned by a mobster, I guess I don't. Italy is a small country—everyone knows one another's business. The only way to do something in private is to be protected."

"But..." I began.

"You must let me tell the whole story!" Paulette protested. "Gardino has three children in America. His fourth, a son named Antonio who took his mother's last name, still lives in Italy. Antonio and Gilberto were roommates in college, and now they are partners in the engineering firm. He has nothing to do with his father's business, but he is totally supportive of the mission of the convent. Antonio persuaded his father to donate the entire town to El Donne as a tax write-off, and *El Convento di Nostra Signora Della Grazia Perpetua* has been granted a lease for 1,000 lira per year in perpetuity."

"How many dollars is that?" I asked.

"Less than $2.00," she said.

Socorro stood up and clapped. "Paulette, you have outdone my story entirely. That's amazing."

The rest of us were sitting with our mouths open.

"You'll have a whole *town*?" Françoise asked.

Paulette smiled. "Along with the convent, there are several houses and several shops, a well, and an electrical system that is run by harnessing the water in the river that runs through the town. There will be enough space for a whole committee of sisters. We'll just need to do the renovations and build the cableway."

"But..." I didn't want to be the only one who saw the obvious fly in the ointment.

"And in support of his son's engineering work, Tito Gardino himself is donating the funds we'll need to create a transportation system—for invited guests only," Paulette added triumphantly.

"And this is all legal?" Sophie asked.

"All but the abortions."

I had wanted to operate outside of the laws of men, but I must confess, I never imagined getting quite so far outside.

CHAPTER 20

IT IS BARBARIC

I was proud that Socorro and Paulette took charge of our abortion services during the rest of their visit. They made the appointments, counseled with the patients, and used the magical herbs to complete the abortions. Once they left, we set about to weave new threads into the fabric of our care.

With the magical herbs Socorro brought, our practice of abortion was transformed. We used the Abra powder to determine the length of pregnancies, and the *Corazon de Gracia* to end the life of the embryo or fetus and cause it to pass easily and painlessly from the woman's body overnight. The one thing we added was an honest discussion of what the embryo or fetus was going to look like. Many of the women who came to us didn't live on a farm. They didn't have any way to be familiar with the appearance of a developing pregnancy. After much discussion, we decided not to use the *moscocero* to make them forget, so we needed to help them come to terms with what they were doing. Sophie used her Brownie Star Flash camera to take pictures of the embryos at different stages to use in our counseling. Women's responses ranged from curiosity to sorrow when they saw their own pregnancies, but, as we'd hoped, none of them were shocked. As we had decided after Lucie had a patient whose attempt to bury the tissue in her church's yard brought a constable from Lyon to our door, the pregnancies were all buried in our consecrated ground or burned, leaving no trace.

I was terribly torn about having a safe and easy method of abortion that we could only use with our patients. All the women in Paris needed it. All the women in the world. But I was equally grateful that we had it, and would have enough for whatever future I could imagine for Our Lady.

We had a long and difficult discussion about the T'ana tradition of marking the woman with a burn on her chest or a scar on her hand. I thought it was very important for women to have a tangible sign of their process of healing. And to have a subtle way to recognize others who shared their experience.

"I don't like it," Françoise said. "The women would consider a scar to be some kind of punishment. And the Church does not allow cremation. We simply cannot consider this 'to the sky' business."

Sophie sighed. "I'm not sure how I feel. I understand your concern, Françoise. Some of the women we see are already looking for their penance. But I am also thinking about how strange it is that, after an abortion, it is as though something momentous never even happened. The woman is so often changed, yet she has no way to mark the change."

"I'm thinking about that, too, Sophie," I said. "We agree it is our interpretation of things that creates our reality. What if we don't offer the cremation, and frame the scarring as something like a badge of courage? I love the part where the healing of the scar is seen as a way to meter the healing of the soul. Didn't they say something about turning to the future when the scar begins to fade? The women we see don't have any way to say to themselves, 'I have mourned enough, and it is time to move on with my life.' In a way, this might give them an end to the punishment."

"But Jane, this is France, not Peru. We don't scar ourselves. It's not how we do things," Françoise insisted. "It is barbaric."

"That's a pretty strong word!" I responded.

"That's how I *feel*. Hearing about this in a story from another culture is a very different thing from doing it. Besides, how could you inflict more pain on women who are already dealing with so much?" Françoise said.

"It may not make sense, but that is one of the things I like about the idea. The abortion is so easy and quick that it almost doesn't seem real. The wound gives them something concrete. When they want to pretend the whole thing never happened, it brings them back to reality—but in a gentle way. I don't want to be part of one more experience that a woman has to keep a secret from herself. We would help them make an interpretation of the scar that empowers them and helps them recognize that they are not alone. They will acknowledge that—they are one of many women who have made this choice," I said.

"I wonder how much the scarring hurts?" Sophie asked.

"Let's find out," I said. "I want you to try this on me—both the burn and the cut on the palm."

"Jane, you wouldn't want that on you!" Françoise insisted.

"I would. I'm serious. I want to, today. Now."

Sophie went to the shed for a spade, and we had a perfectly good fire right in the kitchen oven. It felt right to have marks on my body initiating me into the tribe of women who have made the sacred choice to end the life within them. Sophie came back into the kitchen and washed the little shovel with soap and hot water. Then she got a bottle of alcohol and sanitized it further.

"I'm sure these rituals are not supposed to end in infection!" she said. She honed the edge with a whetstone from the kitchen drawer.

"I cannot stay to watch this," Françoise said. "It is not right. I'll see you tomorrow when this foolishness is over."

"My darling Françoise, would you stay if I asked you to? I need this for myself, no matter what we decide about our patients. I have been doing this work for so long in secret. I want—I *need* an outward sign. A symbol. I guess I could find a sailor who would give me a tattoo—but this ritual already exists in the world. Maybe not in our part of the world—but there are women who have been doing this for centuries. Please. Please stay for me?"

Françoise looked at me curiously. "Of course, Jane, if it means so much to you. Of course I will stay. But don't ask me to hurt you. I can't do that."

I turned to my beloved partner. "Sophie, can you do it? Can you give me this gift?"

Sophie sat at the kitchen table, looking at the sharp trowel. "I can do it if it is so important to you. But I don't understand why," she winced herself, imagining the pain.

"I'm not sure I can explain. Françoise, you know the mark Claude has on his arm from his time in the German camp?"

"You mean the circle the prisoners scribed on their forearms to show they were together—to show they had survived?" she asked, understanding dawning upon her.

"Yes. They chose that sign so the survivors could identify each other, even if they had been held at other camps. They recognize each other on the street, even when they are strangers—because they are not strangers in a way. Remember when we were at that café and Claude jumped up and embraced the waiter, and the rest of us didn't have any idea why? The tattoo communicated without the need for words. It reminded him that he is not alone," I said.

"That makes sense to me, but I still don't like it," Françoise said.

"This has been my work, my world, for so many years. I have earned those marks," I said quietly.

"Do you want the fire first, or the cut?" Sophie asked.

"The fire."

"All right. Are you ready?"

"Wait a minute. What is it the Wise Women said?"

Sophie answered. "As long as you have this scar, you will honor the life returned to the One. Each time you see the scar, you will remember your love and courage and goodness. When the scar has faded, you will turn your face toward the future, but this nascent life will always look down upon you and protect you."

"That is so comforting to think of the life being a protector," I said. I was almost ready. But there was one more thing. "I want to think about the women. There have been so many over all these years. I want to do this in their honor."

I sat still and closed my eyes. I thought of Mimi, and Jeanette, and Kikuyo, and Catalina, and Charlotte, and Lucy, and Coco, and Ricki, and Gertrude, and Françoise. And me. Then I said, "I am ready."

Sophie opened the door of the fireplace and used tongs to pull out an ember.

"I am scared that I don't know how to do this," she lamented.

"It's okay. Just touch my chest here above my heart," I said, pulling my blouse open and bearing the left side.

Sophie took a deep breath. The searing heat only lasted for a moment. With a little cry, she dropped the ember back into the fire.

"Are you all right?" she cried. "Was that all right?"

I smiled at her and Françoise. "Just perfect. Isn't it paradoxical that making these marks with love is so different from harming someone violently, just as lovingly ending an inchoate life—a life that has barely begun—is so different from killing out of anger?"

Sophie insisted on putting a bandage with antiseptic on the small burn.

It was more difficult for her to execute the cut.

"Make a shallow cut on my left hand," I requested.

Sophie wiped the blade with alcohol. Then she did it—one quick swipe, and the thin line of blood blossomed on my palm. Again, she bandaged me up. Her brow was furrowed, and she shook her head.

"I don't know how those women have the guts to do this," Sophie said. "It was terrible hurting you."

"I know, love. I am sorry. But I can't say thank you enough."

"Jane, you come from a different country. You can't understand how foreign this would be to French women," Françoise said.

"Maybe," I said. "But perhaps it would make sense to them. It would obviously be important for the woman to make her own choice of whether to be marked."

"That would be a little bit better," Françoise answered. "But I just don't think I could ever do it, do you, Jane? Sophie did it because she loves you so much." Sophie smiled a wan smile. "Could you do that to other women?"

"I think so," I answered. "I want to sit with this and then we can talk about it again."

As my scars healed, I reflected on all my years caring for women and the things they had taught me about love and pain and sacrifice and courage. In an emotional evening, I argued strongly that women should get to choose.

"We do whatever we can to make this experience less painful for women," Sophie said. "How can we include an experience that is painful?"

"We each need our own sadness as well as our own joy," I countered. "Otherwise we lead only half a life." I was better at articulating wisdom than I was living it. I had spent much of my life avoiding my pain.

Having it as a choice converted even Françoise. We decided to give each woman the option of the gentle scarring across her palm accompanied by much discussion about what it would mean to her to bear a mark of her abortion. Most women wanted it. The few times a woman told us that she deserved it as punishment, we didn't do it, and we realized we needed to work with the woman longer so that she could own her goodness as well as her choice. When it was chosen, we agreed that I would slide the spade gently across the palm. Sophie was there with the bandage, and Françoise held their other hand. Françoise told me that remembering Claude's experience had convinced her that I was right. She understood it, but still didn't like it.

Whether they chose the scar or not, the women who came on the same day felt bound together, just as they had in Peru. Most of the women who were helped at Our Lady could recognize each other from the slender scar. We had already instituted the tradition of the patient digging the grave. It was very different to have the woman with the spade in her hand—the same spade that would mark her hand—choosing where to dig, than it would have been for any church or minister to preside over a funeral. It didn't feel like a funeral. It was a return to earth—part of the circle. Each of the women we saw chose one stone to mark the place and one to take with her.

CHAPTER 21

BERNADETTE

Our Lady, Winter 1961

Brother Timothy surprised us with a visit one afternoon. Françoise was in Alençon with her aunt, so it was just me and Sophie at Our Lady. With him was a young nun—maybe in her early twenties—whom he introduced as Sister Bernadette. She was pale, her skin nearly matching her white wimple and collar. She wore a dark brown robe made of rough homespun fabric. I couldn't help but compare it to the beautifully tailored habit I still wore when our patients needed forgiveness from the church. The sister nodded hello to us but didn't say anything.

"Sister Bernadette is observing silence. Sophie, would you be so kind as to show her the gardens?"

Tim wasn't subtle. It was cold out, and there wasn't much in the garden to look at. Obviously, he wanted to talk to me alone.

Sophie didn't miss a beat and said, "Of course. Won't you come with me, Sister Bernadette?"

We sat down at our usual conference center—the kitchen table.

"Can I get you some coffee or tea?" I asked.

"What I want is whiskey, but it is a bit early, even for me," the Brother said. "I would love some tea."

He spoke as I was putting the kettle on to boil.

"I am very fond of you and Sophie," he began ominously, "but it was all I could do to come here today. I prayed about this, and I must confess that I am still not certain whether I am doing the right thing."

"Tim, this sounds serious. What is it? What's wrong?"

"It is my dear Sister Bernadette. We have been friends for a long time. I haven't seen her for two years and I know something is very, very wrong. Sister Bernadette is in charge of her convent's finances, and she has always been one of the smartest, happiest, and most lively people I know. On this visit, I found her in silence, eating almost nothing, and withdrawn to the point of being a recluse. She had abandoned her regular duties and refused to speak.

Her Mother Superior has chosen to interpret this as a sign of piety, but remember that my mother was a healer. I learned enough from her to fear it is something else entirely.

"I was told that she stopped speaking abruptly several months ago. I am afraid the source of her silence is that some man has gotten to her. This young woman is truly an innocent. She has been at the cloister since she was twelve years old and knows little of the world. It took all my ingenuity to persuade her to come with me, but I don't know if I will be able to forgive myself for doing so. The convent is the only family she has. There is nothing more important to her than her vows, but my intuition tells me that has been violated and she may be with child."

I poured the tea and sat down beside him.

"Brother Tim, there is no sin in bringing her here. We will see if we can discover the reason for her withdrawal. If it is as you think, it will be Sister Bernadette who is responsible for whatever comes next. Does she realize what you suspect?" I asked.

"No. And this may be one of those rare occasions when the power of denial has overcome the power of reason. She may not even *be* aware of what is happening. I have great faith in you, Jane, and I am certain you will be able to reach her as no one else could."

"I will do what I can, Tim. But I can't make miracles."

"I beg to differ," he said, smiling.

I went out into the garden and invited Sophie and Sister Bernadette to come back in. Over the Sister's shoulder, Sophie shot me a questioning look.

"I'll tell you later," I mouthed.

Bernadette obediently went into the bathroom as I instructed and emerged with a sample of urine. She didn't ask any questions, which made me suspect that at some deep level, she recognized what was happening. I took her into the library and told her I'd be back soon. As I left the room, she sat down with a coffee-table book of illustrations of the beautiful, stained glass work of Louis Tiffany.

Sophie came into the laboratory and stood behind me as I dropped a tiny bit of Abra powder into the urine and shook the vial. Although there was some blood in the sample, it changed to a deep blue color. Sophie handed me the chart with the gradations of color, and we both gasped. Sister Bernadette was five months pregnant.

"This is what Brother Tim was afraid of." I told Sophie everything he had said.

"Jane, what will she do?" Sophie asked.

"The first question is whether we can help her face this reality," I answered. "*My* worry is that her terror has got her stuck in denial. It seems that whatever trauma she has experienced has literally struck her dumb. We can't even ask her to make a decision if she is protecting herself by being numb."

"Can you get her to face what is happening to her?" Sophie asked, touching my arm.

"I thought of something that might work. It is definitely a time for Our Lady."

As I was changing into my trusty habit, I considered my idea to encourage Bernadette to talk with me and to bring her back to her adult self. One of the guidelines I had learned over the years was that if I was self-conscious, I was doomed. My only hope was to focus outward—on her—and to follow my instincts.

While Sophie put dinner together, I went to see Bernadette in the library. She stood up as I entered the room and gave the kind of little bow she might give to a nun of superior rank.

"Sit down, Sister," I said, firmly. I had already decided that I needed to embody the quintessential adult, as well as the epitome of religious compassion.

Bernadette looked at me vacantly but sat down.

"I am Mother Jane, Our Lady of Perpetual Grace," I said, looking her directly in the eye. "I need your help."

She tilted her head slightly, but otherwise made no move.

"Brother Timothy has told me that you are in charge of the financial matters of your convent?"

Bernadette nodded but didn't say anything. I recognized I'd have to be patient and deliberate.

"I need your counsel," I said, looking serious. "I am working with some merchants in our village who are at war with each other over the division of proceeds for their wares. The tanners are demanding the largest share of the price of goods, but the leatherworkers say that they should be paid the larger share because their work is more exacting. They have come to violence over their dispute, and the Village Elders asked me to intercede."

I almost saw the wheels turning in her mind.

I continued. "At first, I planned to establish the wage by the time it takes to create the piece. But I worried that wouldn't be fair, since the tanner's work is largely soaking, which takes time but not attention. At least, that's what I thought until the tanners invited me to observe their process. Not only was I thoroughly disgusted, but I was also impressed by the volume of chemicals and work and skill it takes to transform a cowhide into a piece of leather. So now I'm not sure what to do."

Bernadette answered softly in a voice rusty from not being used. "Have you ever heard of a mother who told her two children fighting over a piece of cake that one must cut it into pieces, and the other choose which piece he wants?"

My heart raced. At least she was talking. I tried to stay calm. "I'm not sure I understand. How would I apply that bit of wisdom?"

"Well, you'd direct one group to establish percentages to be divided between the tanner and the leatherworker—and then allow the other group to select which percent it wants to apply to its work," Bernadette suggested.

I smiled at her, knowing that a fifty-fifty division was the only likely outcome. "Thank you so much," I said. "You are very smart."

"Mother Jane," Bernadette said next, "I know what you are doing. Thank you."

"What is it you think I am doing?"

"You are helping me remember who I am. I believed—I hoped—that if I retreated into silence, I could make all of it go away. Does Brother Timothy know?"

"He suspects. He is extremely worried about you."

"I hate to sully him with this mess. He is such a lovely man. He has been nothing but kind," Bernadette said, hanging her head.

"Can I assume that this was not the result of a consensual interaction?"

"Yes. I think that would be a mild way to say it. The man took what he wanted and then discarded me like a piece of trash, like an old rag covered with oil."

"Then Brother Tim is not sullied by caring for you. Another person's sin does not tarnish your value."

"You don't understand. Before Brother Timothy asked me to come with him, I was ready to end my life. I would have done that had it not been an even bigger sin than those I have already committed. There is no hope for me."

I took her hands in mine. "Bernadette, I can see that you feel cornered by impossible and unfair circumstances for which I'm certain you bear no blame. I'm sure you see a bleak future before you. Brother Timothy has brought you here to give you one more option."

"I have heard a bit about your special retreats. Surely you realize that my vows make it impossible for me to consider the alternative you present."

"The difficult reality is that you will either take your own life, have an abortion, or have a baby. If you have a baby, you can leave your order and find a way to raise it, or trust someone else to raise it. I'm certain Timothy would find a loving home."

"But no matter what happens, I forfeit my life. I have lived with the Sisters since I was a child. Sin is sin—the circumstances are unimportant. I cannot imagine why the Lord has laid this burden upon me, but it is mine to bear. I cannot be forgiven."

"Sister, have you prayed about this? Have you prayed for a miscarriage?"

Bernadette's eyes looked fiery. "Of course. That is my only hope. If God pitied me enough to take this life from my body, I could return to my order and live the rest of my life in penance. I could keep this terrible secret."

"Many women pray for a miscarriage, but most don't have one. I noticed there was some blood in your urine. Have you been bleeding or cramping?"

"Yes, just in the past few days. But the bleeding is not much. I have been very tired. I assumed that pain is part of this experience, but there was no one I could ask," she said.

"It isn't normal to be in pain. We can give you some medication to help," I offered.

"Thank you, but I am not afraid of suffering," she said. "It is the least of what I deserve."

"Bernadette, I cannot tell you how to untie this Gordian Knot. Do you know that story?" I asked.

She pursed her lips. "I believe the legend is that there was a chariot that portended Alexander the Great's rise as a conqueror. He discovered an ingenious way to detach the chariot from an impossibly knotted cord. Didn't he use his sword to cut through the knot instead of untying it?"

"Yes, that's one version. Another version of the story is that he pulled the pole through the middle of the knot to get it loose. Either way, he redefined the problem of the knot and reinvented a way to the solution."

"Ah, if only I were as brilliant as Alexander," the Sister said with a wry smile. She wiped her eye with the sleeve of her robe.

Sophie came to the door and knocked softly. "I don't mean to interrupt, but dinner is ready whenever you would like it."

I smiled at Bernadette. "I think this is a good place to stop. But Sister, we will do everything we can to make this a safe place for you. Can you…will you stay with us and not retreat back into silence?"

Bernadette looked down, as if ashamed. "Yes. I can do that. Thank you."

Despite everything I had learned, my own memories of three German soldiers in an alley intruded, and I was desperate to rescue her.

CHAPTER 22

TOO OLD FOR A NIGHT LIKE THIS

We ate dinner, with gentle conversation about the Algerian children Brother Timothy was teaching to read, the delicious turnips that Sophie brought up from the root cellar that morning, and the warmth of the fire that frosty winter night. After we finished eating, Bernadette asked to be excused to go to bed. It was evident that she didn't feel well, and Sophie made up a hot water bottle for her. Brother Timothy, Sophie, and I sat in the kitchen and drank wine and talked more about how to help her, but we didn't find any solution. I felt deeply sad and scared. And something else that eluded me.

When Sophie and I were in bed, I said, "I want to save her. I want to give her *Corazon de Gracia* to end this pregnancy, and then I want to give her *moscocero*."

"Jane, you don't. You want to rescue her from the reality of her life, and you know that doesn't work. Adults don't need to be rescued. She hasn't even asked for an abortion, and you *never* want to give *moscocero*. You always say you don't believe in it—that you aren't the one who should decide what memories a woman has—or how she interprets them."

"But this is too terrible," I said, and I surprised myself by crying. "Her life will be ruined."

"You always say that people need their own pain just as much as their joy, and need to make their own sense of it," Sophie said, pulling me into her arms.

"Sophie, I should never have talked to Bernadette. I descended into a hole. I am experiencing her sadness and her shame."

"Chérie," Sophie said softly, "You know it doesn't work like that. When you think you are having someone else's feelings, it means that you are reminded of something in your own life. You are remembering three soldiers in an alley in Paris."

I didn't say anything, but the shame welled up again as I cried. Finally, I lay my head on her shoulder.

In the middle of the night, Bernadette's cries awakened us. Tim, Sophie, and I arrived at her door at the same time, but we motioned to him to stay in the hall. We found her on the floor, soaked in blood and in obvious agony.

Sophie put a hand on her forehead and said, "She is burning up." We got cold, wet cloths to wipe her face. Sophie asked Tim to get some of the cotton pads we kept in the laboratory. When he brought them, she sent him to the kitchen for towels and hot water. Then Sophie knelt behind Bernadette and held her shoulders, and I squatted between her legs.

In a huge gush of blood, Bernadette delivered what I had only read about before—an anencephalic fetus. A large part of the brain and the skull had not developed. It was about twenty weeks by my estimate, just as the Abra had predicted, and showed no signs of life. Sophie looked at it in shock. I'm sure she had no idea what she was seeing. She wrapped the fetus in a towel and put it to the side. Then both of us turned our attention to Bernadette. She was still in pain, and I knew we had to get the afterbirth out as soon as possible, since her fever suggested the possibility of an infection.

I called for Brother Tim to come in and sit behind Bernadette and sent Sophie for the *Corazon de Gracia*. While I waited, I explained briefly what had happened. I couldn't tell if Bernadette was aware of anything, but Tim seemed to understand. Sophie brought a small bowl of *Corazon*. I inserted a couple of grains deep into her vagina, and, as I expected, it stimulated the rapid expulsion of the placenta. The pains subsided after that, although she was still having more bleeding than I was comfortable with. I massaged her uterus externally, and the bleeding slowed. Brother Tim was a champ. He later told us that he had assisted at some of the births his mother attended. Sophie was an angel, as usual. We got Bernadette cleaned up and removed the blood-soaked sheets from the room. She was too exhausted to speak, but she looked up at me with fear and a question in her eyes.

"The baby was born dead. It never could have survived. There was an abnormality that was not your fault. It is not your fault that the baby died. It was not because of your prayers. There is nothing you could have done differently to save it."

Bernadette's face crumpled into itself and she began to cry. In a few minutes, she fell asleep.

We tucked blankets around her, and Sophie and I made a pallet on the floor so that we could sleep nearby. Before I lay down, I took the fetus wrapped in the towel into the storage room. I washed off the blood and examined it to confirm what I had seen. When we did abortions with the T'ana's magic powder, the embryo was usually very small and was always expelled overnight into the cotton pad. We had never had an experience like this.

Bernadette snored softly when Sophie and I finally lay down next to each other. We were both wrung out, but we had to talk about it for a little while.

In a whisper, I explained to Sophie about a defect in the neural tube.

"Should we have examined her right away?" Sophie asked me. "Could we have avoided this terrible shock?"

"We wouldn't have had any way to know that the baby wouldn't live," I answered. "But I should have examined her because she told me she had been having some cramping and bleeding. Perhaps I could have prepared her for this possibility. She told me that she had prayed for a miscarriage. I wonder what she will make of this," I said.

"Will she be all right? There was a lot of bleeding."

"I think she will be fine," I said. "If I am right, the *Corazon de Gracia* will strengthen her. We'll see. Of course, she will stay as long as she needs to."

"Oh, my dear Jane. Are you still wishing to give her *moscocero*? When this is all over with?"

"No. Tomorrow we will tell her everything and give her the choice to see the baby, and search for some way to find the blessing that is always next to the wound."

"Jane," Sophie said, "I have never seen one this developed. It looked like a baby."

"Yes, my dear," I said. "As pregnancy progresses, it only makes sense that the fetus looks more and more like a baby, even though it is not fully developed and cannot survive independent of the woman's body."

"How very sad."

"It is sad," I said. "Did it change your thoughts about our work?"

Sophie thought for a moment. "No," she said firmly.

I kissed her, and we fell asleep.

In the morning, Bernadette woke before we did. She was sitting in bed, very still. I was worried that she had relapsed into the silent lost person we had met just the afternoon before. When she saw we were awake, she said, "I have so many questions."

"Of course," I answered. "I will explain everything the best I can. But first, how are you?"

"It's strange—I am stronger than I have been in months. It seems wrong, but I am feeling very good. But last night is like a terrible dream. I think I remember what you said—that there was something wrong with the baby?"

"Yes. It wasn't normal—it couldn't have survived. I'll explain the best I can after we are all dressed," I answered.

"Can I see it?" Bernadette asked.

Sophie looked at me hesitantly—and I nodded. "Of course," Sophie said.

"Is it a girl or a boy?"

"A girl," Sophie answered gently.

There were tears in Bernadette's eyes.

"Are you strong enough to get up?" I asked.

"Yes."

"Then we'll leave you to get dressed. You'll probably bleed for several days—even a week or two—but it shouldn't be heavy. There are some pads on the table," I said, getting up and gathering the bedclothes that Sophie and I had brought in.

Sophie stretched, and it was obvious that sleeping on the floor had made her back hurt, just as mine did. At forty, I was too old for nights like this! We returned to our room and dressed.

"She seems so well," Sophie said, pulling her sweater over her head. "After a miscarriage—that far along—I expected her to be weak."

"I did, too," I agreed. "I can only imagine it was the *Corazon de Gracia* that made the difference. Remember the story Socorro told us about the woman who had cancer and seemed to recover after having the *Corazon*? But still, we'll take it easy with her. She has been through a lot."

Sophie finished before me and began preparing breakfast. I hesitated, wondering whether I needed to put on the habit. I decided that Bernadette didn't need Our Lady for her next step, so I put on my comfortable overalls.

The familiar smell of coffee was very soothing. Brother Tim was already at the table when I got there, and Bernadette joined us a few minutes later. We sat with our coffee steaming in front of us. Sophie brought in a platter of scrambled eggs and toast, and we helped ourselves.

Finally, Sister Bernadette said, "I am so sorry for putting all of you through that last night. Thank you—thank you for saving me."

Brother Tim put his hand on hers. "I speak for us all when I say there is no need to be sorry. In fact, I am hereby going to outlaw *sorry* from our vocabulary today. Otherwise, we won't be able to stand it."

Bernadette smiled wanly. She pushed her scrambled eggs around her plate.

Sophie said, "It would be good if you ate something. Is there anything else you'd prefer?"

"No. Thank you. This is delicious. I just don't seem to have much of an appetite," she said. "But I want to see the baby. I want you to explain it all to me—what happened? And I want to tell you the story."

"There is time for all of that," I said. "Where do you want to start?"

"The story," she said. And she began.

CHAPTER 23

A SMALL, THOUGH REVERED, PART OF HIS BODY

"We Carmelites are cloistered, but I was given special dispensation to go into the village to get paper I needed for my accounting. On my walk back to the convent, a peddler came by in his wagon. He offered to drive me back, and I accepted, thinking him kind. Faster than I can imagine, he knocked me off the wagon, threw himself on me, and wrenched my robes over my head. He pulled off my underwear and relieved himself inside me, then pushed me over a small embankment on the side of the road and drove off, whistling.

"To say I was in shock would have been to put it too gently. I literally could not fathom what had happened, so I decided to forget that it ever had. I pulled myself back together—I wasn't hurt, only bruised a little—and I walked back to the convent. I buried myself in my work and didn't let myself think of it again until one of the sisters asked me to order sanitary products, and I realized, to my dawning horror, that I had not made use of them. That's when I stopped talking. I withdrew from convent life and was waiting for the wrath of God to descend on me.

"At first, I searched for the lesson that was being given, wondering if I was being tested, like Job. But finally I understood that I was being punished. I should have prevented that man from taking me, or I should have died in the effort. I realized that everyone would know that I had sinned and that I would be damned forever. I expected God to smite me for my impurity, and I waited and watched for that to happen, but it didn't, so I took that as a sign that I should end my own life. The only way I could imagine doing it was to hang myself, but I didn't know how to go about it. I was in the barn searching for a stout rope when Brother found me."

"Oh, Bernadette. I am so sorry," Sophie said, glancing at Tim to forgive her use of the forbidden *sorry*. "You must have been terrified."

"It might have been better if I was. I was so numb it was as if I was going through the motions."

"I am glad I found you in time. Even without knowing what happened, I had a feeling of what was wrong." He turned to me. "After praying about it, I hoped you and Sophie and Françoise would be my—my saviors," Tim said.

"And you have been *my* saviors!" Bernadette said, looking at us tearfully.

She sighed deeply. "Now that you have heard the story, will you tell me what happened to the baby? Can you explain what went wrong?"

I looked at her seriously. "I'll explain it the best I understand. You were about five months into the pregnancy, so a little over halfway through. Even in normal circumstances, a baby born this early couldn't survive outside your body, but there was an abnormality, something wrong, as you said. There isn't a gentle way to say this. A large part of the baby's brain and skull didn't develop. The condition is called 'anencephaly.' It cannot be diagnosed ahead of time and often results in miscarriage. I am not aware of any case in which an anencephalic baby was born and survived."

"What causes it?" Brother Tim asked.

"No one knows why it happens. From what I understand, it is a defect of the neural tube that surrounds the spine. But I can tell you it's not because of anything you did, or anything you prayed for."

The Sister closed her eyes and sighed.

Brother Tim was holding his prayer book. "Bernadette, I said last rites for the baby. Even though it was not exactly by the book, I knew it would be important to you. And I'll say a funeral blessing as well when we bury her."

"And our churchyard has been consecrated," Sophie added. "So she will rest in hallowed ground."

"You have all been so kind," Bernadette said. Then she looked at me. "It appears that, like Alexander the Great, I have slipped the Gordian Knot. But I don't think that is a sign that I am going to be the ruler of Asia." She gave a rueful laugh.

"Maybe not," I agreed. "But it could mean that you are going to be the wonderful Sister Bernadette who brings light and joy into the lives of all she meets. That is entirely up to you."

Bernadette glanced at Brother Tim.

"I agree completely with Jane," Tim said. Sophie nodded as well.

I said, "I realize your vows include chastity. I am not Catholic, so I will never understand how a man sticking a small, though revered, part of his body, completely uninvited and unwelcome, into a woman, can instantly change her from being good and pure into being a whore! Who gave any man that power? And, to be crude, which I admit I am being, how can a woman's vagina be both so coveted and at the same time so detested? Men seem to want us and hate us in equal measure. I hope you won't let his defilement define you."

Sophie chimed in. "I have never thought of it that way, but it's true. And Bernadette, it was that man's sin, not yours. In this world, I'm afraid the Church would say your sin was being born a woman."

"According to the Church, that is sometimes enough," Brother Timothy added.

"The sin of Eve. Don't all women carry it?" Bernadette asked.

"Ah, another Gordian Knot. How to be female with all the glory and majesty that entails, and still carry the shame imposed on us to keep us obedient and powerless. Pardon me, Sister, but the story of the Garden and the Fall was told by men, and it is used by men. Only you can decide whether it is the true word of God," I said.

Bernadette was crying softly. "You are being very kind. I'm afraid I don't deserve..."

"Don't even say it. Kindness and compassion are exactly what you deserve," Sophie interjected.

"You deserve it from us, and more importantly, from yourself," I added. I could see that Bernadette looked destroyed.

"This is a lot to process," I said gently. "Do you want to take a break?"

"No. I want to see her," Bernadette answered. "Can we see her now?"

And so we did. Sophie went to the storage room, wrapped the baby in a clean towel, and brought her into the library.

Bernadette said, "I want to hold her."

"Of course," Sophie said, and gently handed her the small bundle.

Bernadette opened the covers just enough to see the baby's face. It was a grayish color—not the color of life—but still a sweet face. The sister didn't look at the sad, caved-in skull.

"Poor lamb," Sophie said.

"Yes," Bernadette said. "I am going to name her Agnes—it means pure, and is also associated with the innocent lamb."

"That's beautiful." Sophie said.

Brother Tim said, "We need to bury her, but not just yet. Tell me when you are ready."

"Thanks," Bernadette said. "Would it be all right...? I would like some time alone with her."

"Of course," we said. Brother Tim and Sophie made their way to the kitchen, each saying their own kind of prayer. I stayed behind for a moment.

"May I have a few minutes with you?" I asked.

Bernadette nodded, and we sat and talked about the rituals we had learned from the T'ana women. Then I left her to her grief.

My compatriots were sitting at the kitchen table.

Brother Tim smiled. "That was quite an exegesis, Sister Jane. I must say that every day at Our Lady is a new lesson for me." Sophie nodded in agreement.

"Can we have that whiskey now, Brother?" I asked.

"If there were ever a time, this would be the time," he answered, laughing. "But I am afraid I have a grave to dig, even if a very small one."

I exchanged a knowing look with Sophie.

"We do things a little differently here, Tim," Sophie began.

"I don't even want to guess," the Brother said.

"We learned some things — some rituals—from our friend Socorro, who works with healing women in Peru," I said. "Bernadette wants to dig the grave herself and bury this little one. There are a few more parts of the ritual, but you can certainly add whatever words you want to afterward. Because she is a nun, what you do will be very important to her," I said.

"And because she is a woman, what *you* do will be very important to her," he said, nodding his head. "I understand. I won't get in the way. Tell me when it is time for the Church to have its say."

In a few moments, Bernadette called to us from the library.

"I am ready," she said.

We bundled into our coats and formed a sort of funeral procession with Brother Tim leading, Bernadette carrying the baby, me, then Sophie carrying the burial spade. The cemetery was outside the kitchen door, down a walkway lined with the beautiful white rocks, tumbled smooth by the river, that we used for mementos. It was a cold day, but fortunately the ground was not yet frozen. When we came to an open space, we stopped.

Sophie said, "Bernadette, it is up to you to choose where to bury her." The young nun looked around and finally pointed to a space next to a lilac bush that would bear beautiful blossoms in the spring. We all knelt down. It seemed somehow wrong to be standing up so tall.

I turned to Bernadette. "Do you still want to dig her grave?" I asked. Bernadette nodded, handed the bundle to me, and accepted the spade from Sophie. I continued. "While you are digging, speak out loud any words you want to say to Agnes."

Bernadette started crying and digging.

She said, "Tiny Agnes, my lamb, thank you for blessing me with your presence, and forgive me for my fear of you. Forgive me for having a life that allowed no place for you." She was choking a little as she talked and dug, and I had to put my hand on Tim's arm to keep him from taking the spade and completing the small grave.

"Now," I continued, "you must listen to how this spirit answers your prayer. Close your eyes and hear her voice."

Bernadette closed her eyes, and in a moment began to weep and smile at the same time, like a sun shower. "She has told me that she forgives me and loves me. She has said that God sent her to be with me for this short time. Now she is meant to be in Heaven. She has told me, as you did, that I must forgive myself."

"Is there anything else you need to say to her?" I asked.

Bernadette shook her head slowly. "I just need to say goodbye."

"Good. Say that in whatever way you want."

Bernadette clasped her hands together, bent her head, and was quiet for a moment.

I could see Brother Timothy out of the corner of my eye. He was transfixed by the conversation. I imagined that it made him think of his mother, who was a healer, called a witch by some.

Then I said, "Now, Bernadette, this is enough digging. Place her into the grave." Bernadette looked at me with fear.

Tim said, "It is all right. This is only her body. She cannot be harmed by being placed in the bosom of the earth. Her spirit soars above us. Her spirit is with God."

Bernadette trembled and took a last glance, then covered the baby's face with the cloth and laid her into the hole.

"While you bury her, is there a song you'd like to sing to her?"

As she filled the hole, she started to sing so softly that I almost didn't recognize the French lullaby, *Fais do do, bebé mon petit chou*—Go to sleep my baby, my little cabbage. I sang that song to Lucie when she was little. *Fais do do*. The sweetness and sadness of the moment made me catch my breath. It was as if all the spirits gathered in the churchyard were holding their hands out to embrace the innocent that was joining them.

When the grave was covered, Brother Tim began to speak, but I signaled to him that it still wasn't time. I nodded to Sophie.

Sophie took the spade from Bernadette and cleaned it on a cloth doused with antiseptic that she had tucked into her waistband. She said, "Do you choose to have the physical reminder of this event that we discussed? A scar across your palm?"

Bernadette nodded.

Sophie said, "Hold out your hand."

Bernadette did. To her and Brother Tim's shock, Sophie drew the edge of the spade across her palm, and a brilliant red line appeared. Bernadette gasped, but didn't cry out. Sophie clasped the hand that was bleeding and held it very tight. She said, "As long as you have this scar, you will honor the life returned to the One. Each time you see the scar, you will feel your love and courage and goodness. When the scar has faded, you will turn your face toward the future, but this spirit will always look down upon you and protect you." She wrapped the wound in a clean cloth. "Now choose two stones, one to lay upon her grave, and the other to take with you. These stones will bind you to this place."

Bernadette bent down and chose a pale white stone that she placed on the grave, and a pink rose quartz that she put in her pocket. When she stood up, Sophie kissed her on the forehead and then motioned to Tim.

"My dear ones," he began, "I can see that a church created by men cannot begin to approximate the power of women's knowing. But Sister Bernadette," he turned to her, "in deference to your allegiance and your vows, I commit the innocent soul of this baby, Agnes, to God. May this soul and the souls of all departed through the grace of God rest in peace." Brother Tim and Sister Bernadette each made the sign of the cross.

We came back into the convent exhausted, yet in a state of deep calm. Without another word, we retired to our respective bedrooms and slept.

When we woke, we shared a quiet meal in the kitchen. Bernadette told me she was feeling well. We helped her and Brother Tim gather their belongings so they could begin the journey back to her convent. Before Bernadette got into the car, she drew Sophie and me into a deep embrace, our foreheads touching. We stood that way for several breaths, and then released each other to our futures. Months later, Brother Tim told us that Bernadette had asked to be released from her cloistered life and had taken a position as a Teaching Sister. She had twenty ebullient six-year-olds under her care.

CHAPTER 24

LUCIE SENDS NEWS

1961-1966

Lucie continued to write regularly. Her letters were full of news of the cataclysmic changes happening in the United States, my home country. Here are just a few snippets.

1961: They invented a pill that you can take once a day to protect from pregnancy. This will change everything for women. They won't even need abortion anymore. If they'd just put it in beer, women wouldn't even have to take the pill! Contraceptive beer could be the best invention in a century!

1962: As a mental health professional, I am consulting with doctors about what criteria the 'Therapeutic Abortion' committees in hospitals should be using to determine whether to permit a woman to have an abortion. When I started, most of them insisted that abortion should be prohibited unless a woman was demonstrably suicidal, but I shared some stories with them and they are loosening up. A woman in Arizona who has been through hell contacted me as a psychological expert. You probably read about her case. Sherri Finkbine is a Romper Room School teacher—it's a television show for children. She took the drug Thalidomide during her pregnancy without knowing that it caused terrible birth defects. It wasn't approved in the United States, but she somehow got it from Europe. The hospital committee in Phoenix agreed to give her a therapeutic abortion, but when she did an interview with a newspaper to warn other pregnant women about the dangers of taking the drug, the hospital backed out. The Finkbines went to court to get permission for the abortion, but they lost. I hoped to send her to you, but they decided that they needed a legal, medical service because of all the media scrutiny, so she flew to Sweden for her abortion. I can't imagine how

Sherri and her family survived with their most intimate life on display. But she seems to be handling it all well. Her case means that, for the first time, Americans are having discussions about abortion with their breakfast newspapers.

1963: I am sending you a copy of The Feminine Mystique by Betty Friedan. It has turned this country upside down. Didn't you tell me you met Simone de Beauvoir once? I got to meet Friedan at a book signing. She is one tough lady. Her book is like the US version of The Second Sex, which is now also selling out of bookstores. Something big is happening here.

November 23, 1963: You must have seen this in the newspapers. Yesterday, our wonderful President Kennedy was killed in Dallas, Texas. I am beyond tears.

May 1965: There has been a terrible outbreak of German measles. The doctors tell me that the illness isn't measles—it is something called rubella. Like Thalidomide, rubella can cause miscarriage or stillbirth—and terrible birth defects if a woman is exposed to it early in pregnancy. I am contacting hospital committees to ask that they relax their rules for what they call 'Therapeutic Abortion'—in other words, abortion that they allow. There are some brave doctors who are openly providing abortions for their patients exposed to rubella. Experiences like this are opening some people's eyes to the need for abortion to be available.

1966: The California Medical Examiners attempted disciplinary action against nine doctors who provided abortions to women with rubella. But they held a hearing and thousands of people—even doctors—defended them, and the charges were dropped. California could be the first state where abortion is legal.

Abortion could be legal. I couldn't fathom it.

CHAPTER 25

THEY DID IT!

October 28ᵗʰ, 1967

The phone rang early. I had just put the water on the stove for coffee, and Sophie was still dressing.

It was Brigitte. She was breathless. "Jane, they did it!"

"Who did what?"

"The British. Parliament has voted to make abortion legal."

"Oh, Brigitte! That is wonderful. Françoise will be here soon with the *Tribune* and we'll read all the details. Will this persuade the ministers to act before France is left hopelessly behind?"

"Matthieu and I hope so. We are working to bring a group of conservative members of the British Parliament who voted in favor of changing the law to meet with some of our conservative ministers. We are going to wine and dine them and hope that some of the British reasoning will rub off on the French."

"Will abortion be legal in Catholic Ireland?" I asked.

"No," Brigitte answered in her usual direct way. "Just England and Wales for now. The rest of the empire is still on its own. But women will be able to travel to the UK from other countries. There are so many French women who will never find Our Lady. At least for the ones with a bit of scratch, this could mean something safer than the mean streets of Paris or the alleys of Marseille."

"Americans will come over, too, I expect. At least the ones with money, as you say. You have been working on this so hard for so long. Surely it is time."

"You may be familiar with the quotation from Rabbi Tarfon, 'You are not obligated to complete the work, but neither are you free to abandon it,'" Brigitte said. "That helps me keep going—doing my little part. But legal abortion in France *has* to be within shouting distance now. After all, England is right next door."

"I'll put a call in to Matthieu later," I said. "Within shouting distance indeed!"

A few months later, Brigitte told me that a good friend of hers was serving on the committee of physicians and hospital administrators charged with creating the regulatory guidelines for abortion provision through the National Health Care.

I asked her how the law would be administered.

"There are certain things that must be ascertained in order for a woman to have an abortion. Two doctors must certify that there is risk to a woman's or her children's mental or physical health if the pregnancy is continued. Abortions are also permitted if there is a risk of severe mental or physical abnormalities in the fetus."

"Do you think…I wonder if they would include a mandate to explore women's emotional and spiritual well-being? Maybe we could talk with them about our experience at Our Lady?"

"I wish. I'm sorry, Jane. I already asked about it. They are overwhelmed trying to thread the needle between the law's proponents and those who opposed it. They don't want to appear either too liberal or too conservative. My friend said there is no way they would venture into the murky waters of the emotions."

"Maybe it's a conversation they would entertain once everything has been in place for a while."

"Maybe. Or maybe Our Lady is going to be unique."

"That's just the problem. I don't want us to be unique. There are women everywhere who have emotional or religious issues they need help working through. We can only see a few of them compared to the need. I am so frustrated. What good does it do to have abortion care legalized if so much of what women need is left unattended?"

Brigitte said, "What good, indeed."

CHAPTER 26

HENRI

Our Lady, 1968

The massive front door of the convent opened and fourteen-year-old Henri strode in looking furious. Over his shoulder, I could see Françoise scurrying behind him. She opened her hands and shook her head—a gesture I took to mean the situation was out of her control. Henri passed me and confronted Sophie.

"You. The most gentle person I have ever met. *You!* How could you?"

I caught up with him and put my hand on his arm, but he brushed it off and wouldn't turn to face me.

I thought Sophie might wilt, but she stood tall. "Henri, it appears there is something you want to talk to me about."

Françoise skidded into the kitchen, out of breath.

"I am so sorry," she panted. "It was all my fault. I didn't know he was in the house."

Henri wheeled around to face her. "You are just sorry I overheard the secret I wasn't supposed to know." Then he turned back to Sophie.

"All this time you said you were helping those women solve their problems. But the problems are *babies*. And you are killing them."

I flashed back to Petite Lucie's observation that Henri wouldn't understand nuance.

"Henri, this isn't Sophie's doing," I began, wanting to take the burden off her.

"No, Jane," Sophie said. "This is as much mine as yours. Henri, sit down and we can talk about this."

"No," he shouted. "I loved you. I trusted you. You are murderers. And you are going to Hell. I don't ever want to talk to any of you again." Henri spun around and was out the front door, slamming it behind him.

Françoise burst into tears and sat at the kitchen table. "I have made a terrible mess of this."

Sophie and I sat on either side of her. "What exactly did he overhear?" I asked.

"I was talking with Dr. Levy about a patient, so he heard all of it. All of it."

CHAPTER 27

OVER LEMONADE

We mourned the loss of Henri from our lives. No amount of coaxing from Françoise could make him reconsider—he refused to talk to us. Even his parents couldn't make him change his mind. So we just missed him.

I continued to write Lucie regularly, but waited a long time for her next letter.

> *July 1968: I'm sorry I haven't written in a while. In the spring, Martin Luther King was murdered, and I fell back into that dark place where I was after Tildy was born. Then, just as my daffodils were coming up in the front yard, Bobby Kennedy was murdered. There is something wrong with this country that allows its leaders to be killed. I don't know if I can stay here.*

I worried about her. In my letters, I urged her to get help when she felt so low, and she did seem to get better. It was fascinating to hear about all the complicated doings of the world outside Our Lady, but I was also relieved that we had the peace of our isolation. Lucie rarely wrote about Tildy and Oliver. She didn't say if things were better in her personal life. That made me aware of how fortunate I was. Sophie was a big part of my happiness. Every day she shared the work, supported my vision of how to help women, cooked amazing meals, encouraged our friendships with Françoise and Claude, and Anne-Marie and her husband, and all the wonderful people in our little village. And she loved me.

One afternoon I sat with a pile of Lucie's letters, lost in a daydream about the past.

"Chérie, are you all right?" Sophie asked me, putting her hand on my shoulder.

I shook my head to get out of my reverie. "I'm okay. I was just thinking about how time goes by. My life is more than half over. I hope my father would have been proud of how I have lived it."

"I know he would have, dearest," she said. "If we could host an event for all the women you have touched with your love over these years, there wouldn't be room for them!"

I smiled. "You always have a way of putting things into perspective," I said, kissing her cheek. "What did I ever do to deserve you?"

By 1968, our kitchen shelves were full of 'recipe' books. On the bottom shelf, I kept my National Geographics. They were too heavy to go anywhere but at the bottom. When I was a child, I would sit on my father's lap. He'd hug me to him and call me *mo chuisle,* Gaelic for 'my pulse.' Then he'd tell me stories about every picture in the magazine. I loved looking at them and imagining the extraordinary places and people I'd never see.

At Our Lady, we had our own adventures. Sophie, Françoise, and I talked constantly about our various patients and the ways we were still tweaking our counseling sessions. I thought we knew pretty much everything there was to know about how to provide excellent abortion care, and I was very proud that we made changes and added new ideas when we had them.

One morning, Sophie asked me and Françoise to sit down with her to listen to some concerns she was having. Sophie and I talked all the time, so I knew it had to be something serious because she hadn't said a word to me.

We were all at the kitchen table, mugs of coffee steaming before us, and Françoise and I were chatting about something. Sophie had a few of the recipe books open, and she cleared her throat to get our attention, like the professor she had once been. As soon as we quieted, she began, and we listened intently. Sophie never asked for anything, so the least we could do was listen.

"I want to talk with you two about a woman I met in the market. You know how careful we are not to say hello to anyone we don't know well, in case she was a patient...well, this woman came right up to me and told me she needed to talk.

"We found a quiet spot at one of the outdoor tables in the café. Over lemonade, she tearfully asked me if it was normal that she had been in misery since she came to us for an abortion *three years ago!* I vaguely remembered her—but not much about her story. Here's her recipe for Boeuf Bourguignon." Sophie turned the book around so that Françoise and I could see it. The date was August, 1964. The patient's name was Nanette, aged 25. According to the coded recipe, she had a one-year-old and a four-year-old. Her husband was fifteen years older than she, and had recently had a heart attack. She didn't think she could cope with caring for him as well as two young children and a new baby. She had been an Our Lady patient, which indicated that she had needed more than the most basic counseling.

"Sophie, I don't know what is going on with her now, but you did everything you possibly could have. Look, you talked with her for more than three hours before her abortion. You..."

Sophie interrupted me. "Jane, I can see this is making you feel defensive, which is exactly what I was afraid of. At first while Nanette was talking to me, I felt that too—and I felt very sad that somehow I had failed her. Even before I came home and looked at the notes, I knew we had spent a lot of time together. But that's not the point. I finally figured out that *I'm* not the point—*she* is."

Françoise jumped in. She always played the role of mediator on the rare occasions when Sophie and I disagreed. "Sophie, tell us the rest of the story," she said, giving me the evil eye for interrupting. "What did you say to her?"

"I didn't know what to say. I could tell she was still hurting, so I just told her honestly that I was sorry about that. And I asked if she thought she had done the wrong thing. At first she said yes, that she had regretted her decision all these years. She stopped going to church because she didn't feel worthy of God's love. She even felt unworthy of her children's love. She was just a wreck. But then, as she talked more, I asked her to remind me why she had thought it would be best not to bring that new life into the world. She told me about how much she loved her husband and how afraid they both were when he had the heart attack. Then she talked about her children, and what they needed from her at the ages of one and four. Honestly, it made me exhausted just to hear about her life.

"It sounded to me like her issues were some of those familiar ones—forgiveness, especially self-forgiveness, and self-worth. There came a point in our conversation when we talked about what she believes God thinks. She said she believes that God has forgiven her, and then she burst into tears again and asked me, 'But do I deserve it?' I told her that she was the only one who could answer that question. That wasn't very satisfying. Then I thought of something that might help her forgive herself. I asked what it was like for her husband, and especially her children, for her to be so miserable. She burst into tears again and said that she tried to hide her feelings from them.

"I told her, 'You know you can't hide anything. Especially from the children. They are like little sponges. They will know that maman is in pain, they just won't know why. And, because they are children, they will most likely believe there is something they have done wrong. That is just the way of children.' Nanette wailed, 'Oh, I don't want to hurt them.'

"I pushed a little bit more. 'What would you need to do in order to be with them—the way you want to?' She answered tearfully, 'I'd...I'd have to forgive myself.'

"I smiled gently at her. 'Yes, you would,' I said. 'Whether you deserve it or not.' I talked with her about the idea that it was her *interpretation* of what she had chosen that was causing so much pain, and I asked if she could imagine any other way to think about what she had done that would allow her to feel like a good woman again. That was hard for her, but she finally came back to all the reasons she decided to have the abortion. But even then, it seemed almost impossible for her to hold on to that. It was as if she was determined to be miserable and give herself the punishment she thought she deserved."

"This is exactly why I have been begging you to use the *moscocero*, Jane," Françoise said. "This is a horrible story. Maybe we shouldn't have done an abortion for this woman."

"Maybe not," Sophie said, "but I could see from my notes that she was adamant about wanting it. She even told me that she would do *anything* not to have the baby. I was afraid she might seek another illegal source—or even harm herself if we didn't do it."

"So, what are you suggesting, Sophie?" I asked, a bit impatiently. I'm afraid I had more of Dr. Nick in me than I would like to admit. "What do you want us to do?"

"I don't know," she admitted, shaking her head. "I just didn't want to be the only one to know this. Maybe we could talk more with each other if this kind of patient comes to us. I don't want to carry the weight of this by myself."

"That's exactly why we stopped doing abortions on women who remain pitiful in spite of our best efforts," I said. "If the woman is still feeling pitiful, then we end up feeling like it was *our* decision, not theirs, and that is not right. As for the *moscocero*," I turned to Françoise, "we have talked about that before. How can women be strengthened by making such an important life decision if they can't remember that they have done it?"

Both Socorro and Paulette were using *moscocero* in their practices in Peru and Italy. It seemed that I was the only impediment to using it in France, but I felt so strongly against it that Françoise and Sophie had capitulated. It was a discussion—you could even say argument—we had been through before. Although I wanted to dismiss Sophie's analysis, an experience in nursing school in California, when my colleague Marisol and I worked to help a woman named Catalina with her impossible decision, hovered just outside my consciousness.

Although Sophie and Françoise usually went along with me, I found that I doubted my decision about using *moscocero*. I kept remembering how much I had wanted to use it for Bernadette, and worried that, in my wish to make women stronger, I was adding to their shame. Finally, I decided that I needed to face my fears and ask about it. I wrote to Bernadette and Sophie's sister Gertrude, and asked them if they wished they could forget everything that happened.

I got a letter back from Bernadette very quickly. She wrote:

Oh, my dear Jane. You will remember how hard I tried to forget what had happened to me. Instead of making me feel better, it made me feel as though I were already dead. Today I believe that all my memories are part of who I am—both the bitter and the sweet. Thanks to you, I have no regrets.

That made me feel much better. But I worried that Gertrude didn't respond, and I had just about decided that I had ruined her life when her letter finally came.

Dear Jane,

   I am sorry it has taken me so long to answer. I have been very busy. I am in charge of all the official events for the Mayor's Office, and we have just dedicated a new park.
   I was a bit surprised at your question because Sophie and I have discussed this many times. Something happened to me when I was with you that I have never quite been able to express. Although I have always been a very strong woman, and have often had a lot on my shoulders, it always seemed like a terrible burden before. Now I am overjoyed when the Mayor, or my children, or my husband, de-pend on me. How can I explain it? I made a choice to live my life on my own terms. To answer your question, I don't wish to forget any of it.

I can't say that their responses totally stilled the second-guessing that was always with me, but they tamped it down a bit—enough for me to carry on.
   The question around using *moscocero* lingered.

CHAPTER 28

STACY

Our Lady, Spring 1968

My heart registered the accent before my brain even made sense of it. I quickened my pace, coming into the kitchen where a young woman was talking animatedly to Sophie. I was right! It was an American.

"I had no idea I was pregnant when I planned this trip. I had been working so hard—I just—you know, wanted a little time off. And then, boom. My boobs are sore, I can't stand to drink milk, and the smell of fish sends me off. Those are all the signs I had before. I know they made abortion legal in England last year, but I wanted to see if there was any possibility other than going over there. And, incredibly, I met a woman who knows a woman who knows a woman...and here I am!" She looked triumphant. "What *is* the deal with this place?" she asked.

Her name was Stacy. In addition to needing an abortion, she told us she belonged to a group of women who found illegal abortionists for women in Detroit, Michigan. I decided not to risk doing a *Corazon de Gracia* herbal abortion on her because I was afraid she would want to share the discovery with her American abortionists. We used the Abra powder the way we always did and determined that she was eight weeks pregnant. She was delighted by our way of keeping records and provided us with the recipe for her mother's famous pumpkin pie. But when it came time for her abortion, I pulled out the never-used-anymore siphon and curette from the storage closet, even though I knew the *Corazon* would be more comfortable. I just couldn't risk information about our magical herbs going back to the United States with Stacy. Despite my misgivings, she was astonished that the procedure was so quick and easy.

Stacy said, "Even though I explain the abortion process to women over and over several times a week, I have never heard of anything like this machine you are using. Oh, I wish you would come visit and demonstrate the procedure. It is so frustrating dealing with these abortionists—they all want so much money, and they are so demanding. And we don't have any way to be sure the women are being well cared for and respected. The women I work with would never believe you are doing the abortions yourselves."

When it was time to dispose of the fetal remains, I wasn't sure what Stacy would make of our usual process. I tried to explain our approach. "Because there is a churchyard here, we bury the remains. It's not a religious ritual—just the most simple and obvious way to take care of the tissue—to return it to the earth. We usually ask the women if they would like to do the burial themselves."

"That's interesting," Stacy said. "I am not attached to this pregnancy—it's not a baby to me or anything like that—but I wouldn't mind knowing where it is. And I'd definitely like to bury it myself. Otherwise, it's my plan never to think about this again."

Sophie looked at her kindly, "Even if this is not a big deal to you, you will probably think about it again. It is a part of your life experience. What if you remembered this as a time you were resourceful and resilient and took care of yourself in a good way?"

"I like that," Stacy answered, looking thoughtful. "I have sometimes wondered how we would do abortions if women invented them. If abortion weren't so furtive and filled with shame for so many women. If we had a graveyard at our disposal, I'm sure some women would like that option. And some of them would take the tissue home and bury it. And some of them would just want us to throw it down the toilet."

Remembering the woman Lucie took care of from Lyon in the very early days of Our Lady, I said, "I wish we were able to make those choices available, but the one time a woman wanted to bury the fetus herself, we ended up with the constable at our door, so we stopped giving that option. I hate to worry about being arrested."

"You are not kidding," Stacy laughed ruefully. "It is scary for all our volunteers. We do our best to divide the services up and move to different locations, but there is always the chance that a woman tells the wrong friend or someone gets suspicious. That daily fear comes with the territory."

When it was time to go to the cemetery, Stacy was very quiet. She dug a shallow hole, placed the small embryo into it, and covered it with dirt. She surprised me by whispering, "Goodbye, little one. I'm sorry it wasn't the right time." She took a stone with her, but decided not to have the scar on her palm. "I don't know how I would explain that to anyone," she said. "I guess I don't feel any need to identify myself physically with this experience. But all the ways you do things are making me look at this a bit differently."

I hesitated to say anything about the T'ana. I had never known any other women who were doing abortions, but I wished I could share those stories with Stacy. "We have learned a lot from rituals that indigenous Wise Women have been doing for many years. For us, this is sacred work," I said. "I don't mean that in the traditional way—connected to a male god. I mean as one of the sacred blood mysteries that are part of the journey of women's lives."

"I've never seen abortion as anything more than survival," Stacy said.

"It is that, and yet so much more," Sophie said. "Don't women deserve more than survival?"

Stacy only stayed with us for two days—she insisted that she was fine to travel and had to rejoin her friends in Provence lest anyone be suspicious of her side trip. She thanked us over and over for helping her, and paid us $200 American. That was significantly less than she would pay in Detroit, and significantly more than most of our patients paid.

After she was gone, Françoise, Sophie, and I sat in the kitchen and talked about her visit.

"I felt so guilty about not using the *Corazon*," I said, "But I think it was the right thing.

Sophie nodded in agreement. "She had a safe, easy abortion—undoubtedly better than anything available in America."

"But this makes me wonder about the future," Françoise said. "It sounds as though the women in Detroit are seeing so many more patients than we are. We can't tell them about the *Corazon de Gracia* herb because they'll want it all, the way Americans always do. Excuse me, chérie," she said, "But you know I am right. It's a shame because even if they didn't have the herbs, it would mean so much to them to use Nick's siphon invention."

"I agree, Françoise. And that's something they could have. Nick would send them one if they wanted. But our situation here is so different from theirs," I mused.

When Stacy had hugged me goodbye, she asked again if I would visit her group. I didn't take the idea seriously until a couple of weeks later when I got her letter repeating the invitation. As I contemplated the trip, I realized that over the years I had become a part of the French countryside—as much as the goats along the road and the vines that covered the walls of the convent. For so many years, I wore a uniform. First, I wore the habit, then the Navy blues, then surgical scrubs, and now the wooden clogs and overalls of a gardener. I have a few garments in my closet for special occasions—like the pretty dress I wore for Lucie's wedding—but Sophie and I lived a very simple life. I couldn't even imagine what kind of clothes I would need to visit Detroit in the spring. It was hard enough to find appropriate clothes when we went to New York to visit Lucie.

"Do I look old?" I asked Sophie one evening, squinting into the small bathroom mirror and holding my wild hair back.

"Of course not, dear. Fifty-five is not old. You are beautiful."

"I should know better than to ask you," I smiled and blew her a kiss. "But if I go to Detroit, what on earth will I wear?"

"*If?* I thought you had decided. Weren't you intrigued? Are you going to let an issue of wardrobe stop you? What would Simone de Beauvoir say?"

"She has nicer clothes!" I laughed.

"But there is so much you could teach them—even more than the siphon. You have a way with patients—and you could tell them about all the things Lucie has shared from her psychology classes. Surely these ideas would be invaluable to the work they are doing."

"Maybe," I said. "If you help me figure out a wardrobe, maybe I will go."

Should I have known it was another chance for failure?

CHAPTER 29

I AM SORRY ABOUT THE BLINDFOLD

Detroit, 1968

Sophie and Françoise helped me cobble together a 'Detroit trousseau,' and off I went. My flight was uneventful, if you can say flying thousands of miles in the air from one continent to another is uneventful. I am still amazed the danged things get off the ground. I arrived early in the morning. The plan was that at the end of the day, I would check into a small hotel in the center of town near the places they were working. I couldn't imagine they moved around and did their work in different apartments every day in order to stay safe from the authorities. Quite a feat of organization.

I took a cab from the airport to a rundown apartment building where Stacy lived. She welcomed me with a cup of American coffee, which I found I had missed, and stowed my suitcase behind the couch. Stacy explained we would begin by my sitting in on some counseling. About an hour after I arrived, we saw our first patient—a young mother of two, named Natalie, whose husband was in Vietnam. "He came back on leave for three days, and now here I am!" she said, shrugging her shoulders. "There's no way I can have a baby now." Stacy asked the requisite medical history questions and estimated the woman was about eight weeks based on the time she was with her husband. I noticed she wrote the basic information on a small blue index card, but didn't seem to take any other notes.

Stacy explained the procedure. I was very impressed that her group seemed to share Dr. Levy's insistence on full information. She described the process of going to one address and being blindfolded and taken to another address. And she said the fee would be $600.

"Thank goodness my mother gave me money to get my roof fixed," Natalie said. "This is way more important. We can live with buckets for the time being." When Stacy seemed satisfied that all the necessary information had been given and received, she instructed Natalie to call her the following morning for the address. The woman thanked her and left.

A soft knock on the door revealed the second patient—a young black woman who introduced herself as Ricki and told us she was a college student. Stacy asked the same basic medical questions—age, date of last period, etc. It appeared Ricki was about nine weeks pregnant.

"Are you certain about your decision?" Stacy asked the nervous-looking young woman.

Ricki answered, "I am very sure. I am the first person in my family to go to college, and I hope to go on to study architecture. Having a baby now would make that impossible. And besides, I am not with the father anymore. We had been dating for three years, but when I told him I thought I was pregnant, he said this is on me. He hasn't returned any of my calls since."

Stacy smiled warmly. "I am so sorry. Unfortunately, I hear it all too often."

Ricki wiped her eyes with her sleeve, holding her head down.

"Are you okay?" Stacy asked.

"Yes, I am fine," Ricki answered, her voice stronger. "I just want to get this over with."

Stacy again explained the procedure: Ricki would come back in two days to a location they would tell her over the phone. Then she would be blindfolded and driven to another place where the abortion would be done. She would be given a packet of antibiotics and a medicine to take after the procedure to help her uterus return to its normal, small size.

"Is it a real doctor?" Ricki asked, hopefully.

"It is a practitioner who has had a lot of experience," Stacy answered, a bit defensively. I was sure it was a response she had rehearsed. "I am sorry about the blindfold," Stacy said. "But I'm sure you can understand the abortionist can't risk having anyone identify him. You know, of course, this is against the law. In the unlikely case anyone asks, you will need to remain silent. No one will be able to tell that you had an abortion—afterward, it will be like a period—or a miscarriage in case someone knows you have been pregnant."

"No one knows except the guy," Ricki said.

"Okay. But did you tell him you were going to have an abortion?"

"No. He told *me* that's what I should do. No one else knows."

"That's just as well. The fewer people who know, the better. If there is a friend you really trust to keep a secret, bring her with you, but she'll need to wait at the first location. It usually takes about two hours. As I told you, the abortion itself takes less than 15 minutes, but we drive women back and forth in small groups, so that's why it can take so long. Any questions?"

Ricki looked desolate. "I wanted to ask about the money. They told me six hundred dollars?"

Stacy answered, "Will that be a problem?"

"I have $150. I hope I can borrow the rest from my brother, but I can't tell him what it's for. My family is Southern Baptist. I am the baby of the family, and I have always been the good girl. I just can't tell him."

"Would he trust you enough to lend it to you without knowing why?"

"I hope so," Ricki answered timidly.

"Some women in your situation say they need to borrow money to help a friend," Stacy suggested.

"That might work," Ricki said. "Thanks."

"If you can't get it all, call me," Stacy said. "We will figure something out."

CHAPTER 30

STOP WHEN YOU ARE DONE, AND DON'T STOP UNTIL YOU ARE DONE

Stacy put her hands together as if she had completed a project and said, "Well, okay. We are finished with this part."

But I looked at Ricki and recognized we were not. Dr. Levy taught me the most basic rule of doing an abortion. He said, "Stop when you are done, and don't stop until you are done." It was a humorous reminder to be patient enough to wait for the tug against the instruments as the uterus closed down and you could feel the ridged texture of a clean uterine wall. The same advice applies to the emotional aspects of an abortion. When it came to counseling, what Lucie had taught me to look for is a sense of peace. I wasn't getting that from Ricki.

It was clear I was not supposed to speak, but I couldn't un-know what I knew, so I asked, "Ricki, do you believe in God?"

Stacy immediately gave me a warning look, but Ricki burst into tears and, trembling, said, "Yes, and I am afraid he will punish me for this. Will I go to hell?"

Stacy looked alarmed as I continued.

"Tell me about God," I said, placing my hand on her arm.

"Well, for me, it has always been Jesus by my side. He was with me when my mother died, and he took her to heaven. He is loving above everything, and he takes care of us even when we cannot take care of ourselves."

I was focused on Ricki, but I could sense Stacy move back a bit to give me room to slide my chair right in front of the young woman.

"Is Jesus always with you?" I asked.

"Always," Ricki said.

"Is he with you right now?"

Ricki's eyes filled with tears. She didn't say anything. Then, with a huge sigh, she said, "I didn't imagine he would be here with me, but he is."

"How is he caring for you right now?"

Ricki closed her eyes and said, "He has enfolded me in his arms. His heart is beating against mine. He has whispered to me he loves me and I am forgiven."

I sighed my own deep sigh, and we sat like that for a moment. Stacy was squirming in her chair, but she had the good sense to be quiet. Finally, Ricki opened her eyes. She reached over and hugged me, and, of course, I hugged her back. And then, I could feel that we were, indeed, done.

Later in the evening, when we were sharing a bottle of wine in her kitchen, Stacy told me that once volunteers were trained, no one sat in on their sessions, so she was at liberty to explore the woman's deeper feelings if she wanted to.

"Sometimes I work with women who are struggling with their religious beliefs—especially Catholics and Baptists—but I wouldn't have any idea what to say to them. I am an atheist," she said.

"So am I," I offered.

"But you talked about her religion. About Jesus. How can I? What would I say?"

"I don't talk about religion all the time—only when I sense that's what is difficult for the woman. Just follow their lead, as I did with Ricki."

"How did you get it was hard for her?" Stacy asked.

"For one thing, she mentioned she was a Baptist. There are an awful lot of strict lessons for women in that church. But it was when she said she had always been the good girl. Did you see her face? It was as if she was apologizing to us."

"I did notice that. I hoped she would be all right. But I was glad you asked her about it."

"She probably would have been all right. But I guess I want more than 'all right' for the women I see. To be honest, I do this exploration as much for myself as for the patients. This work has been my life. I want to do it with integrity. I don't want any regrets, or any fears I may have missed something important—that I avoided something because I was uncomfortable."

Stacy nodded in understanding.

"If I'm exploring a woman's religious faith, I want to understand what she believes about God and forgiveness and sin and all of it. So I might ask questions like, 'Do you believe in a loving, forgiving God, or is your God more like an angry daddy?' Often they laugh or cry when they realize they made their own father into God. I might ask if they have prayed for a miscarriage. If the woman says she has, it suggests she really doesn't want a baby. I ask her how having a miscarriage would be different from having an abortion—and she almost always says it wouldn't be her fault. Women don't think they are equipped to make decisions about life and death, although women have done that throughout time. One of my patients said, 'It is not only my right, it is my *responsibility* to decide when to bring a new life into the world through my body.' I try to remind them the idea of sin can be just another way of saying we are human—that we are imperfect."

"That is very compassionate," Stacy said.

"There is so much judgment in this world—and extra for women. I'm not showing them any more compassion than I would like to receive myself."

Stacy furrowed her brow. "I have always seen abortion as a means of survival," she said.

I laughed. "I remember you told me that the first day I met you. Perhaps it is because it is connected to the convent for me, but I have always thought of abortion as sacred."

"That doesn't make any sense," Stacy insisted. "The Catholic Church is completely opposed to abortion. You should hear some of the things the Detroit Bishop has said about the murder of innocent lives, and going to hell any time the subject is mentioned. And the priests talk about it from the pulpit. I have had Catholic patients who tell me they understand they are damned to hell, but they still need to have an abortion. I guarantee you, there is nothing sacred about it!"

"The way I am using the word 'sacred' isn't anything to do with a church. One of the meanings of sacred is 'set apart.' A woman who is making this decision is set apart from her usual life, and if she has enough support, she is surrounded by grace. It is a holy mystery. Holy equals whole. The opportunity for a woman to be whole. That is what abortion is to me."

"Abortion is a ritual? Isn't that a little…well…a little primitive?"

"Primitive? Perhaps. But if you mean unsophisticated, you are overlooking the many rituals we live by every day, whether we are religious or not. Look at what we say when someone sneezes; our handshakes; our marriages and graduations."

"I guess those are rituals," Stacy agreed. She refilled her glass, and then mine.

"More than just rituals. For many women, these are what ethnographers call 'rites of passage'—events that change us in deep ways we can't explain."

I noticed there was a battered dictionary on the bookshelf next to the sofa.

"Let's see what Webster's has to say about it." I thumbed through to the r's. "This one works—'A ritual is a set of acts repeated in a precise manner.' If that doesn't describe an abortion, I don't know what does." We both laughed.

"I've never heard anyone talk like this before," Stacy said thoughtfully. "I remember you said abortion is sacred when I was with you at Our Lady. But I'm not sure I really understand."

"I don't pretend to be an expert," I said, "but I have done a lot of reading about ancient women. My friends and I are learning from a group of Wise Women in Peru. They speak of honoring the blood mysteries."

"Sounds creepy. What does it mean?"

I returned the Webster's to its shelf and moved my pillow to settle in on the sofa.

"The mystery is that women bleed in these transformational rites of passage: menstruation, childbirth, miscarriage, and abortion—but they do not die. Men can't figure out what to make of it. In medieval times, that fact was used to turn what was once, perhaps, a reverence for women, into fear and hatred of the feminine. And we still live with the residual effects. What do you imagine these laws against abortion are about?"

"It is the church and the government telling us what is moral and what is not."

"And yet, have you ever talked with a woman who is not doing the most moral thing she can figure out to do?"

Stacy was silent for a moment. She took a sip of her wine and said, "That's true. But if the laws aren't about morality, what are they about?"

"Control, pure and simple," I answered with a sigh.

I'm not sure why I poured my heart out to this woman I hardly knew. But as I went on, I found myself almost in tears.

"Abortion is not as simple as moral or immoral," I continued. "It is not like a line with good at one end and bad at the other end. Abortion is more like a circle. It encompasses many contradictions—grief and relief, loss and joy, goodness and exigency, sacrifice and self-love. And abortion is an experience that can be messy and bloody, and all too human. It is an experience with ragged edges. By that I mean that it is rarely simple—there are so many things the woman tries to consider—her relationship with the man, beliefs about motherhood, her deepest yearnings and dreams, worries about having enough, religious teachings, loyalty to self and family, fear of the unknown, the wish to do the *right* thing. But there is one common aspect I've found in all the decisions—can you guess what it is?"

"Desperation?" Stacy answered. "That is what I have usually seen. It is so painful."

"Yes. I have often seen that too. Yet underneath it—underneath the desperation and fear, and the shame and anger, is love. Love every time."

"What do you mean?" Stacy said, looking confused.

"Why does a woman choose an abortion? Because she loves the not-to-be child so much that she cannot and will not bring it into a bad situation. Because she loves herself enough to recognize it is not good for her to give birth to a baby that she doesn't want. Because she loves the children she already has too much to put them at risk when resources are already stretched too far. Sometimes even because she loves the man she is involved with, more than she loves herself. Love isn't simple, but one way or another, it is always about love."

We talked for several hours more until I was exhausted. So many times I wanted to tell her about the *Corazon de Gracia*, but I knew I shouldn't. So I told her the things I had thought about my work for all those years. We talked until it was too late for me to go to a hotel. She made up her couch for me, and I fell into a deep sleep punctuated by dreams of the faces and stories of the women whose lives abortion had braided with mine.

CHAPTER 31

NOT LADIES, NOT PATIENTS, NOT DOCTORS

Early the next morning, there was a knock on the door. Stacy opened it to two women who introduced themselves briefly as Libby and Sarah. Stacy explained that they were administrators in the organization. They ushered Stacy into the next room, leaving me sitting by myself at the kitchen table, wondering what was up. They spoke in hushed tones, but I could still hear them.

Stacy said, "She did a great job on my abortion in France—and it was so fast. She has come all this way—I trust her."

"I'm glad you trust her, but we need to know at least as much about her as we do about the other abortionists," Sarah replied, sounding authoritative.

Libby chimed in, "That makes sense."

I got up from the kitchen table and poked my head around the corner. I said, "Ladies, I am more than happy to share my qualifications with you. It will take a little while to tell you about my background. Can we make a pot of coffee?"

"We can talk over coffee," Sarah said, "but we're not *ladies* by any stretch of the word."

"I'm sorry," I said. "I have been out of the country for a long time, and I am a little old-fashioned, at least in my vocabulary. How should I address you?"

They looked perplexed, so I just continued.

"It's good you care about your patients."

Stacy looked hesitantly at her compatriots.

It was Sarah who corrected me again. "We don't call them patients. They aren't sick, and we aren't doctors," she said firmly.

"Got it," I said. "Not ladies, not patients, not doctors."

"Right," Sarah said. "So tell us about yourself. How did you get into this?"

I let out a long sigh. "It all started in Paris with ten little girls."

I told them about my Aunt Mathilde's boarding school, my seven-year-old students, smuggling little Jewish girls out of Paris, and helping Dr. Levy provide abortion care. Then I told them how I got my RN in the Navy. At the word 'Navy,' Libby sputtered. Then I said I had worked with Dr. Nicos Ariti in Alameda. "He runs the Navy's Civilian Services in Japan. And he invented the device I look forward to showing you." I gestured to the flight bag I hadn't yet opened. "Dr. Nick insisted on providing abortion care to the poorest women in both Alameda and Kyoto." I continued, "When I left the Navy"—my ears burned as I remembered how I left the Navy in disgrace—"I did some teaching." My summer class with Oliver and Lucie surely qualified as teaching. "Then I decided to go back to France. I had access to a renovated convent outside of Paris, and I began my practice there. It is a different pace from yours, though. We usually care for fewer than ten patients a week."

Libby looked shocked. "Then I guess you haven't seen much of a range of cases," she said.

"Perhaps I wasn't clear in my story," I answered, trying not to sound defensive. I was only fifty-five, but with these intense young women, I might as well have been a hundred. "Abortion care has been my work for thirty years. I have been performing abortions myself for over twenty years. In California, we saw about 35 women for abortions every week. In Japan, we cared for about 100 abortion pa—we did about 100 abortions a week. I'm guessing I've seen just about every kind of abortion case there is."

Stacy asked quietly, "Have you ever had a death?"

I had the sense she was asking as much out of her own fear as out of any evaluation of my skills.

"Only once. I assisted the doctor in caring for a woman who became septic after another abortionist had performed some kind of procedure on her. She died."

There was a moment of silence—who knows whether in memory of the dead woman, or in anticipation of the unthinkable happening to them.

"My current work is different in scale," I said, "but from the counseling I observed, it's clear we agree on some standards."

"What do you mean?" Libby asked. Stacy looked nervous. She didn't need to tell me to keep my part of Ricki's work to myself.

"Well, first of all, you share information. You want the woman to understand the procedure and the risks it entails. Unless things have changed dramatically in this country, that is not the usual way medicine is practiced."

"You are right," Sarah said. "We want women to be empowered by this experience, not further victimized."

Libby added, "And we want them to be our partners. After all, this is their life. We are providing a service, but the last thing we want to do is to patronize them."

"Exactly how my first teacher, Dr. Levy, would explain it." Skeptical looks passed between them. In their experience of doctors, patronization was *de rigueur*. "It was Levy who taught me the importance of giving women full information. It appears to me you are also concerned about knowing whether the woman is confident about her decision."

"Yes...that is critical," Libby said urgently. "How can we risk what we are risking if she isn't sure she wants an abortion?" They all nodded vigorously.

"I agree completely," I said.

Stacy added, "And we must be clear she is not being pressured by someone else. We learned that the hard way."

"That is also important to us," I said. "And you give this excellent information about birth control," I said, pointing to the newsprint *Birth Control Handbook* put out by McGill University in Montreal. "I will be sure to order some."

"They are great," Stacy said, trying to keep the conversation enthusiastic. "Those handbooks were written and put out as a protest by students."

"The women I see will appreciate this information," I responded, trying to keep the enthusiasm alive.

Libby looked at me defiantly and said, "But you're just doing abortions for women who are rich. The ones who can afford to come to your hotel thing for a week? How much do you charge?"

"On the contrary. Most of the women who come to us are—I can't think of the right way to explain it compared to American society. They are poor, but working hard for the little they earn. In Europe, it is common and inexpensive to travel within your country and even from one country to the next. And it is common for women to take time every year for a religious retreat, which is why they are able to come to our convent, Our Lady of Perpetual Grace, for anywhere from three days to a week."

"They are with you for three days?" Libby asked, incredulous.

"Yes. We are fortunate. It gives us a lot of time to work with each woman, especially those who need more attention."

"But it is like a hotel, right? I mean, you feed them and everything?" Libby asked, still defiant. It was obvious to me I hadn't won her over with either my skill or my charm.

"Yes, we eat together. And to answer your question, they pay what they can. It is important for the woman to pay something, so she has a stake in the process. We ask for a larger donation from wealthy women, and a smaller donation from women with fewer resources. It seems we have that in common, too." I turned to Stacy. "I noticed in counseling, you told the woman you would work something out if she wasn't able to find all the money." Stacy blushed. She told me later she had been criticized for being too soft about finances. After all, they had to pay the men who did the abortions.

I continued, "Because we perform the abortions ourselves, and we only take a small salary, we can provide care for no charge at all when we need to. Our most frequent donation is about 150 francs."

Libby looked surprised. She said, "I wish *we* could only charge $150."

I laughed. "That translates to about 30 dollars, which includes her room and board. When we started Our Lady in 1951, we figured out how much we would need to cover our costs. As we added things, like a telephone, we increased our fee. Since we ask for more from our wealthy clients, there has always been plenty." They all looked surprised. I was happy to finally have something to impress the skeptical Libby.

"That's wonderful," Stacy said, happy her French 'show and tell' project, as I obviously was, finally had some merit. "So, can you show us the gizmo you used on me? I told everyone how quickly you did my abortion, and no one believes me!"

Imagining I had passed the hazing stage, I unzipped my bag and pulled out the gizmo. I liked that name better than USA—*Uterine Siphon Apparatus*—and resolved to introduce the moniker to my Paris team, as I was now thinking about Françoise, Sophie, and, occasionally still, Levy.

I explained the mechanism and how it worked, and asked Stacy to bring a bowl of water. She placed it on the table in front of me. I put the thin metal siphon tube into the water and pulled back on the syringe, creating a vacuum. The bowl emptied and the small glass jar filled. The three women gasped in wonder. I showed them how the gasket prevented air from being introduced into the uterus, and that was that. They were ready to see it in action.

"I assume your doctors work the same way I was taught before I had the siphon—to dilate the cervix and use forceps to empty the uterus, and then do curettage? With this gizmo, the forceps are rarely needed, and I only do a gentle curettage to ascertain the walls of the uterus are clean."

The women looked at each other. After a moment, Libby said unsteadily, "Yes, that is the way they do it." I wasn't convinced she had any idea how her practitioners were doing abortions. Later, Stacy told me that none of them, for all their bravado, had actually seen an abortion being done. Stacy's personal experience of having one made her an expert among her peers.

I decided to take a risk and talk about counseling. "Because France is a Catholic country, there is a lot of talk about sin. We provide services to women who need emotional support to be certain about their decisions."

In spite of Stacy's warning look, I was determined to wade deeper into what was obviously dangerous territory. I continued. "We see women who doubt their own morality, women who don't believe they are valuable enough for their wishes to matter, women who think God is a mean and punishing father, women who will do anything to try to keep their man, and women who say they are going to be damned for having an abortion, yet tell us they must do it anyway. You are fortunate to live in a secular country where women don't have to struggle with ideas like that. It can be very painful."

Stacy looked hesitantly at Libby and Sarah. "That happens here, too, sometimes," she said, very obviously not mentioning Ricki.

Libby explained, "We don't believe in making women justify their decisions to us. If they want to tell their story, of course we will listen."

"But what do you do if they are experiencing confusion or conflict?" I asked.

Libby said, "We listen."

"You listen?" I asked. I felt a bit chastened because, before learning from Lucie, that's probably how I would have answered.

"That's all psychiatrists do, isn't it? I mean...I don't know about it myself, but that's what people say, anyway," Sarah said, blushing fiercely.

I was not able to hold my counsel.

"But if you don't offer any way to interpret having an abortion other than as a sin or a tragedy, how are they empowered?" I asked, gently. "My colleague Lucie calls it 'reframing.' It means giving women new imagery and alternative language that they won't hear in church. I worked for years without having any idea what a difference that can make to women. And over the years we have learned from every pa—from every woman."

Libby and Sarah didn't seem impressed by anything that had happened 'over the years.'

"Lucie began changing the way we talk with women way back in 1951." Their collective gasp represented the realization that I probably was 105 years old.

Libby collected herself. "We are not interested in being social workers. We want to provide a service the patriarchy has denied women—an opportunity to decide for themselves whether to become mothers. That's all." The conversation seemed to be over.

The process of being cleared to do an abortion was not finished, even after I had passed that job interview, as I thought of it. They explained that they had several doctors they referred to, and the abortions were done in hotels or apartments on a different day from the counseling session. I suggested that I could provide care for Ricki, the woman whose counseling session I had watched, because she already knew me. They accepted that idea. Stacy pointed out that it made sense to have me care for her because Ricki might be having trouble with the fee. They all agreed on that, too. The problem appeared to be getting approval for the scheme from farther up the chain of command.

"We need this device," Stacy argued. "It would make the abortions faster, easier, and safer."

"But they would need to persuade the abortionist to use it," Libby argued. "It is almost impossible to get him to do anything differently."

"But what if he still gets his money, and it is easier for him?" Stacy tried again.

Sarah weighed in. "Let's set up this abortion and get the higher-ups to come and watch it."

So it was agreed that we would contact Ricki and she would come back to Stacy's apartment the next day instead of doing the usual blindfold two-step. I'd have the gizmo and the sterilized instruments I needed, and they would set it up so that the women who ran the show would come along. When I went for a walk outside Stacy's apartment, I picked up a small white stone and put it in my pocket.

CHAPTER 32

HE IS STILL WITH ME

The next morning a small group gathered in Stacy's apartment: Ricki, the administrators, Sarah and Libby, and two women I had not met who seemed to be even more senior in the organization. They looked a bit surprised when Ricki hugged me, but no one said anything. When Stacy took Ricki into the bedroom to get her ready, the older one, a petite brunette with weathered skin, shook my hand and said, "I'm Candy, so good to meet you. Libby and Sarah have told us so much about you." She turned to the woman next to her, who was a bit larger, with long, wild hair, wearing a brightly flowered muumuu. "This is Angela. She and I work most closely with the doctors—I mean, the abortionists we use. We would be the ones to introduce anything new to them, as difficult as you can imagine it would be," she said, laughing.

I liked her immediately. I said hello to Angela, and we walked together into the kitchen so I could wash my hands and put on gloves.

Ricki's abortion went very easily. Candy and Angela were shocked at how fast it was and how comfortable Ricki was.

Candy took me to the side and said, "There is so little bleeding. We hardly needed the sheet. Are you sure it is complete? It is just terrible when women have retained tissue. They call us in the middle of the night, and there isn't much we can do except tell them to use a heating pad and hope the tissue passes."

"I am quite sure it is complete. That's the beauty of the gizmo. I realize you didn't get to hear my story, but I have been performing abortions for over twenty years."

"I don't mean to question your expertise," Candy said. "But from what I hear, your setup is very different from ours. If there was a problem, the woman would still be with you."

"You're right. I didn't mean to discount your appropriate concern. Come into the kitchen and we'll check the tissue. Dr. Nick taught me how important this is. I'm sure your practitioners always do it." Of course, I had no such belief, but I didn't want to make them any more defensive than they already were.

We left Ricki lying on the bed with a blanket and a heating pad. I carried the bottle with what the doctors call 'products of conception' to the sink and asked for a glass dish. Stacy climbed on a stepstool and brought down a Pyrex pie plate.

"This is perfect," I said. "Do you have a strainer you don't mind me using?"

Stacy said, "You can use this one," gesturing to a colander hanging on a hook above the stove.

"Before I begin, I want to acknowledge that this clinical part of an abortion can seem disrespectful or even callous. But, as with any medical procedure, it is essential. I am not a religious person, but I like to begin by saying, 'Little spirit, I am sorry it was not the right time for you to be born.'" It was what Stacy said as she was burying the embryo in our churchyard after her abortion at Our Lady.

Stacy glanced at me, and I could see a tear in her eye.

Candy made a face and said, "That doesn't sound like something any of our practitioners would say."

"I understand. It's just for me."

"I don't mean to be rude, but can we get on with this? What exactly are we doing?" Angela asked, looking over my shoulder.

"We are checking to be sure the abortion is complete," I said. "We start by pouring the contents of the uterus through the strainer and then washing out any blood and fluid." I used the spray attachment on the sink. "Then we empty the tissue into the glass container and add some water. You'll see that the tissue floats."

Stacy and Candy moved closer.

"I'm holding the plate out over the sink so there is light behind it. That allows us to identify the essential elements of the pregnancy. This is the embryo," I pointed to the translucent tissue. It was about an inch and a half long.

Stacy's mouth was open. "That's it?" she asked.

Angela pushed closer. "Is that the head?"

"Yes," I answered. "You can see the eyes, right here."

"Oh my," Candy said. "I have never seen one whole like this."

"With this gizmo, the embryonic tissue often comes out intact, just like this."

I remembered the first time I had seen an embryo and slowed down to give them time to absorb the complex experience.

"This tissue with the dark areas is called decidua—it is the lining of the uterus that is loose enough to slough off because of the suction. And this white fluffy stuff that looks like tiny roots is called chorionic villi. It is evidence of placental tissue."

Their attention was still fixed on the embryo.

"As you are aware, there are several reasons it is important to do this kind of examination. First, you want to be sure there was a pregnancy in the uterus, because a positive pregnancy test without tissue might indicate an ectopic pregnancy—a pregnancy growing in the fallopian tube or somewhere else outside the uterus. In that case, it is critical that the woman get immediate medical care, because an ectopic pregnancy can rupture and be life-threatening."

Candy gave Angela a meaningful look. I guessed it meant she didn't think anyone they worked with was paying any attention to that possibility.

"But those are pretty rare, aren't they?" Angela asked hopefully.

"Yes—relatively rare. But still important to rule out," I answered firmly. If I was going to teach them, I was determined to teach them correctly.

"So, what else are you looking for?" Angela asked.

"I want to determine that the size of the embryo corresponds to my estimate of the length of pregnancy. And most importantly, I want to be sure the tissue is complete—that there is a spine, limbs, and a calvarium—or skull. That is the best way for me to be sure there is no retained tissue which could cause problems later, whether because of infection or pain. In an earlier pregnancy, I'd just be looking for the translucent tissue that is the sac, and some darker evidence of decidua—the sloughed-off uterine lining."

Stacy looked at the two other women. "Are the doctors, is he—is *he* checking for these things?" she asked, warily.

Candy answered, "I'm sure he is doing whatever he thinks is needed." And that settled that.

"So, everything is in order here, and I am confident Ricki will be fine. What is your procedure for disposing of the tissue?" I asked.

"We do what any woman would do if she had an early miscarriage," Candy said. "It goes into the toilet. Do you have a problem with that?" she asked, obviously a bit defensive.

"Not at all," I answered.

"Tell them what you do, Jane," Stacy said.

"As you said, our situation is very different from yours," I answered. "Because we are working in an old convent, there is a churchyard where nuns were buried. We give the woman the opportunity to bury the embryo. Don't misunderstand—it's not like a funeral. We are not religious in any way. But many women seem to find it comforting to know where it is. It's a bit like leaving a part of themselves in a safe place."

"Sometimes women ask if they can take it with them," Stacy said.

"We used to allow that, until we had a policeman at our doorstep," I said, ruefully.

"Police are one of our main concerns," Angela said. "We work so hard to keep the cops away."

"And I'm sure you do a great job," I said, encouraging her. "I guess we just think the more satisfied the woman is—the more she feels certain she has made the best decision she can—the less likely we are to have trouble." That is the closest I came to saying I thought they ought to do more of an emotional exploration.

Stacy disposed of the tissue and washed everything out, putting the objects we used aside so they could be used for another tissue examination, if they could convince anyone it was a good idea.

We trooped back into the bedroom, and I told Ricki she could get dressed. In a few minutes, she appeared, clearly ready to go. She was smiling at me.

"He is still with me, even now," she said.

I smiled back and nodded. As I gave her a goodbye hug, I slipped the small white stone I had picked up into her hand and whispered, "This is to remember your love and courage."

CHAPTER 33

IGNORING THE HOLE

1968, on the way back to France

On the flight home, I sat tucked into my window seat, sipping a whiskey sour and musing over the experience. I guess it is natural to become used to one's own habits. I was surprised at how the Detroit women did things, and they were surprised at how we did things. I thought about their rule that they wouldn't ask a woman her reasons for wanting an abortion. That seemed strange to me, since there were other things they insisted upon discussing. I wondered if they were afraid of the emotions that spilled out when you asked those questions. While there are many women who are certain and confident of their decision, there are some who are struggling. It's as if they are in a deep hole. It seemed to me the key to counseling in abortion—or perhaps any counseling—is to listen and to interact, to hear about what is difficult for the women, but not to be drawn into or overwhelmed by the complexities of their life's story. After all, the women themselves are often already overwhelmed by it. They need someone outside holding a ladder, not another person coming down into the hole with them. They *need* the ladder and an invitation to come back out. To me, it seemed these Detroit women had decided to ignore the hole altogether. And yet they performed an incredible service. They helped more women get abortions in a month than we would in a year. I wanted to talk about it with Lucie. I kept wondering, *Is any abortion a good abortion?*

Henri sprang to mind, as he so often did. No amount of counseling or emotional resolution would have made abortion more acceptable to him. Henri was an ache in my heart that would never go away.

I got in so late that Sophie and I didn't even talk. She woke as I slid into bed and gave me a kiss. So my stories about Detroit had to wait until the following morning's meeting.

Sophie understood what I hoped to do—even more than Lucie or Françoise—to help women find some kind of wholeness in the process of choosing whether or not to have a baby. In every conversation, she supported my vision and challenged me to do more.

Françoise was taking croissants out of the bag and putting them in a rattan basket. She joined us at the kitchen table.

Sophie began. "What did you learn in Detroit, chérie?"

I sighed a deep sigh. "I have been wondering how to make sense of it all. The most important thing I realized is that it is essential to provide the kinds of conversations we have when women are troubled."

"So they were doing the same kind of thing?" Françoise asked, buttering a roll.

"No. They don't do *anything* like what we do. In fact, they don't even believe in asking questions about how the woman is feeling. They said something about 'not being social workers,'" I replied, showing some of the frustration I had been experiencing. "I talked a bit more deeply with a patient named Ricki, but only because the process intrigued the counselor."

"But I don't understand," Sophie said. "Aren't these the feminists Lucie wrote us about? The ones who care about women? How could they do abortions without helping the women be at peace?"

"I had that question, too, until I realized that I did that for years with Levy. We were always nice, and we wanted to put women at ease, but in those early years, Levy and I never asked—not once—how they felt. If they had the courage and wherewithal to find us, we left it at that. But I later recognized that when Levy asked me to wear the habit, he sensed the woman needed something more. And perhaps it helped. I always hoped the women were all right afterward, but Levy's main concern was their physical health."

"Well, I have told you how much the habit helped me," Françoise said. "I was a scared little girl. I can't imagine how I would have gotten through it without those kind words. I still keep them in my mind and remember them when I am afraid. But it was more than the words—it was knowing I had forgiveness from someone recognized by the church."

"I know. And that always worried me because I didn't want to trick you. Addie confronted me about that." I was reluctant to say her name, but Sophie seemed all right. "You might have been the first woman Levy realized needed that habit, but not the last. Many times, I wished I had something like it when I worked with Dr. Nick. In some ways, he was so great, but he didn't understand. Even when I tried to tell him some women needed help with their emotional response to having an abortion, he brushed me off and essentially said if they wanted an abortion, they would just have to deal with whatever it brought up for them. He figured that because we took a risk providing an illegal service, the least they could do was to be happy about it. And if they weren't happy, it was their problem.

"Fortunately, I did enough of the abortions myself to take extra time when I saw women who needed it. But until I watched how Lucie worked with Gertrude, I only guessed at how to help a woman go deeper into her own feelings.

And I certainly didn't trust my intuition the way I do now—to sense when a woman needs more. I have a lot of judgments about those Detroit women not even wanting to learn if a woman is troubled, but I also understand. They are seeing so many patients—and in such an impossible situation—moving from one apartment to another, constantly worrying about the police, and dealing with the men who do the abortions and therefore wield the power. They don't have the time or energy to do the kind of counseling we do. And most of the time, the women are okay, I think. At least I hope."

"But you counseled a woman? They let you?" Sophie asked.

"They didn't exactly let me—I was sitting in on her session and I sensed she needed to talk about religion, so I just sort of butted in."

"I can't even imagine!" Sophie said, laughing.

"I am glad I did," I said, batting her on the shoulder. "I know it made a difference. And the counselor—it was Stacy—remember, the woman who came to us? I think she was glad, too. She wanted to know more about how we did it. I hope she'll be able to persuade the other counselors to at least check in with women about their feelings. Somebody has to understand how important this is."

"Maybe they will," Françoise said.

"What else?" Sophie asked.

"Well, one thing I liked about what they did is they don't call anyone a patient. They said, 'They are not sick, and we are not doctors.'"

"Hmm. I guess it is true. 'They are not sick and we are not doctors,'" Françoise repeated. "So what do they call them, then?"

"Women, I guess," I answered.

"Well, that's not very warm," Françoise said, with a look on her face that told me she was coming up with something. "What if we called them guests?" she asked.

"Hmm. I like it," Sophie said. "That fits in much better with the retreat idea, and I hate calling them retreatants. Such a creepy word."

"I like it too," I said. "Guests it is, from now on." We went on to review the recipes from the past week and the guest reservations for the week to come.

Still, my failure hung around my neck like an albatross.

Stacy kept in touch with me by mail. As she feared, the abortionists had no interest in the suction device I had demonstrated, even though I promised that Dr. Nick would send them one. The women in charge never seemed to want to learn what Stacy was doing in counseling, even though she reported that one of the abortionists had said to her, "What are you doing differently? When you have talked to them, there is not all that crying and shaking." It was not the last time I was frustrated with the choices that some of my abortion-providing colleagues made about the best ways to provide care.

CHAPTER 34

SHE IS *ALMOST* THIRTEEN

Our Lady, Spring 1969

Sophie and I lived a quiet country life, with only the *International Herald Tribune,* our central source of news of the day, so we were always rather thrilled with Lucie's letters. I was only getting mail from her sporadically. I knew from experience that meant something was very wrong. Lucie wrote that she was unhappy, but she didn't tell me why. I think some of it stemmed from her growing involvement in the women's movement, which Oliver was dead-set against. The movement was afoot in France as well, but in a much more subdued way. After all, Françoise's 'Aunt Simmi' wrote *Le Deuxieme Sexe* way back in 1949.

Lucie mailed me a signed copy of Betty Friedan's *The Feminine Mystique,* which I found much more approachable and more of a call to arms than de Beauvoir's rather dense and scholarly tome.

When we didn't get a letter or even a card for weeks, I finally telephoned. Lucie was crying and trying to talk at the same time, so I was not able to understand her well—as if a torrent of thoughts and feelings had been unleashed. I didn't interrupt or attempt to make sense of all of it. I just let her cry and talk.

"I can't stay with him. I just want to kill myself. He doesn't want a partner; he just wants me to be a pretty wife—an arm piece for him. I am a therapist—a professional—but he has decided *that* is not appropriate for the wife of an important doctor. He wants me to stop working, even though it is the only good thing in my life. He doesn't want me to publish my work. Of course I love Tildy. She is my daughter—but I don't really *like* her. She is *his* child—prissy and opinionated. I have my own separate money, but he wants to tell me how I should spend it. I never should have let myself get tied down.

"If only I had listened to you, Jane. But back then, I was afraid he would leave me if I didn't agree to have a baby. He convinced me that it would make us happy again. But by the time I was pregnant, he started to get even more demanding. He said it was his right as a husband and father to decide where his heir would be born—and that his *son,* he said that all the time—as if he could somehow command the baby to be a boy, had the right to be born in the United States of America, the best country in the world. You remember his grandfather died around that time, so he inherited money, and his father had been begging him to come into the practice for years. So we returned to America. Oliver's parents gave us a house in the suburbs, because that is where successful people live. It was too far from your mother and the Goldfarbs for me to feel that I had any real family there. I was so alone. I had such a hard time when Tildy was born, like a black curtain was drawn between me and my life. I didn't get out of bed for weeks. When you and Sophie and Levy came to visit, you saved my life.

"After my month at River Oaks, things got better. I have done my best to be a good wife to Oliver. Thank goodness you found Dr. Mindy for me. She suggested that I try to remember what brought us together in the first place. For that, I had to banish a host of terrible memories. Instead, I brought out the photo album from our wedding. Remember? All those wonderful and quirky pictures his uncle took? That helped. We both looked so young—but I saw love in those photographs that I haven't felt for a long time.

"I was never confident as a mother. But it is not all my fault. Tildy is a difficult and cranky child. I'm sure it didn't help that I wasn't there to care for her at first, but I did my best. And she had a very good nanny. I didn't like having a maid, so I fired Clara. I tried to keep up with the housework myself, but the living room was always scattered with toys and journals. Oliver got angry if everything didn't look like a picture in a magazine, and he wanted to be able to bring his colleagues home for dinner at a moment's notice."

I interrupted. "Surely you could hire some help again, Lucie? Oliver has plenty of money, doesn't he?"

"Help? Oh, yes, I finally agreed to that. We hired a lovely young girl. She helped with the housework and cooking so that I could take classes in the city. We even had a small apartment built onto the house for her. Barbara has been with us for several years, and Tildy loves her. I guess she is not the only one. When I walked in on Oliver and Barbara in our bedroom, I realized I had to leave. I packed a bag and I am going to go to a hotel. Oliver didn't even try to convince me to stay. They will be better off without me."

"Lucie, I am so sorry. You must be frantic," I said, stating the obvious.

"You know, I almost don't care anymore. Remember I wrote to you about that speak-out in Greenwich Village with women telling about their abortions. Oliver begged me not to go. But I'm so glad I did. The hall was packed with women—standing, sitting, crying, yelling. They had a microphone, and woman after woman told their stories of going to Mexico, or Scandinavia, or using a knitting needle, or finding someone to help them, like I did. You can't imagine the experience of telling my secret to a room full of women who were also telling their secrets. I am thirty-nine years old and I feel free for the first time in…well, maybe ever. I am so angry about what has been done to women. It will be hard to leave my patients, but I just have to. I'm coming back, Jane. I'm coming back to live with you and Sophie at Our Lady."

"That's wonderful. There is plenty of room for you and Tildy."

"Only me. Aren't you listening to me? I am not bringing her."

"But Lucie, Tildy is much too young. She is only twelve. She needs you," I said. "You can't really be thinking of leaving her."

"I don't want to talk about it," Lucie said coldly. "Tildy is almost thirteen, and she is better off without me."

CHAPTER 35

A NOTE FROM ABBIE

Milagro, New Mexico, 2016

Dear Reader, (Oh I hope there will be readers!) Please forgive me for in-terrupting the story—and at a time of such tension! My name is Abbie. I am Lucie's granddaughter—Tildy's daughter. Jane has insisted that I insert my own story here to explain how these memoirs came to be. It's a bit funny, be-cause Jane also insisted that when I gathered her stories hopefully to share with a wider audience, she wanted it to be about her ideas, not about her life. "No one cares about my comings and goings," she said. I had to convince her that the story of her life is what brings her ideas alive and gives them meaning. And then she had to convince me to share about my *life. So, here goes nothing.*

As you are aware, Grand-Mère Lucie, as I called her, married Oliver, the young medical student who nearly killed her. (Actually, I never heard anything about that part of the story.) Perhaps their relationship represented an exam-ple of the idea that opposites attract. Grandpapa was a serious man. When I think of him, I remember the smell of his pipe. They named my mother Mathilde, after Jane Smith's courageous Aunt Mathilde, whom the Nazis killed during the war. Mother was always called Tildy. When my mother was about thirteen, Grand-Mère moved back to France. My mother shared very little about her childhood, but when I was a teenager, I overheard her telling one of her friends about it.

"My mother abandoned me when I was a child. I'll never understand how she could have done that," my mother said, sipping a glass of the red wine that she only had when my father was away on business, intoxicants of any kind being forbidden in our Southern Baptist household.

Her friend, Nancy, gave a sigh. "That's awful. Did she tell you why she did such a terrible thing? Did she ever apologize?"

My mother gave the sigh of a martyr. "You'll never believe what she said."
My mother set her glass down so hard that I heard the wine slosh. Mother lowered her voice, and I pulled back into the doorframe to be sure she wouldn't see me. "She told me that at thirteen, I was old enough to take care

of myself." My mother sniffled just a little bit—something that only happened when she drank wine. She made a point of never crying. I almost wanted to go into the room and put my arms around her, but I knew better.

Even Nancy knew enough to keep her distance, but she said, "Oh Tildy. I am so sorry."

"It's certainly not the worst thing that ever happened to anyone," my mother said tartly. "Thank goodness I had Phyllis Schlafly as a role model, or I'd never have known how to be a good mother." My mother wasn't one to underestimate her own talents. "My father had a nice girlfriend, and my mother's leaving taught me a lot about self-reliance. That has come in handy as a preacher's wife!" I couldn't see her face, but I pictured the wry smile that always accompanied Mother's comments about the 'cross to bear' of being a preacher's wife. Before she said any more, she stood up and said, "No use in dwelling on the past. I hope you'll keep this between us?" Privacy was paramount to my mother. There was anxiety in her voice—the fear that she had shared too much.

"Of course," Nancy answered, also standing up. "You are privy to enough of my secrets to depend on my discretion." Nancy gathered her purse and coat. "I need to get along, dear. I left Herb's dinner in the refrigerator, but he may not be smart enough to get it into the oven properly." The two women chuckled about their bumbling husbands, as women of that time did. I slipped back into my bedroom, realizing I had just learned more about my mother's inner life than she had ever revealed to me.

Now that I am finally doing my own therapy, I understand my mother's fury at Grand-Mère. They were equally redoubtable, but in different directions. Mother's great rebellion was to become as conservative as Lucie was liberal. I grew up in a very strict household. We lived in Dallas, where my mother attended Southern Methodist University and then married my father, a Southern Baptist preacher. For years, I only knew of my grandmother from birthday cards and Christmas presents. My mother's stony silence demonstrated a clear warning not to ask any questions. But when I was twelve, my Grandpapa, who lived in New York City, died of a sudden heart attack, and Lucie came to the States for his funeral. Grand-Mère and Grandpapa had never gotten divorced—I gleaned that much from the snippets of adult conversation I overheard. My mother said that they had still loved each other, but "simply couldn't abide sharing the same space."

Grand-Mère Lucie was a force of nature, and I fell in love with her immediately. She was sixty-two, but she didn't seem old to me. She wore loose, flowing pants that reminded me of the harem girls in my Arabian Nights stories. She stayed at the Plaza Hotel and told me that the famous children's book character, Eloise, lived on the same floor she did. I remember that I wasn't certain whether or not she was teasing. My parents and I stayed at Mother's family home in Connecticut, and took the train into the city for the funeral and for one large luncheon held at the Plaza. At both events, Grand-Mère insisted that I sit beside her. It was early spring, and still cold in New York. I can vividly remember the little black wool coat my mother bought me at Saks Fifth Avenue to wear to the funeral. Grand-Mère stood out in her bright pink Chanel suit in the middle of a sea of black. No one seemed to mind, except my parents, who were horrified. "That's Lucie," is what her friends said over and over in fond voices. An endless stream of people wanted to kiss her on both cheeks—people who hadn't seen her since she went back to France. But she kept me by her side, which seemed to infuriate my mother. Perhaps that's why she did it.

The funeral and everything are sort of a blur in my mind, but I'll never forget the conversation Grand-Mère and I had in the hotel ladies' room. I had never seen a bathroom like it. There was an entire sitting room with little fabric-covered chairs like the ones in my mother's dressing room. Grand-Mère sat me down across from her, held my hands, and said, "Chérie—would you like to come for a visit to France?"

I knew she was my grandmother, but in some ways, she seemed like a movie star. I can still smell her perfume—always Chanel # 5. I have no idea if anyone even wears it anymore. Big hair was the one thing she and my mother always agreed on. (My mother still has her hair all teased up and sprayed once a week in the beauty parlor of the nursing home that I am supposed to refer to as a 'Memory Lodge.' Alzheimer's is a bitch.) Anyway, I couldn't even imagine that she wanted me to go with her. I was excited to find my mother and ask her, even though part of me already anticipated the 'no.' I dragged Grand-Mère by the hand to find my parents, an aggressiveness that certainly wasn't typical behavior for me.

I was out of breath by the time we found her. "Mama, can I visit France with Grand-Mère? I promise I will be very, very, very good if you will let me go." Although my father stood right behind her, it hadn't even occurred to me to address the request to him.

My mother was taken aback. She stared at my grandmother while directing her answer at me. "Abigail, your grandmother is far too busy to take care of a child."

Of course, I now understand the many layers of meaning in that sentence.

"Nonsense, Mathilde. I have plenty of time. Abigail is such a special child. I'm sure she will be no trouble at all." More layers. "It is time she saw the country that is in her blood—in both your blood. Her summer vacation is coming up and she can fly back with me. Mathilde, I insist."

"Abbie is too young to be exposed to your life," my mother said with an ugly look on her face. The coldness between them took my breath away. I wondered if they had ever loved each other—and it frightened me to think that

my mother could ever feel that way about me.

"Nonsense, again. We will stay in the apartment in the city. I will show her the sights that every young woman should see—the glories of Paris, the beauty of the South of France. If we have time, we could even go to Switzerland. It will be part of her education."

My father broke the impasse. He didn't usually disagree with my mother, but he loved me, and I was jumping up and down to go.

"Tildy, dear one, I think we should let her go. Just for a few weeks. It will be educational for her to see other ways of living. She's a good girl, and you have taught her well. We have nothing to be worried about."

My parents always quoted Bible verses about how the man was in charge of everything, but it was Mother who made the decisions, so this was a miracle. I think that since my father said it in public, my mother had to agree, or else she wasn't being an obedient wife.

My mother glared at her mother. "No visits to the country. No going to your so-called 'cloister,'" she demanded. "She is not to meet any of those people. Do you promise?"

Grand-Mère looked pained and said, "Of course, chérie."

Grand-mere winked at me. That part sailed right over my head.

So it happened that I spent more than a month with Grand-Mère. We stayed in her cozy apartment in Paris. We visited the Arc de Triomphe, Sacré Coeur, and Notre Dame, and my favorite, the Eiffel Tower. She had friends everywhere, so we spent time with a family who lived on the beach in Sête in the South of France. I still can remember the pommes frites. Grand-Mère gave me a thick, tattered paperback called The Longest Day, *which I read on our tour bus ride to Normandy. The book was about the D-Day landing—history that I only vaguely knew about. Grand-Mère told me the briefest version of how she and Dr. Levy and Jane Smith came to America during the war. I had heard of the famous Miss Smith, but had no idea how instrumental she was in my family's survival.*

"Chérie, I should have named your mother Jane, and perhaps she would have had a bit more backbone," Grand-Mère said.

Frankly, the idea of my mother having any more backbone terrified me.

My favorite part of the whole trip involved taking the train to Switzerland and then riding the funicular up a steep mountain, where we stayed at a hotel built inside a glacier.

Grand-Mère shared her wisdom freely.

"Chérie, you must always speak honestly (she pronounced the 'h') about your heart's truth."

Some part of me believed her, but there was no place for the truth of my heart in my mother's household! So I hid that tidbit away in a secret part of me that I am just now discovering.

She also said, "Find the courage—like 'coeur' the French word for heart——to make the life you want for yourself."

That was also a hard one for me. The only thing less welcome in my family than the truth was anyone wanting anything different from what my mother wanted. Although Grand-Mère occasionally asked questions about my life, I never gave more than a noncommittal answer. I thought it was somehow my responsibility to protect my mother.

Every day was a new adventure with Grand-Mère. It was impossible to believe that she and my mother were related, let alone that one had raised the other. One time, my Grand-Mère looked at me with an unusual wistfulness and said, "There are some women who should not have children. I am one of them."

I had never heard anything like that in my life.

As an only child, I excelled in amusing myself. Reading was my favorite way, and my grandmother had an extensive library. One of the books I loved was The World According to Garp. *I didn't understand all of it, and my grand-mother told me not to tell my mother that I had read it. It gave me an insight into a world I had never seen—a world of strong, independent women. My grandmother's world. No matter where we traveled, it seemed that women recognized her and wanted her approval. I wondered if my Grand-Mère had fashioned herself as a kind of Jenny Fields—a godmother of women.*

A month is a long time for a twelve-year-old, and I was terribly homesick, so even though I was having a wonderful time, I was glad to go home. In the ensuing years, my grandmother and I became pen pals of sorts. About once a month, I looked forward to receiving an envelope with my name written with a flourish in the black fountain pen she always used. She once told me that a woman's handwriting should be as elegant and distinctive as her perfume. All during my growing up, my mother never wore perfume, and I was never allowed to wear it. But I secretly bought a small bottle of Chanel #5 eau de toilette and hid it in the back of my closet so that I was able to evoke Grand-Mère whenever I needed her. Although our letters made me feel connected to her, we both just stopped writing after a while. I never saw her again.

CHAPTER 36

MORE FROM ABBIE

My mother wasn't merely conservative—she was a card-carrying member of Phyllis Schlafly's ultra-right Eagle Forum, *named so because 'eagles mate for life.' In my twenties, I tried hard to be the daughter my mother wanted— quiet, pious, studious, obedient, self-effacing. But in her letters, my grand-mother encouraged me to be loud, alive, brave, and important. That other self—what I thought of as my Lucie self—hid within me, biding her time. Now in my thirties, I am on a journey to find that part of myself. Mother's hypocrisy was unbelievable. I struggle every day to be less angry with my mother for trying to mold me into the perfect, passive woman, especially when she did whatever she wanted.*

By the time Grand-Mère died in the spring of 2013, Mother was only fifty-seven, but she already lived at the Memory Lodge, lost to early-onset Alz-heimer's disease. It is hard to believe that my mother is about the same age now as Grand-Mère was when I visited her. Perhaps it is confusion that makes Mother seem so much older—or a life filled with fear and resentment. My father has lunch with her every Sunday, even though she doesn't have any idea who he is. I go sometimes. But it is painful to mourn for someone about whom you have such mixed feelings—to mourn for someone who doesn't remember who you are—to mourn for them before they are dead.

To my surprise, Grand-Mère left me a chunk of money and all her personal effects. I was teaching sociology at my local community college when she died, and we had already adjourned for the break between the spring and summer semester. And so I spent another month in France, this time at Notre Dame de la Grace Perpetuelle. I couldn't imagine what to expect from the convent, since I had been forbidden to go there as a child, but it buzzed like a hive with some mysterious activity. Lucie set up Our Lady as a non-profit or-ganization and left it in the hands of the women who ran it.

When I arrived, I was welcomed by Sister Lydia. During my visit, the var-ious sisters went about their work, while I concentrated on sorting through my grandmother's papers. I arrived in time for the memorial, planned by the sisters and Lucie's friends who wrote to me about the arrangements. They called it a celebration of life. I had never heard of a funeral called a celebra-tion. They waited to hold the service until a few weeks after her death so that admirers from all over the world could be there.

The chapel at the convent was packed. The main eulogy was given by a woman named Petite Lucie who said she owed her very existence to my grand-mother. Dozens of other people spoke, including two women in their eighties who shared stories about having been at Miss Smith's school in Paris with her in the 1930s. At the reception, those two elderly women cornered me. They introduced themselves as Socorro and Paulette. Socorro spoke with an accent I couldn't quite place and seemed to be profoundly deaf. Paulette told me that she lived in Italy, and ran the 'Our Lady Convent' in San Miracolo, and that Socorro ran the convent in Peru. I smiled and nodded at them as if I had any idea that the Convent of Our Lady of Perpetual Grace was some kind of in-ternational franchise. Paulette recognized my confusion and got very quiet. She whispered loudly to Socorro in Spanish, "Ella no lo sabe." My high school Spanish was pitiful, but enough for me to realize that she said, "She doesn't know." At that mysterious comment, I smiled and nodded again when they both said how much they had loved my grandmother.

As I turned to extricate myself from the awkward conversation, Paulette took my arm and said, "You must talk with Jane. She is too old to travel, but she will meet with you. She will tell you her story. Our story. Your grand-mother's story. Jane lives in New Mexico in the cloister there. The village is called Milagro. Her address will be in your grandmother's papers." It didn't occur to me that the famous Miss Smith could still be alive.

I couldn't fathom how to sort through all Grand-Mère's papers. On top of the desk, several piles of old letters were bound in ribbons. On one of the piles, a huge paperback book, Cider House Rules, *was like the cherry on top of an ice-cream sundae. A note in my grandmother's handwriting was paper-clipped to the cover. It read, 'Darling Abbie—I am so glad you are here. I hoped you would come. I'm not certain how much you have realized about my work—it is all here in my papers. Before you go any farther, I want you to read this book. I remember how much you loved Garp. This is by the same author and I think it will help you understand. I mean it. Stop right now and read this book.'*

I was tempted to open the letters and find out the mystery that everyone but me seemed to know. But even dead, my grandmother was powerful enough to make me follow her instructions. Perhaps I was still the good little girl I had always been. I brewed a cup of green tea in the kitchenette adjoining her bedroom, then went out the French doors to the porch that opened onto a beautiful view of the gardens. And I read. John Irving grabbed me immedi-ately and didn't let go. I read through dinner. One of the sisters kindly brought me a tray with a grilled cheese sandwich and a cup of soup made from freshly-

picked tomatoes. I read most of the night—finally falling asleep around three a.m., and emerging late in the morning for a cup of coffee. I read all that day—I don't remember if I ate—and I came to the end at about midnight.

When I finished the book, I held it to my chest, sobbing. I didn't want it to be over. I didn't want to leave the characters behind—the "princes of Maine and Kings of New England." I didn't want to leave my Grand-Mère behind. Still holding the huge book like a talisman, I pulled the enormous pile of Jane's letters into my lap. In between anecdotes and pleasantries, I read the history of the extraordinary lives Jane and my grandmother lived—and I learned about the work they did in four countries—providing abortion care in spite of the laws of men. Because women could come and go in the cloisters with no one paying much attention, they provided abortion in plain sight.

I sat on my Grand-Mère's bed with the letters all around me and just cried. I cried for all the things I never knew about her life. I cried because I felt so stupid and worthless compared to these amazing women. I cried because I was still pretty sure that abortion was murder, as I had been taught. And I cried because I also knew it was grace.

I found a tattered black leather address book, and sure enough, Jane Smith's contact information was written in my grandmother's hand in bold black ink. I packed up all the most important papers in a steamer trunk and said farewell to the sisters whom I now recognized as her colleagues. I drove home to Connecticut, resolved to meet the amazing Miss Smith.

I wrote to Jane, introducing myself and asking if I could visit her. I got a positive reply right away. I was financially independent for the first time in my life, so I resigned my teaching position. I asked my dear neighbor to take care of my plants, packed my little blue Toyota Corolla, and headed on my longest ever road trip from Connecticut to New Mexico. I had no idea what I would find when I got there, or how long I would stay.

Meeting Jane was like being with my grandmother all over again. And like my grandmother, Jane lived in a wing of an active cloister. I knocked on the enormous wooden front door, and a short, plump nun in her mid-seventies opened it. There were sisters in habits, and other women passing in and out.

"Welcome. I am Sister Bernadette. You must be Abigail. Jane will be delighted you are here." She clasped my hands in both of hers and made a little bow, like a benediction. Then she beckoned me to follow her down the hall.

Sister Bernadette tapped lightly on the door as we came to the sitting room. She turned to me and smiled. "I don't know why I still knock," she said. "Jane is partially deaf. You'll have to speak up," she said, in an encouraging way. And there, sitting in an easy chair festooned with what looked to be silk scarves, was Jane. She wasn't exactly elegant—but she was so commanding a presence that at first I felt as though I were meeting royalty. The adobe building seemed ancient and medieval, but Jane's space was beautiful, with rugs and tapestries that I later learned were Navajo and Peruvian, covering the walls with color and design.

Bernadette motioned for me to sit down. When she opened her hands, I noticed a fine scar across her palm.

"Jane, I'll be back in a bit with lunch," she said in a loud voice. "We are very busy today, but ring if you need anything and I can come right back." And then it was just me and Jane. Me and the legend.

I was an adult—I had met important people before—I had been a teacher. Yet I was tongue-tied. Jane looked at me and smiled so broadly.

"Welcome, my dear," she said. "You look so very much like your grandmother."

Dear Reader, thank you for your indulgence in giving me the chance to tell how my story fits into the puzzle.

CHAPTER 37

LUCIE RETURNS

France, 1969

Lucie came back to Our Lady in the summer of 1969. She rented a small apartment in Paris and spent part of the week there to manage her private therapy practice, and the other part working with us at Our Lady. It struck me that Lucie seemed to be able to help other people solve their relationship problems when she had, at the age of thirty-seven, basically given up on her own.

I hated to see Lucie in pain, whether from a broken wrist, postpartum depression, or the failure of her marriage. On her first visit back to Our Lady, she curled up next to me on the sofa, lay her head on my shoulder, and wept.

"I'm sorry, Mam'selle. I tried. I tried. I didn't know how to be a good wife. When I found him in our bed with Barbara, it just about killed me."

I put my arm around her shoulder. It was touching to be called by the nickname she invented when I first met her as a seven-year-old.

She continued sniffling. "I was never a good mother to Tildy. What kind of woman leaves her own child?"

I remembered my old roommate from nursing school, Clarice, asking that same question about a child she placed for adoption.

"How can I forgive myself? What am I supposed to do now?" she whimpered. Even as an adult, Lucie had the capacity to be thirty, going on thirteen, going on seven. I didn't have words to soothe her.

Stories have always been important to me. In Paris, I told my seven-year-olds stories of Harriet Tubman, Joan of Arc, Queen Esther, and Marie Curie to teach them that women make a difference in the world. I've shared stories of women for the same reason. Stories give us empathy for ourselves and others. We cannot judge another's life if we have not walked her path. A story was just what she needed.

"Shh," I whispered into her ear. "*Écoute, mon trésor*"—my treasure.

"Once upon a time, there was a wonderful little girl named Lucie. She was a student in Paris at Madame Mathilde Smith's school. Lucie was smart, funny, and very, very brave. Once she climbed a linden tree just to see more of the world, and when she fell and broke her wrist, she hardly cried at all.

"At first, Lucie had nine classmates, and together they did everything in two straight lines. But then the world lost its mind, and one by one all the other girls were sent away—leaving Lucie behind. Many other little girls came and went, passing through the school on their way to safety. Even if she knew them only for a short while, they became like family to her.

"Lucie's own mother had died when she was very small, so she had only her papa, whom she loved dearly, though he was far away. When bad men killed him, Lucie was taken into the hearts of Mademoiselle Jane Smith, who loved her as if she were her own daughter, and Dr. Bernard Levy, who loved her like a true father.

"In those days, the Nazis occupied Paris, and it became dangerous to remain, especially for Jewish girls like Lucie. So Jane, Levy, and Lucie sailed across the ocean to New York, where Hymie and Sadie Goldfarb—and their cocker spaniel, Rosie—became her new family. Lucie did well in school and made many friends.

"She grew up and fell in love with a kind, clever man named Oliver. Together they sailed back to France and got married. Oliver, like his father and grandfather before him, became a doctor. After a few years, he wished to work in America, so they returned to the United States. Lucie gave birth to a daughter, whom she named Mathilde after the brave woman who had run her school. They called the baby Tildy.

"Lucie loved her daughter, but after the birth, she struggled. It wasn't her fault—she simply could not feel close to her baby. With time and help, she did much healing, and she even learned how to help others heal too. But being a mother never came easily to her.

"Lucie remained fiercely independent, just as she had been as a child. She liked to do things her own way. Oliver, more traditional, wanted her to do things his way. He was unhappy with her becoming a professional woman. When Lucie chose to continue her studies despite his disapproval, she hired a young woman named Barbara to help with Tildy. The more Lucie pursued her dreams, the more she told herself Tildy was happier with Barbara.

"Eventually, Lucie and Oliver grew too unhappy together. One day, Lucie made the heartbreaking choice to leave her daughter in Oliver and Barbara's care and returned to France.

"Lucie went on to help many people as a therapist. She knew well that sometimes it is easier to help others heal than to heal oneself. And she also knew that the losses she had suffered as a child still shaped her as an adult.

"I cannot say what Lucie's future will hold, or whether she will ever forgive herself. But I do know this: she has her good days and her bad days, and she takes care of her problems the best she knows how."

Lucie mouthed the ending just as she had as a child.

Oliver was furious with Lucie for leaving. Despite his 'indiscretion,' as he called his liaison with Barbara, he never imagined Lucie would have the nerve to leave. Barbara stayed on with him and Tildy, but Lucie refused to give Oliver a divorce.

She said, "Oliver broke the glass when we stood under the chuppah. That means our vows are indestructible. I don't care what he does with his life, but he is not going to make a mockery of our wedding!"

Tildy was furious and hurt that her mother had left her, her sense of betrayal no doubt egged on by her father. Tildy was also arrogant, righteous, and self-involved, like Oliver. Lucie traveled to New York when Oliver died and met her granddaughter, Abbie, for the first time. They adored each other. Spending that month in France together was the closest Lucie came to a rapprochement with her daughter. Her failure as a mother grieved her until the end of her life.

CHAPTER 38

THE CHURCH HAS A LOT TO ANSWER FOR

Our Lady, 1969-1973

At Our Lady, we settled on scheduling three or four guests to come on Monday afternoons, often accompanied by Lucie. The bus arrived at about 3 p.m., and it took about an hour for our guests to walk to us, shepherded by Jet, our black and white Shetland Sheepdog who had stepped into Gracie's pawprints. We evaluated those guests on Monday afternoon and counseled them on Tuesday during the day. They ingested their *Corazon de Gracia* on Tuesday afternoon, passed their pregnancies on Tuesday night. They left us Wednesday afternoon, catching the same bus that dropped off the next three or four women, who were with us on Wednesday, Thursday, and Friday. We attempted to keep Saturday and Sunday free for ourselves, although we were rarely completely successful. While the *Corazon de Gracia* made abortion simple, human beings remained, invariably, complex.

Sophie and I rarely quarreled or even disagreed about anything, but one morning, while Sophie, Lucie, Françoise and I drank coffee and discussed the day's guests, the earnest expression on her face told me she planned to bring up a subject about which we had already had a bit of a clash.

"I want to talk about the women who can't forgive themselves," she said, seriously. "Lucie, do you have any ideas?"

"Sophie, we have already been over this," I said impatiently. "You can't claim a secret formula to predict how women will feel after their abortions. Most of them handle this experience well. Honestly, it is only the few who stand out."

"Wait a minute, Jane," Lucie said. "I read some of Sophie's notes. I agree with you that most women are fine, but some aren't. Let her finish," she said, putting her hand on my arm. Lucie always cautioned me about my impatience.

"You need to know about this, Jane. I am not trying to tell you what to do," Sophie continued, buoyed by Lucie's support. "I flagged the recipes of some of the guests who seemed certain enough about their abortions beforehand, but who were miserably regretful soon after. I say certain enough because some of them may be saying what they imagine we want to hear. Do you remember Fanny from a few weeks ago? She was in her late thirties with flaming red hair?"

Françoise nodded, gravely.

I didn't really remember her, but I nodded too, just to be agreeable.

"At first she told me she already had two children and was too old for another one, so she was certain she wanted an abortion. But the next day, after she had already taken the *Corazon*, she told me something astonishing. She said when she arrived and met all of us, she decided if *I* were her counselor, she would complete the abortion, but if any of you was assigned to her, she would have a baby. Like casting the dice."

Françoise sat back in her chair. "I have never heard anything like that."

Lucie and I had to agree that we hadn't either.

"She had already taken the medication, so there wasn't anything to do but to assure her I would support her no matter what happened. She passed an eight-week embryo overnight. We looked at it together in the morning, and she seemed all right. She even said goodbye and sang a lullaby. We laid the embryo to rest with some flowers, and she took a stone, though she decided against the scar. Then she took a nap. She woke up wailing."

Françoise nodded again. "Her screaming scared everyone," Françoise said. "I was afraid she was dying. After she stopped screaming, she started crying. I don't know which was worse."

"I examined her to see if there was something wrong, but I didn't find anything. When she finally stopped crying, all she would say is that she had murdered her baby."

"I don't remember that—surely I would remember something like that," I said, eyes wide.

"I don't either," Lucie said. "Perhaps it happened on the day you and I were in Paris?"

"I meant to tell you about it," Sophie said. "I'm sorry."

"That is a pretty important experience to forget to tell me about," I said, looking from Sophie to Françoise. I didn't mean to sound blaming, but I am quite sure that I did.

"That's why we are telling you *now*," Sophie insisted. "And I am trying to explain how it fits in with the other women I am worried about."

Sophie had a pile of recipe books on the kitchen table. We gave her our full attention, and she opened the books to patient records to which she had taped a piece of colored paper. She pointed out things on the pages and then went back to her notes.

"I went through almost two years of records. There aren't many, but the women who were distraught after their abortions share some important things in common." She turned a page around. This was her list:

1. They are usually over 30 years old
2. They are already mothers
3. They doubt every decision they have made in their lives
4. They think they should be perfect
5. They keep changing their minds about what to do
6. They are extremely anxious
7. They are visiting their midwives as well as us
8. They had a painful or difficult childhood—even if they don't acknowledge that at first
9. They go into a kind of emotional hell after their abortion

"It is the fifth issue that is most indicative of this kind of guest. She is…what is that word when you are *so* mixed up?" Sophie looked at me.

"Confused?" I suggested.

"No—more than that—it means of two minds."

"Ambivalent?" Lucie suggested.

"*Ce'st ça!*" Sophie said, excitedly. "Exactly. They are so ambivalent. Just like I said, this woman, Fanny, was prepared to make her decision based on chance. It must be terrifying to be so uncertain. These are all guests who appeared to be 'certain enough'—but I followed up with some of them and they refused to talk to me. Women who had been so grateful and relieved when they left us were hostile—furious. They blamed us for pressuring them into an abortion, and said they would never do such a terrible thing."

"How many did you flag in two years?" I asked.

"Only fourteen—out of almost nine hundred. It seems like a small percent, but it may be many more. Just like that woman I told you about a few years ago who found me at the market, these women think we are evil, so they'd never contact us afterward. The most disturbing thing is their claim that *they* didn't do this—some wicked 'not them' part had an abortion. Most of them were anxious before their abortion, and I am afraid they expected that ending the pregnancy would end the anxiety, but instead, it got worse. They lost all sense of their own goodness. They doubt and judge themselves, and they are in emotional hell and can't figure out how to get out."

Lucie folded her arms across her chest, and I noticed there were tears in her eyes. She said, "This sounds so much like me when I was pregnant with Tildy. Although I don't fit all your criteria, I recognize many of those traits. I was surely stuck in a kind of spiritual hell. I was never so afraid in my life—no, it wasn't fear, it was anxiety. It was chronic, and not about any specific thing, so it was very hard to deal with."

Sophie looked at her and said softly, "Lucie, you have never talked much about that time. We were all so worried about you. But then, when you got back from treatment, it almost seemed like you wanted to just forget that it ever happened."

"You're right. I did want to forget it. The kindness of the staff at the treatment center helped me come back to myself—but I still don't know why I had such a terrible reaction to childbirth, just as you don't know why these women have such a terrible reaction to having an abortion. That is still a mystery, and it frightens me because I'm afraid it could happen again."

Sophie put her arm around Lucie. "I'm so glad you are talking about it now. I wonder if there is anything these two experiences have in common?"

I laughed gently. "In some ways they have everything in common—whether or not to have a baby."

"Yes," Françoise said, "But most women aren't so confused about what they want. And they are not so sad and ashamed afterward. I wonder what makes these women different?"

Lucie reflected a minute, then said, "They sound like patients with more than one personality. I certainly wondered if that's what was wrong with me. Before Tildy was born, I thought I would go mad trying to negotiate the two disparate voices in my head. One said, 'You are so ungrateful. You should be happy to have a baby' and the other said, 'You will die if you have a baby.' I didn't know which one was real."

"That's what these women told me!" Sophie exclaimed. "Two voices. Both are very punitive. No wonder the woman is in hell, but it is a hell of her own making."

"If the misery is coming from their interpretation of the situation, couldn't they change it?" Françoise asked.

"That's what I wondered," Sophie said. "I tried to suggest some different meanings they could give to their experience and their choice, but they seem determined to punish themselves."

"I'm remembering my own experience," Lucie mused. "In a crisis, we sometimes revert to our most childlike selves. In this case, the child part learned that God is a mean old man who is supposed to punish them. It is very difficult to re-frame a belief as deep and foundational as that."

Sophie said, "That is so right! And many times with these women, it's like I am talking with a little girl, not a grown woman. When they are punishing themselves, it is the voice of a very mean father that is coming out of their mouths. They attribute it to God—and say they are not worthy of forgiveness."

"*Mon Dieu*," Françoise said. "The Church has a lot to answer for."

"I agree," Lucie said. "The idea that they are sinful is drummed into them from such an early age. And the oldest patterns are the hardest to reverse. This reversion into a child-like state could be caused by anything that triggers a memory of an old trauma—so I wonder if it could be useful to ask these patients—sorry, I mean these 'guests'—about any difficulties in their childhoods?"

"Yes, I do that," Sophie answered. "A woman may have moral turmoil over the nature of abortion. But it almost always seems there are also some deep emotional hurts—one of their parents died, or abused alcohol, or a sibling died and they blamed themselves for it," Sophie said. "And they are somehow stuck at the age when that most terrible thing happened."

"I felt just like that when I had Tildy—like a lost little girl—stuck at the age when my mother died. The people at the treatment center helped me grow up again. That's what made me want to be a counselor."

"How do you help other women who are little and lost?" I asked.

"I call the therapy I do *growing up inside*," Lucie explained. "But it is a process. I'm not sure how it could be helpful for a woman who is trying to decide about an abortion because there is not enough time. I'm sorry that there aren't any easy answers. Sophie, if you are worried about their reactions to abortion, have you considered not providing the service to them?"

Sophie paused.

"Is that what you are suggesting?" I asked.

Sophie looked at Lucie. "What would you have done all those years ago if someone had refused you an abortion?" she asked.

"To tell you the truth, I would have kept looking until I found a place that would do it. But I wasn't ambivalent about the abortion. I never had an emotional problem before or after it—except nearly dying because it was done by someone who did not know how," she laughed wryly.

"Right," Sophie said. "But in my experience, when a woman has decided on abortion, she won't let anything stand in her way. I certainly don't want to say no and force them to go somewhere else—somewhere their feelings won't be taken into account. Somewhere they could die. I just don't know what to do. Talking with these women makes me so upset. They are accusing us of hurting them—the last thing I want to do. One woman told me that she was in hell, and that she would never have had an abortion if she had known how it would be afterward. Another guest I tracked down told me that she would give anything to go back before her abortion."

I interjected, "I know the kind of woman you are talking about, Sophie. Before her abortion, she acknowledges she is ambivalent, but if I suggest she shouldn't go through with an abortion, she practically falls on her knees and begs me to do it."

"What do you think we should do, Sophie?" Françoise asked.

"We can at least keep these characteristics in mind. When a guest comes to us who fits in with this profile, we could at least warn her that she might have a very hard time afterward. And then we can keep trying to find ways to help these women find peace no matter what they decide. Since most of our guests are here in secret, they may have no one to even talk to."

"Of course, that violates all the rules of counseling," Lucie said, laughing. "The point is to allow the patient to come to an understanding on her own."

"But when there isn't time for that, and when we know what is likely to happen—how terrible it may be—don't we owe it to them to tell them that's what they might expect?" Sophie asked, nearly crying.

"Do you ever ask them what they are expecting after their abortion? Oh, I'm sorry, of course I know you do," Françoise asked.

"No, Françoise—it is a very good question. When I have asked, they have told me that they are afraid they might regret having an abortion, but they think they would regret having a baby more. Lucie, I have even used that exercise that you suggested—writing themselves a letter to say all their reasons for having an abortion. The patients who did that told me afterward that it wasn't them who wrote those letters."

"What did they mean, 'it wasn't them?'" Françoise asked.

"They couldn't explain it. They just said, 'I would never have done anything like that.'"

"You've got something important here, Sophie," Lucie said. "I'd like to see if I can help. Do you imagine any of these women would talk to me?"

And so, Lucie began providing ongoing therapy for some of the women still in distress after their abortions.

It also happened that the New York legislature legalized abortion shortly after Lucie came back. We could hardly believe the April 11th, 1970 headline in the *International Herald Tribune* that Françoise brought every morning with the bread and pastries from the local bakery. It was a tense fight in the New York legislature, finally decided by an assemblyman named George Michaels, who sacrificed his political career to do what he thought was right. Brigitte and Matthieu Neuville were still working hard to change the law in France, only to be disappointed by the lack of political support.

In 1971, we surprisingly had some healing of an old wound.

There was a knock at the door. I opened it to find Henri. It had been nearly four years since I'd seen him.

"Jane," he said.

"Henri."

A young woman stood behind him.

He said, "This is Amelie. I bumped into her at the bus stop and she asked directions, so I walked with her."

His voice had deepened. This eighteen-year-old Henri was no longer a boy. I had to resist my impulse to throw my arms around him, or to go running into the garden to tell Sophie he was at the door. Sophie, especially, was still mourning the loss of her favorite boy from our lives.

"Thank you, Henri," I said. "Would either of you like some coffee?"

Amelie answered, "Not for me, thanks. Is there a place I can put my things? And a bathroom?"

"I'm sorry. Of course, I'll show you to your room. Would you like to lie down and have a little nap?"

"I would love that."

"Henri, you know where the coffee is if you'd like some." I showed the young woman to her room and returned to the kitchen, wondering if Henri would disappear as surprisingly as he had come. He was still there, heating water on the stove.

"Let me get Sophie. She'll be so glad to see you."

"No. Wait. I want to talk to you."

We sat in silence as he poured the hot water over the grounds, then stirred them. He pushed the plunger to force the coffee to the bottom of the carafe and poured two mugs. I felt as though I was in the presence of a wild animal that I could spook with the slightest wrong move. Who was this boy who knew how to make coffee? Who knew how to keep silent?

"Do you want milk?" he asked.

"Black is fine." He handed me a mug, and I took a sip.

"I do want to see Sophie. To apologize. But I want to talk to you first."

"Okay."

"I have been meaning to come for a while. Seeing Amelie at the bus stop was just a good excuse."

"Okay." The ball was in his court.

"I...She talked with me on our walk here...about her life. About why she is doing it."

"I hope you..."

"I didn't say anything bad to her, if that's what you are wondering. I'm seeing it...I'm seeing everything differently."

"Henri, I hope you know how much I have always loved you. I realize that what we do is very hard for some people. You don't owe me any explanation."

"I want to explain. I know it has been a long time. I have been talking with Aunt Françoise and Uncle Claude about this for the past few months. They have been helping me understand. But I couldn't face you. And...especially Aunt Sophie. Françoise says I had her on a pedestal like a saint, so it's been hard for me to see her as a regular person."

"I understand. I have that problem myself sometimes."

We shared a little laugh.

"Aunt Françoise told me about how she met you. That she was supposed to be marrying a Nazi or something, but she got pregnant. Claude said her family could have been killed if the Germans learned about it. That her parents took her to Dr. Levy, and you helped. Was it really like that? The Nazis and all?"

"Yes. They took anything they wanted and hurt anyone who got in their way."

"But Françoise's parents were really going to make her marry one of them?"

"Her parents were good people. They were doing the best thing they could think of to keep their family safe. It is hard to explain something that doesn't make any sense."

"So how did you know how to help Dr. Levy?"

"I didn't. Your Aunt Françoise's abortion was the first one I had ever seen. You know how persuasive Dr. Levy can be. He convinced me I should help and told me what to do. I was wearing my teacher's uniform that was modeled after a nun's habit, so Françoise thought I was giving her a holy benediction when I held her hand. She was so terrified that Levy thought the comfort of a non-judgmental nun would help her. We still do that now when a woman is having a hard time."

"You pretend to be a nun?"

"Essentially, yes."

"There's an awful lot I still don't understand. It is illegal, right?"

"Yes."

"Weren't you scared?"

"I was scared to death. But when I heard Françoise's story, I thought I needed to help."

"I have thought about what I said to Sophie about a million times. *Is* it killing babies?"

"I don't have an answer for you. Some people believe it is. The Church teaches that it is. I see it differently, maybe because I wasn't raised Catholic. Maybe because I'm a woman and I know that all the rules were written by men. When a woman is pregnant, I know something is developing that would be a baby if it is born. But when it is still inside the woman, I think she has to decide whether to bring it into the world. And yes, what we do is a kind of killing. Even though that is a hard word, it is honest. A decision as serious as this one deserves our honesty. But what has made you think about this?"

"Aunt Françoise kept trying to talk with me, but I didn't want to. She begged me to talk with you and Sophie, but I just couldn't. You were everything to me and I was so shocked when I understood what you were doing. I was so...I just couldn't believe it. When Aunt Françoise told me her story, I had to listen. And Uncle Claude helped me—to understand it differently."

"Do you want to talk to Sophie now?"

"Yes, but I'm scared. Will she love me if I still don't agree with her?"

"Yes. I guarantee you she will. We have both missed you so much, but she has been especially sad. She is going to be amazed at how you have grown up."

"Jane?"

"Yes?"

"Manon's daughter, Petite Lucie, thinks the way you do."

"Really? How do you know?"

"We've gotten to be sort of pen pals. I really like her."

"I'm glad. I like her too."

"Will you get Sophie?"

"Yes. She's out in the garden. I'll get her now."

I took a step toward the side door, then stopped. "Would you like to go find her yourself?"

Something between fear and excitement flashed across his face. "Yes," he said. "Thanks."

It was all I could do to stay in the kitchen and let them have their time. I did the lunch dishes. I swept the already-clean floor. I re-read the newspaper from the day before. I heated the oven and cut up a baguette to make croutons. After forever, Sophie and Henri came in, smiling, arms around each other's shoulders. I hadn't noticed how tall he was—a lot taller than Sophie. Almost as tall as I am.

I asked, "Would you like to stay to dinner?"

"No, *merci*. I'm working on a report for school." He kissed Sophie and then me on the cheek. "I'll see you soon," he said.

Sophie smiled. "Make it sooner than four years, buddy." What had been a tragedy had become the subject of teasing.

"I promise," he said, as he went out the door like he'd never stopped coming and going from the convent.

Sophie and I looked at each other, and collapsed onto the kitchen chairs.

"He wants to be a doctor now," she said, smiling.

"And he and Petite Lucie have formed some kind of relationship. That's something I might have dreamed of, but I never imagined it could happen."

"As I recall, she was pretty condescending about him last time we were all together," Sophie said.

"I remember. She said he didn't have nuance."

We laughed, remembering how surprised we were that she had even known that concept at the age of twelve.

In April, we were astonished by the courage of Simone de Beauvoir and 342 other women who published their names as having had illegal abortions, still punishable by up to ten years in prison. Françoise was positively crowing about her brave Aunt Simmi.

The first issue of *Ms. Magazine* was published in the United States in early 1972. On the cover was a sort of weeping multi-armed Kali Goddess in a dress with a baby in her belly. She juggled work, cooking, cleaning, beauty, laundry, and carpool—just the normal tasks of a typical American woman. Even though the magazine took a month to get to us, Sophie, Lucie, Françoise, and I all found it terribly exciting. The world was changing.

In May, the *Tribune* brought the terrible news that seven members of the abortion group I visited in Detroit were arrested. I hated imagining Candy, Stacy, Amelia, and the others behind bars. They took huge risks every day in order to take care of women. Stacy wrote to me later that they had all been bailed out and awaited trial. At Our Lady, we felt pretty safe from the authorities, since we hadn't used instruments to provide abortion care for years. Even if the police raided the convent, there would be no evidence of what we were doing. We didn't think anyone would believe we were producing abortions with herbal medicine. But reading about the arrests made all of our hearts beat faster.

Then the unimaginable.

Françoise had already come, carrying croissants and the newspaper, when the phone rang.

I was in a good mood. My coffee was in front of me with a chocolate-covered croissant on a plate, so I answered cheerfully.

"*Bonjour, Notre Dame de la Grace Perpetuelle.*"

It was Brigitte. "Jane. Have you heard?"

The newspaper was folded in half, the top headlines showing.

"Lyndon Johnson died?"

"No, silly. Not that. Read the bottom half of the paper."

I was used to reading the newspaper by folding it in half so it didn't take up so much room on the table, so I flipped it over.

The headline read, "Highest Court in U.S. Declares Early Abortion a Constitutional Right."

I gasped.

Brigitte spoke again. "The Supreme Court in your country has made abortion legal with one bang of the gavel. Do you realize that Matthieu and I have been working for fifteen years to make that happen in France? *Fifteen years*, with no results."

"Wait, wait. I need to tell Sophie and Françoise. Brigitte, let me call you back."

I called out to both of them. "It's happened! It has finally happened."

Sophie ran into the kitchen from the bedroom and Françoise from the pantry.

"What is it, Jane?" Françoise puffed. "What's wrong?"

"Look at the newspaper."

Françoise wrinkled her brow. "I glanced at it when I bought it. The American who was president died." She wrinkled her brow. "Why do you care? Did you know him?"

I reached out and took her hands and swung her around.

"No. Look at the bottom half of the paper."

Sophie and Françoise moved to the table and read over my shoulder.

"I can't believe it," Sophie said. "Jane, did you have any idea this was going to happen?"

"A couple of years ago, Matthieu told me they heard a case from Texas, but didn't make a ruling. I don't really understand how it works, but their decision covers the whole country. Abortion is legal in America!"

All I could think about was my friends who had been arrested in Detroit for helping women. I thought about the terror of moving from one apartment to another every day—of blindfolding their patients and knowing the men they depended on to do the abortions were not real doctors. All of that would be over.

After some tears of celebration, I remembered Brigitte and called her back. She sounded glum.

"Brigitte—what is wrong with you? Isn't this what we have been working for?"

"Mademoiselle Jane, how was this so easy and fast in America?"

"It wasn't. Good people in my country have been working on this for years. Lucie wrote to us about doctors in California who tried to get the laws liberalized as early as 1966. But of course this is hard. You are still pretending to be reactionary in order to persuade the conservatives. Perhaps it is time to stop that and be who you really are?"

"I don't mean to sound defeatist. I'm not going to abandon a strategy that has us closer than we have ever been. It's just hard."

The women in Detroit got to celebrate twice. In February, all charges against them were dropped because Roe v. Wade made the Michigan law invalid. Many years later, when I read various accounts of those women who risked so much to help others, I was proud to learn they had started to do abortions themselves—and had even begun using a version of the vacuum gizmo I had shown them.

By then, Lucie lived with us almost full-time. Manon told Lucie about her wish to work with us.

"I am not Sophie or Jane. Hell, I'm not even Françoise," Manon said, laughing. "I'm rough-cut. But my unfinished edges allow me to feel things and share things that are deeper than what is allowed by custom. I won't be scared off by women who are too raw to speak in anything but curses, or by those who can't do anything but bellow. Our Lady gave me a life. I'd like to repay that debt."

Lucie embraced her, and with Manon's arrival, a new energy came to the convent. As I had imagined, the two women became the best of friends. They had a lot in common. They were almost the same age, had both lived in Paris as children, and each had a daughter. But there the difference was painful.

While Manon was in constant touch with her beautiful 'Petite Lucie,' as we called her, our Lucie never got letters from her daughter. Petite Lucie visited often because of her blooming relationship with Henri. She did her best to play the loving daughter to both women, but it was hurtful for Lucie to see what a wonderful relationship they had.

Manon had an incredible head for business, and she helped us put our financial affairs in order. Brother Tim had only reluctantly let her leave her position managing his parish office. Françoise spent more and more time in Alençon with her family, so Lucie and Manon took a larger role in the running of the convent. That gave Sophie and me some time to travel. Even though she was having a terrible time with indigestion, she was a trooper. We had a wonderful trip to Peru, to visit Socorro's *Convento de Nuestra Señora de la Gracia Perpetua*, and to Italy to visit Paulette's cloister, *Convento di Nostra Signora della Grazia Perpetua*. They were very different, but both beautiful and both busy. Sophie constantly reminded me that so many women were being helped because of my vision. But my glass-half-empty mind kept reminding me of how many women across the globe remained at the mercy of the criminal laws of men.

CHAPTER 39

SUCCESS OR FAILURE?

Our Lady, and New York City, 1974

After Roe v. Wade, Stacy, the abortion counselor from the illegal Detroit underground abortion network I had visited, secured enough financial backing to open a clinic. She wrote to me now and then, but I was surprised when she called. She got right to the point.

"There is a new organization bringing all the abortion providers in the country together to create standards," she said breathlessly. "It's called National Physicians Network."

"That's good, isn't it?"

"It *is*. I want you to meet with the board. They are gathering at a clinic in New York City. I got you a fifteen-minute slot on their agenda."

"Why?"

"I want you to tell them about your work. About women's hearts. At my clinic, we're counseling the way you do at Our Lady. So many women need that help. The board won't listen to me, but you are so experienced. Besides, I can't go. My nephew is getting married. So you must come!"

Sophie and Françoise, listening in, nodded furiously.

"I've also booked you with the board of Family Matters, the group that provides birth control and gynecology to women all over the country. They don't do abortions yet, but I'm guessing they will. The National Physician's Network is holding a national conference on Sunday, and you're on a panel," Stacy declared, obviously proud of herself.

"And you made all these commitments without asking me?"

"I'm sorry. I had to before the schedules were booked up. It's just a coincidence that both boards are meeting in New York, and the meetings are on Saturday and Sunday, so you won't miss seeing patients. This is a chance to convince them right from the beginning."

Sophie and Françoise were poking me and vigorously mouthing "Say yes!"

I sighed. "Fine. Mail me the details. At least I'll get to see my mother." I acted as if I could barely be bothered, but my heart was dancing. And I was terrified.

I mapped my trip: Friday flight to New York, meetings Saturday morning, train to Connecticut to stay with my mother, train back to the city for the panel on Sunday, red-eye home. Sophie helped me polish my talk and typed it up so I wouldn't be as nervous. She even made me business cards, creating elegant borders with her pinking shears.

At the last minute, I decided to bring the Uterine Siphon Apparatus. I wasn't going to give them the T'ana women's magic Abra or *Corazon de Gracia*, but at least I could share Nick's invention that had already made abortion so much safer for women on three continents.

I didn't sleep much the night before my flight, which was scheduled to leave from the new Charles de Gaulle Airport outside of Paris. I was fidgeting too much to drive, so Sophie navigated the unfamiliar route. At the enormous airport, she kissed me goodbye and wished me luck. I tried to sleep on the flight, but I was going over and over my presentation. So much rested on my ability to convince them. My track record was grim. I failed to convince Dr. Nick. I failed to convince the women doing illegal abortions in Detroit. I failed to convince Addie. I failed to convince the Paris illegal abortionist, Madame Trédivic. The officials in the UK didn't even give me a chance.

I registered at my hotel and tucked myself into bed without incident. I woke up at 8:00 a.m. and scrambled to get ready for my 10:00 a.m. meeting. The organization was meeting very close to my hotel. Although I grew up an hour outside the city, I didn't have any experience navigating New York. In lieu of getting on a subway or bus where I feared I might disappear, I asked the doorman for directions and walked the twenty blocks to the clinic.

I had never been to a legal abortion clinic before. The various apartments where Stacy's underground organization met with its patients in Detroit didn't count. The clinics in Alameda and Kyoto were sub rosa. Somehow, I thought the convent didn't count either.

The clinic was on the fifth floor of a skyscraper. The clinic's name, Your Choice, was printed right on the list of businesses in the elevator. I smiled to think they were able to do their work out in the open, paid for by insurance, without interference from the police or the politicians. It was truly something to aspire to. I entered the clinic to see a registration desk with three women checking in patients and answering the phone. When I gave my name, I was instructed to sit down. I was glad I had a moment to wait and take it all in. The walls were pale pink; the carpets were hunter green. It was an elegant decor with wicker chairs and sofas upholstered in a floral pattern. On the walls were posters that said, "We honor your choices," and "Thank you for trusting us with your care." One had the smiling face of a woman holding her hands out in welcome. Another poster with two women talking said, "We won't tell anyone, but you can."

A woman came and took me back to a large meeting room. The meeting was already in progress, with evidence of breakfast—coffee and doughnuts— on plates haphazardly strewn about the table. A tall man with white hair stood to great me.

"I'm Dr. Bernie Schwartz, chair of the board. Welcome." I shook his hand. He motioned to an empty chair, and I sat down. He introduced the other seven members of the board. I noticed they were all doctors except one. Her name was Lily Booth, and she gave me an especially wide smile.

Dr. Schwartz said, "There are 20 minutes scheduled for your presentation. Please begin."

I introduced myself briefly, then started with the special surprise of the Uterine Suction Apparatus. I pulled it out of my bag with a flourish. I expected the perplexed looks on their faces and went directly into an explanation of the function of the device, giving my old colleague, Dr. Nick, full credit for its invention.

"My dear Miss Smith," Dr. Schwartz interrupted, "surely this is some kind of joke?"

It was my turn to look perplexed.

"You really don't know?" he asked, trying not to laugh.

I was rescued by the non-doctor, Lily. "We are very fortunate to have an electric version of your—your apparatus."

"Electric?" My eyes were wide.

"I think there is time to show you. Come with me," Dr. Schwartz said.

Only Lily chose to accompany us, the other doctors laughing among themselves. We walked down the hall to an open door. For the first time, I saw a vacuum aspiration machine. It worked under the same principles as the USA, but as the doctor siphoned water out of a cup, I saw their machine was much more efficient. It still didn't hold a candle to the T'ana's *Corazon de Gracia*, but I had to admit it was more impressive than our homemade device. I blushed from head to toe and wished *I* could be siphoned up into a cup.

"I'm certain you meant well," Lily said. "It must be difficult for you to keep track of the latest medical advances."

We trooped back into the meeting room, and I tucked the USA back into its bag as if it were a disobedient child. I sat down in my chair, my shoulders slumped, thoroughly defeated.

"Was that all, Miss Smith?" Dr. Schwartz asked.

"Didn't you have something else to share?" Lily said hopefully.

I imagined what Sophie and Françoise would say. I cleared my throat and said, "Yes. If there is still time." Schwartz nodded at me, so I pulled the papers out of my bag and proceeded to describe three decades of experience and the lessons we had learned in caring for women. After I had described our basic protocols, I included the all-important disclaimer.

"Of course, not all patients need the same amount of emotional care. But we believe we have made a significant difference in the lives of the women who do."

Even before I was done, there were hands up around the table. I thought that was a good sign until Dr. Schwartz pointed to a beefy man with black hair and a red face, who began in a patronizing tone.

"Miss Smith, is it?"

It sounded like an accusation.

"Yes, Jane Smith."

"You live in France, but I take it from your lack of accent that you were born here?"

Somehow I felt as though I had been caught in a lie.

"Yes. I have lived in the countryside outside Paris since 1950."

"Ah. Then it's no surprise you are so behind the times. France is dominated by Catholicism, I believe. And America is a secular country. It's obvious why you need to do extra in your practice. But all that is not needed here."

I started to protest that a Baptist woman I worked with in Detroit had needed it, but a woman with shiny blond hair and the face of a model piggy-backed on her colleague's comments.

"Your practice is illegal in France, is it not?" She asked her question as though that fact discounted my three decades of experience.

"Yes."

"It's different here."

Before I could say anything else, a tall, thin man said, "Perhaps you need this where you come from. Perhaps those women are confused, but here, women are clear about what they want. If they don't believe in abortion, they won't have one. In America, we call that freedom."

They were all smiling and congratulating themselves when Dr. Schwartz said, "I'm sorry. That's all the time we have. We wish you the best." With that, he stood up to signal that it was time for me to leave. And leave I did.

It was fortunate that there was a small park across the street. I'm not sure how I got there, but I was sitting on a bench almost in tears when the board member, Lily, sat down next to me.

"I'm so sorry," she said. "They are just awful. They only put me on the board so they could claim they have input from clinic staff, but they don't listen to anything I say any more than they listened to you. They are all full of themselves and think they know everything."

I smiled gratefully, and she continued.

"The doctors who own clinics are mostly the renegades—the pioneers. It is wonderful that they are willing to help women and work in a largely ignored or vilified field. But most of them think they are God's gift. I'm a friend of

Stacy's, and we are hoping to do the kind of work you are talking about at my clinic. The counselors want to do it, but we are limited to 15 minutes for each patient. That is supposed to include everything—explaining the procedure, going over possible complications, and talking about aftercare. We need to learn so much more about how to do it. And if our owners don't agree, we'll never have the time."

I realized I hadn't even imagined how clinics worked in "legal abortion" America. I hadn't thought that, in addition to the many wonderful people who only wanted to give good care, there could be owners who only thought of making money. It reminded me of teaching the illegal abortionist, Madame Trévidic, who only had time to end pregnancies as expeditiously as possible.

Lily reached out and took my hand. "I am embarrassed they didn't listen to you. But there will be another chance at the conference. The panel won't be doctors—it will be counselors and clinic administrators—the people who see patients every day. They must recognize what you are talking about. They *have* to listen."

I thanked her for her supportive words, holding back my tears. "I am supposed to talk to the board of Family Matters this afternoon. Do you think they will be any more responsive?"

Lily shrugged her shoulders. "I wish I did. They don't even do abortions yet, so all they think about is medical care. They think they are rescuing women from disaster by giving them birth control. But obviously, disaster still strikes. That's why we're here."

"Are they all as paternalistic?"

"Most of them are. I don't know the Family Matters people. It's possible they are different." She looked at her watch. "I've got to get back to the meeting or they will send the police into the ladies' room after me. Good luck this afternoon."

Lily patted my arm and left me sitting on the bench.

Stacy had emphasized how great it was that there would be time for lunch between the two presentations, but I had no appetite. I sat on that bench forever, reading and re-reading the presentation Sophie had typed for me. I couldn't find anything to change, but I added an introduction that acknowledged some of the differences between France and America, and included stories from California and Kyoto to demonstrate that emotional and spiritual needs were part of every woman's makeup. I sat there a bit too long, so I had to take a cab to the next address.

Another skyscraper. This time I rode the elevator to the eleventh floor. The reception area was more businesslike than the clinic. I remembered that this was the headquarters of a very large corporation. Who knows how Stacy even got me on their agenda?

At exactly 1 p.m., a young woman came into the waiting room, looked down at her clipboard, and called my name. I followed behind her like the tail of a kite. She handed me off to a man standing in the hallway outside a door that had the word 'Conference' on it. He was also carrying a clipboard. He smiled at me and said, "Good morning, Miss Smith. I'm afraid we had to add a few unexpected items to our agenda, so we'll need to limit your remarks to 10 minutes."

He was so formal, the only thing I could think to say was, "Thank you." At the same time, my mind weighed the benefits of speaking very fast versus leaving out some examples. At least I wasn't going to make the mistake of showing them Nick's abortion apparatus. He led me into a large room with floor-to-ceiling glass windows that made me queasy, and introduced me. No one stood up to shake my hand. There were no other introductions. No one offered me a chair. I felt like a contestant in a spelling bee.

I was the only woman in the room.

After an embarrassing pause, I began. These folks didn't even let me get five minutes in before they spoke. No one raised a hand. They all talked over each other.

"Miss, um, I think you are in the wrong place. We are discussing medical protocols. We don't even provide the service of voluntary termination of pregnancy."

Another said, "You think women are so weak they can't figure out what they want?"

"You are making your patients confused—asking all these questions. Planting these ideas in their heads. If they want something, they will tell you."

"You should be speaking at a seminary," another man said, laughing. "Or to a gathering of shrinks."

Another man looked down the table at the person I guessed was the chairman. "Why are we wasting our time on this?"

The chairman took charge and stood up. By now, I understood this was akin to being hauled off the stage with a shepherd's crook. I stood up myself and said a quick thank you and got out the door as quickly as I could.

Ignoring Françoise's voice in my head urging me to be frugal, I took a cab to Grand Central Station. As a child living in Connecticut, we occasionally came into the city to go to a museum or see a show, so I was familiar with the majesty of Grand Central Station. I sat on a bench and gazed upwards like a tourist while busy travelers rushed by, not taking any notice of the magic all around them. I was awed by the European-style sculptures at the entrance, and the iconic blue ceiling with gilded illustrations of constellations and celestial figures.

Trains were frequent, so I just sat until I found some self-forgiveness. I hated the idea of telling my mother, let alone Lucie, Sophie, and Françoise, that I had failed. Failed myself. Failed them. Failed women.

I found a pay phone and told my mother when to expect me. At the age of 86, she still lived in our family home. My two cousins, Sibyl and Hannah, had moved in with her to act as caregivers. Mom's mind was still sharp.

"My train gets in at 4 p.m. I'll take a cab to the house."

"Nonsense. Sibbie will pick you up. Hannah is making fried chicken for dinner. We will be so glad to see you. It has been too long. Now remind me, what have you been doing in the city?"

What, indeed? I gave a vague rundown of my meetings, avoiding my sense that the trip had been for nothing.

My mother read between the lines. We had agreed not to keep secrets from each other.

"Darling, what is it that you are not saying?" she asked.

I started to cry like a seven-year-old. "I failed totally in my mission of persuading other abortion providers to attend to the emotional and spiritual well-being of their patients."

"I'm so sorry, Jane."

"Thanks." I sniffled and blew my nose. "But I can't wait to see you and the girls."

"You can tell us all about it when you get here. Sibbie will be in the station wagon."

I slept on the hour-long train ride, my head against the window. My dreams were populated with women who had worked so hard to resolve their feelings about being pregnant. Back in my nursing school days, I met Catalina, who had feared her recently dead uncle's spirit wanted to come back into the world through her pregnancy. In one of my first forays into spiritual healing, we brought her uncle and Jesus into the counseling session, and she asked for and received their forgiveness. I remembered the young woman in Japan who wanted a baby because she was starving for love. She had an abortion. Afterward, I got her a puppy. I thought of Manon, the young prostitute who feared she would not be a good mother, but decided to have the baby. The women in Peru whose stories Socorro told. Women who transformed from confusion to certainty about their decisions. None of them could have done that alone. Not because they were stupid or weak, but because they didn't know how. As much as anything else, we gave them tools to use in every area of their lives. Tools to make decisions with both their heads and their hearts.

It had started to rain by the time I got off at the Stamford station. I was happy to see my cousin, wearing one of those old-lady clear plastic rain hats that look like shower caps. I loved Sibbie, but at 40, she looked as old as me. It depressed me that I was half-a century old and had not realized my goals for the world. Sibbie gave me a strong hug, and we scurried to the car.

I was so happy to see my mother. We had a big hug and kiss. We'd been writing each other every week for many years, but a letter just isn't the same.

I put my small suitcase in the bedroom, and Hannah announced dinner was ready. Her fried chicken, mashed potatoes, and green beans were perfection. Almost enough to make up for a day of failure.

"Sweetheart, you said on the phone that you'd failed. What is it you are trying to do?"

I hadn't written much about the trip. Just that I had meetings and was going to get to spend the night. For years and years, my mother and I had kept secrets from each other, pretending that everything was fine. That all came to a head back in 1958, and since then we have been close. But I was feeling very ashamed just then.

"A friend suggested I come to try to convince some of the leaders in women's health care to include attention to women's emotional and spiritual needs as well as their medical needs. The way we do it at Our Lady. Most of the people I was presenting to were doctors, and they either didn't think counseling was necessary, or even imagined it was our fault when patients were in turmoil—as if the questions we asked *created* the uncertainties women struggled with."

My mother was indignant. "Surely they recognize that a question as serious as whether to have a baby is complicated. Women are not machines."

"I agree," Sibbie said. "I can see how passionate you are about this, Jane. Your mother has told us so much about the amazing work you do at your convent."

"They gave me only a few minutes for my presentations. I hardly had a chance to be passionate." I sighed.

"I'm sorry about that, darling. But this sad, slumped-over version of you is not likely to persuade anyone. You said you have another chance?"

My mother had become a self-help junkie and served as an ersatz motivational coach for her friends.

"I'm on a big panel tomorrow afternoon. There are three other women talking about things that are so boring I can't even imagine. And then me. Talking about something that is crucial to every woman who comes for abortion care—the opportunity to explore her deepest feelings and to find her truest self."

Hannah was clearing the table, but she stopped and said, "If you tell it to them that way, they can't help but listen."

"I planned to share some stories about the women we have worked with."

My mother piped up. "That patient Charlotte is a story you should tell. The one who said she felt like a dead squirrel when she first came to the convent. It was like magic when she found the strength to tell her parents about her abortion. I'll never forget her."

"I won't either. But you're right. I need to dive right into what this way of working does for women. I want to touch the audience's hearts, not just their heads."

I woke early, had breakfast, and Sibbie took me to meet the 9:00 a.m. train. It was heartbreaking to say goodbye to my mother—we both recognized it might be our last time together. I arrived at the conference hotel at 10:30 a.m., registered and put on my ID badge, and found an unused room to work on what I wanted to say. I emerged at the sound of people in the hallway.

There was a podium at the front of the room with the names of the presenters. We said hello to each other as we took our seats. A moderator introduced each of us, and the presentations began. I would like to say that I paid attention at all to the other women's talks, but I didn't. When the moderator said my name, I stood up. None of the other presenters had stood, but I needed to pace, like I always did when I was having my best thoughts.

"I assisted with my first abortion in 1939." There were gasps I had anticipated. Most of the people in the room were not yet born in 1939. "I had no idea what I was doing. I only knew that a frightened woman needed help. I held her hand and, though it may sound strange, I prayed with her. Because that is what she needed." I was pacing across the stage.

"Since that evening, I have worked with hundreds of women in Paris, California, and Kyoto, Japan. They spoke different languages, but their hearts were the same.

"You are probably aware that about ten percent of the women who come to your clinic don't really need you. They are mature and confident in their decision, and they simply need abortion care. Your kindness is the icing on the cake. About eighty percent of the women you see are sure of their decision, but have some fears or beliefs they need help to reframe in order for them to have a sense of peace about their choice. You also know that if you are given 15 minutes total to work with a woman, you will not even be able to find out what those issues are, let alone help her re-frame them."

The room went deathly quiet. I had told the truth. They all wondered where I would go from there.

"From my decades of experience, about ten percent of the women you see are deeply troubled about what choice to make. They may have been raised as a Catholic, or Baptist, or some other fundamentalist religion that hates and fears women and labels birth control and abortion as sins—even sins that merit excommunication from the community of the church. They may have been adopted, or not be at all clear about the morality of ending a pregnancy. They may have been hoping the man involved would marry them—perhaps still imagining that he would come back to them if they had a baby. They may be a teenager—or really any age—without the skills to make such a significant and life-altering decision. They may want to have a baby but be afraid of the judgment of their family and the larger society. You know them. You know what I mean, because sometimes you have found some way to take a bit more time with them than you are allowed. And yet, you never had enough time. Whether they had an abortion or not, these are the ones you take home in your hearts and minds. These are the ones that make you doubt yourself. And even doubt whether you are doing the right thing." I noticed that a woman in the front row was crying.

"And there are some women you aren't even aware of. Women who are so deeply ambivalent about abortion that they will roll dice, or consult psychics, or ask anybody else what to do. These women who are split require special care. If they have an abortion, they will go into their own version of hell, and you won't know because they will never call the clinic that they now think is evil."

I was almost done. "No matter which of these women we are talking about, they need to be seen and heard. Every woman needs care that fits her situation. And you need the time to do your sacred job with both art and skill. Abortion is not just a medical experience any more than birth is. No matter what choice is made, pregnancy involves every part of a woman's life. A decision this significant needs to be made with both the woman's head—her logic, and her heart—her love. And you need to be trained to be open to a woman who is having her own deep feelings without losing yourself. If you don't have a boundary, you will either do this work like a robot—without ever risking—or you will burn out."

The moderator attempted to get my attention to tell me our time had elapsed. I ignored her. Women were already making a long line behind the microphone for the question-and-answer period. The moderator said, "We must stop. It is time for the lunch break." Behind me, one of the other panelists said, "Let her speak."

I continued. "And is this good enough? Is this what you dreamed of doing? Fifteen minutes to meet the needs of each woman? Is this only about money? Will you be silent as women are all being treated the same instead of being served as individuals? Are their feelings too dangerous? Is this what feminism has come to? Making abortion care a conveyor belt instead of providing each woman what she needs? The vast majority of abortion care doctors are men, and the vast majority of clinic owners are men, but women are the gatekeepers of that care. You have the power to make a difference."

I stood there for a second before I registered the standing ovation. Even the other panelists were standing and clapping. The moderator took the microphone and said, "Thank you. Yes, thank you. Please—it's time to break for lunch in the La Guardia Room. Our next session will begin at 2 p.m. sharp." She turned the microphone off, so I hopped down from the stage and approached the women standing in line who didn't seem to mind missing lunch. I had them drag the chairs out from the rows so they could sit in a circle.

The clinic staff members shared their grief and frustration at not having enough time with the patients who needed it. I passed out all the business cards Sophie had so lovingly created that I hadn't even bothered to take out of my bag at the earlier meetings. I encouraged them to remember they had power if they worked together. I even thought they might start an organization specifically for abortion counselors, since the doctors had already staked out their territory. I felt like a union organizer. Before I knew it, I had to say good-bye to get a taxi to the airport.

On the flight home, I wondered if the trip had been a success or a failure. The people in charge were not interested in what I had to say. But the women who actually worked with the patients understood exactly what I meant.

Could that be enough?

The year passed uneventfully. We did our work as we always had—aware that our safety from arrest depended on our relationship with Inspector Chastain and others in the gendarmerie for whom we had done favors. Then change finally came to France.

When there was a knock on the door one January morning, I guessed it would be Brigitte. Her years in government had led her to tame her frizzy hair into a polished chignon. She wore a bit of makeup, and her suit was crisply tailored. This time we had some warning. Matthieu called the afternoon before and told us what time we needed to listen to the radio. At the convent, that was more difficult than it sounded. The thick stone walls built to keep the outside world at bay did just that. Henri did something magical that allowed us to set the radio up outdoors. We bundled up in our warmest coats and sat around the rickety old wooden table as if it were a campfire. The coverage of the final vote in favor of what they were already calling the 'Veil Act' was riveting. Sophie went into the kitchen during a boring part and brought back hot chocolate for me, Françoise, Brigitte, Henri, Lucie, and the three guests— the word we used for our patients—who were sitting with us. Acting Health Minister Simone Veil announced from the podium that abortion would be legal in France. It was too important for whoops of joy. We were just stunned. January 17th, 1975. It was as if a new world had begun.

"Finally, finally, finally," Brigitte said.

"Yes, dear friend. You did it. These years of working so hard have paid off."

"My niece Lydia is in nursing school now. She's already told me she wants to help do abortions."

"I know. She told me too. She will be wonderful. But, Brigitte, you know they won't be doing abortions the way we do."

"Of course. They won't have your magic Peruvian fairy dust."

"I don't just mean that. They won't be doing all the talking and crying and exploring feelings we do."

"Why not?" Brigitte asked.

"That's not how doctors work. They deal with the body, not the spirit."

"But I don't understand. Some of the stories you have told me—some women—maybe all women, need more than that. They deserve more than just a medical procedure. Why even make it legal if they are going to do it wrong?"

Her question, if not in those exact words, haunted me for the rest of my life.

Two weeks later, I was surprised to see Brigitte once more at the front door. "Come in, old friend."

"Jane, I have a gift I have owed you for a long time."

"Brigitte, you don't owe me anything."

"A gift for women, then. Consider it a gift for women."

She handed me a document rolled up like a scroll and tied with a ribbon. "Get Sophie and Françoise in here. I want them to see this too."

I gathered my colleagues, and we sat at the kitchen table as I unrolled the paper. Sophie read aloud over my shoulder. "Hear ye, hear ye. As of February 10th, 1975, Our Lady of Perpetual Grace Convent shall be considered free from any and all legal restrictions or regulations. It shall hereby and in perpetuity provide medical care under the auspices of the Bureau of Traditional Medicine and shall be free from any and all interference or scrutiny."

Sophie and I gasped. Françoise laughed heartily. Brigitte grinned. The government's recognition of us at Our Lady as practitioners of Traditional Healing Arts protected us from anyone who sought to accuse us of providing illegal abortion care before the law was changed. In addition to the get-out-of-jail-free document we framed and hung by the front door, Brigitte gave me a photo of herself and Matthieu Neuville standing behind Simone Veil. Levy came to visit and brought a bottle of champagne to celebrate. The world *was* changing.

CHAPTER 40

STOP ALL THE CLOCKS

Our Lady, 1977

"He was my North, my South, my East and West,
My working week and my Sunday rest,
My noon, my midnight, my talk, my song;
I thought that love would last forever: I was wrong."

-W.H. Auden
From "Stop All the Clocks"

In 1977, just before Christmas, Sophie was diagnosed with pancreatic cancer. She died on March 18th at the age of 54.

That's all I can bear to say about it.

CHAPTER 41

LIFE GOES ON

Our Lady, 1978

Everyone I loved was there for me. Brother Timothy came and stayed for weeks. Lucie, Manon, and Françoise acted like emotional pillows—trying to soften my fall. I was not able to appreciate any of them then, and I hoped they would forgive me. I almost couldn't stand to be at the convent. Every room, the gardens, the kitchen, even the chores reminded me of Sophie, and broke me.

I lost interest in everything. There was no reason for me to be in any one place over any other. There was no reason for me to be. I could so easily have slid back into the bottle of my post-Betty misery, but Lucie loved me too much to let me.

"No more wine tonight, Jane," she'd say, gently taking the bottle away and hiding it in a high cupboard. It went on like that for weeks—with me just going through the motions—doing what I had to do to survive. I didn't think anything could be good again.

In my emotional absence, Lucie and Manon took over the daily running of Our Lady. You might think that once abortion was legal in France, women would stop coming to us. But under the new law, abortions required an overnight hospital stay. It wasn't necessary, but it was a concession to government conservatives. Even though getting an abortion took three days with us, some women preferred the intimacy and warmth of the cloister.

I was sixty-four, but I felt like I was a hundred and sixty-four. I rattled around feeling sorry for myself. Once, when I was telling Manon how insignificant I was, she reminded me about the three women I had counseled that week.

"Don't they count for anything, Jane?" she asked. "You changed their lives."

"I forgot about them," I answered.

It took months for me to begin to feel like myself. One afternoon, I got a call from Brother Tim.

"I'm sending you someone very special," he said mysteriously.

"A patient?"

"No. It's someone who wants to help. She is a friend of Sister Bernadette's."

"You didn't tell her about what we do here—how we do it, did you?"

"Jane, you are still afraid? You are safe from the law now. Brigitte has seen to that."

"You're right. But I am still wary of outsiders. Most people can't understand how we approach our work."

"I haven't talked about it, but I'm afraid that Sister Bernadette, I mean Bernadette—I can never remember that she is no longer a nun—anyway, Bernadette may have shared just a bit. I believe that's why this woman wants to come. She wants to help women."

"We don't need any help. We are doing just fine. Are you sure I can trust her?"

"Jane, are you becoming paranoid in your old age? Of course I am sure. And she is absolutely great. You are going to love her."

"This may not be the best time," I said. "Manon is away visiting her daughter."

"You and Lucie and Françoise can handle a visitor," Tim said, laughing. "And you'll see, she's wonderful. She can do a little of everything. Her name is Zaza. She'll be on the Wednesday bus along with the patients."

On Wednesday afternoon, four women came to the door. Lucie greeted them, and the patients introduced themselves. There was a short, rather plump young woman with curly red hair who introduced herself as Yvette, a teenager named Monique who had short black hair and lots of makeup and was smoking furiously, and a tall, stocky woman in her late twenties named Clara, who wore her blonde hair in a pageboy with a fringe. Lucie ushered them to their rooms. Standing quietly behind on the steps was a slender woman of medium height with skin the color of mahogany. She had dark brown hair pulled back with a ribbon. Her gaze was intense, her eyes almost black.

"You must be Jane," she said, coming up the stairs and holding out her hand. I shook it. I was so surprised that I am afraid I stared at her. I couldn't remember a woman of African descent ever coming to the convent.

"Oh no, he didn't tell you! That Tim. I warned him against surprising you, but he has worked with us for so long I'm afraid he no longer notices our color."

"Oh, I am so sorry to stare. It is a perfectly lovely surprise. It *is* unusual to see anyone with your beautiful dark skin around here," I said, embarrassed. I thought of my dear friend Sally, the only Black nurse years ago in my class at the Naval Academy. "Please come in." She carried her small suitcase inside.

"That's all right. Thank you for being honest about it. Some people just pretend they didn't even notice. That is much more awkward." She hesitated for a moment. "I wanted to say how sorry I was to hear about Sophie," she said gently, putting the suitcase down.

"How do you know about her?"

"Brother Tim loves you all, and he and Bernadette have told me a lot about you over the years."

"Thank you," I said, my eyes involuntarily filling with tears. The others knew enough not to talk about Sophie, but I must admit that I relished hearing her name spoken. Lucie came back and said that our three guests were taking a nap before dinner.

The woman reached out her hand to Lucie. "You must be Lucie. Brother Timothy has talked about you so much that it's as though I already know you. My name is Zaza. I am so delighted to meet you. I am here to help if you will have me."

"Then let's start out right!" Lucie said, giving her a hug.

Zaza returned the embrace, but with what I interpreted as a bit of reserve. In her exuberance, Lucie didn't even notice.

"Leave your suitcase here. We'll put it away later. While our guests are napping, we can get to know each other. Tell us all about you. Why has Brother Tim sent you to us?" Lucie swooped us all into the kitchen. "Sit, sit, sit," she said, and we sat around the long table.

"Are you hungry? Would you like something to drink?" I asked, trying to think what Sophie would do.

"I'd love a glass of water, thank you," she said.

I got a glass of water for her, and Lucie poured two glasses of red wine, gesturing to ascertain that Zaza didn't want any.

"No thanks. I don't drink alcohol," Zaza said, almost apologetically.

Once we each had a glass in front of us, Zaza was quiet again.

Lucie prompted her. "Tell us about yourself," she said, more sedately than usual.

Zaza took a sip of water, then a deep breath. She closed her eyes for a moment and then began the tale of her life.

"My parents came to Paris in the 1950s, fleeing the political unrest in Algeria. Algeria is officially part of France, but its darker inhabitants, especially those who were Muslim, like my parents, didn't receive a warm welcome. I was the first of what became nine children. My mother somehow arranged a scholarship for me to attend a Catholic boarding school because she wanted a better life for me than she and my father had.

"When I was thirteen, my parents and siblings moved to a camp sponsored by the government for Algerian workers who were brought over after the war when there weren't enough French men to fill the jobs. My entire family died when typhus swept through the crowded community. It wiped out most of the camp so quickly that the outbreak was over before I even learned about it. The school kept me on, out of pity, I guess. There was nowhere else for me to go."

"Oh, my goodness," Lucie exclaimed. "That is so awful."

Zaza continued. "Thank you. Many days, I wondered why I survived. I wondered if they died because I wanted too much—if Allah was punishing me for being with the Catholics. I wept for my family and for myself. I met Brother Tim when I was just finishing high school. He arranged for me to be trained as a nurse and even found a job for me at a hospital. Later I began working with him to care for people at the camp. But again, I wanted more. Allah, forgive me for wanting more."

I smiled. "The original sin of women."

"Yes, exactly that," Zaza smiled too.

"How do we fit in?" Lucie asked.

"It is all because of Bernadette. Just after she left the order, she took the same nurse's training that I did, and she became my dear friend. We confided our deepest secrets to each other, and she told me about her time here with you."

I was wary. Even though Brother Tim and Bernadette had sent her to us, I still wasn't convinced I should trust her.

Zaza continued, "I miss my family—my mother most of all. She defied everyone to send me to school—she didn't want me to marry young and have baby after baby like she did. I always wondered if she might have survived the epidemic if she hadn't been depleted by having so many children. I am very grateful for my education. I love the people at the camp, but somehow I want something different. People sometimes yell at me that I should go back to where I came from—but I was born in Paris. I lived all of my forty-two years in this country. My parents were French citizens. I am as French as they are. Perhaps I am searching for somewhere to truly belong."

"Tim said you wanted to help us?" I said.

"Yes. When Bernadette told me about this place, I had a funny idea that Our Lady of Notre Dame could be my home. Please forgive me for being presumptuous. Timothy thought I should call you—to at least ask if I could come, but I wanted to present myself and risk your honest response. I just took a chance." She looked at me apologetically. "I hope I haven't made a mistake."

Lucie took her hand. "Not at all—we are so glad you're here, aren't we, Jane?" she said, impulsively.

"It is wonderful that you have already made friends with Lucie. She's our toughest customer, but we are a team here, so we'll need to talk with Manon and Françoise," I said, looking sideways at Lucie.

"Of course, I understand," Zaza said.

We had a light supper of cold cuts, bread, and cheese, and made an early night of it.

The following morning, Lucie took Zaza and our three guests for an outing in the village. Françoise appeared, as usual, with some fresh bread, vegetables, and roasting chickens to make for dinner. After Sophie died, we had been taking turns cooking, with varying degrees of success. None of us cooked the way Sophie did. Françoise put the groceries away and sat down with me at the table with a cup of fresh coffee. At least we were all good at making coffee.

CHAPTER 42

WHAT KIND OF NAME IS THAT?

"Where is everyone?" Françoise asked, sipping her coffee. "Don't we have guests today?"

"Remember, Manon is still away, but there are three guests. Lucie has taken them into the village."

"She likes to get a sense of them before we begin, doesn't she?" Françoise mused.

"You're right. And there is another visitor. Brother Tim and Sister Bernadette have sent a young woman who wants to work with us. I think she is delightful and would make a wonderful addition to our team, but, of course, I told her that we would all need to agree. Her name is Zaza Bashir."

"What kind of name is that?" Françoise asked, making a strange face.

"Her family came here from Algeria," I answered. "Is that what you are asking?"

"She is '*pied noir*'?" Françoise demanded. Her tone changed. "We cannot have someone like that here, Jane. They are not like us."

"I am not sure what you mean. This woman is French—she was born in Paris. Her family is Muslim, but she attended Catholic school."

"It doesn't matter. If she is dark, no guest would let her touch them. You don't understand—they are not like us."

My heart was pounding. "Françoise, I have never heard you talk like this before. Don't you remember that we fought a war over exactly that sentiment? 'They are not like us?' I realize there are French who blame the war on the Jews. Is that what you think? That the Jews are not like us?"

Françoise stood up so suddenly that she knocked her chair over. "How dare you, Jane. No one has ever accused me this way. You know me better than that."

"I *thought* I did," I answered angrily.

With that, Françoise set her jaw and said, "It's obvious that I am not wanted here." She grabbed her coat and purse and stormed out of the kitchen.

I sat stunned for a few minutes, waiting for tears to come. But they didn't. I was more shocked than sad, but also confused. I righted the chair Françoise had knocked over, and did what I often did in those days. I took my coffee out to the garden and sat on a stool near the white roses where we had scattered Sophie's ashes.

"Sophie, what should I do? I can't break our home apart on account of a stranger. But what about Françoise's reaction? I can't simply pretend this is all right."

I listened for Sophie's answers, as our guests listen for the voice of God.

My darling, I am so sorry. There are many prejudices—all based on fear. Just because you don't have one kind doesn't mean you don't have another. And like other expressions of hatred, prejudice is a heavy burden to carry. I am sure Françoise will find herself. Don't send Zaza away. She is supposed to be here.

"I think so too, although I can't explain why. But I don't want to tell Lucie about Françoise's prejudice. I have a ridiculous impulse to protect her."

You don't need to tell Lucie. Let's see how it all plays out.

As always, I felt much better after I had talked with Sophie.

Lucie and our guests got back in time for lunch. The four looked as though they had been friends forever. I had put together a simple ratatouille from the fresh vegetables Françoise brought with her that morning. Lucie was telling them about the history of the cloisters, with lots of jokes and quips, and the guests were laughing and asking questions. As I listened to the conversation, I sensed there was something about Zaza that inspired trust. She wasn't as talkative as Lucie, but she radiated kindness. They were a powerful team. I couldn't recall a time when all our guests were as at ease.

We sat down for lunch, and the stew wasn't half bad. Zaza was polite about it.

"This is lovely," she exclaimed. "Do you like to cook? It is one of my favorite things."

I had to admit that it was one of my least favorite things, but I accepted her compliment.

"But where is Françoise?" Lucie asked, sounding disappointed. "I can't wait for her to meet Zaza."

I hated to lie, but it seemed the only thing to do, so I said, "She isn't feeling well. I'm sure we will see her tomorrow."

Lucie turned to Zaza. "You are going to adore Françoise. In many ways, she is the reason we are all here. She is just the best."

Zaza smiled at the anticipation of meeting the wonderful Françoise.

After a dessert of sliced apples slathered with Brie cheese, I explained to our guests how the rest of their visit would be structured. Since it was just Lucie and me doing the counseling, we would take two shifts. Lucie took Monique into a room that was large enough for Zaza to observe her. Clara said she'd be happy to explore the gardens, so I worked with Yvette. We did our usual pregnancy tests with Abra powder and found that Monique was nine weeks pregnant, and Yvette was seven weeks. Neither seemed to have any difficulties with the choice of abortion, so there wouldn't be any more work needed.

Lucie wanted to give Zaza a chance to ask questions, so I took Clara into counseling. She was twenty-seven, married with two children. She was confident about her decision not to have another child. She had had a miscarriage before, so I was happy to assure her that our process would be quicker, easier, and less uncomfortable than that. Our magic powder told us that she was eleven weeks. After Clara and I were finished talking, we all gathered together in the garden and completed the ceremony of taking the *Corazon de Gracia*. Since our roses were in bloom, we honored the T'ana tradition of the orchids by giving each guest her grain of *Corazon* on a tender white petal. Zaza's eyes were lit up, and I could only imagine how surprised she would be to learn the magic of our process, so different from her nursing school training.

It was Lucie's turn to make dinner. She hated cooking even more than I did.

"I guess I'm making chicken again," Lucie said. "Couldn't we go into the village for something?" She rolled her eyes and laughed. "I'm simply not much of a cook."

"I would be happy to put something together," Zaza piped up.

"That would be wonderful!" Lucie said.

I thought it was bad manners that she so readily accepted Zaza's offer.

"Lucie, Zaza is a guest," I said.

"Jane, honestly, I would love it. I never get a chance to cook for people. If I weren't a nurse, I would be a chef," Zaza insisted. She said she didn't need any help, and I happily relented.

While Zaza was busy in the kitchen, I pulled Lucie to the side. I wasn't sure how to broach the subject, but I had to tell her not to assume that Zaza would stay with us.

"Manon and Françoise still need to weigh in," I said.

"Well, sure they do, but why wouldn't they want her to stay? She's great. You've seen how she interacts with the guests. It is as though she has been doing this all her life. She's smart and intuitive, and she will make a wonderful counselor. She's been through a lot, but she's not a victim about it. It has made her more compassionate."

"Is it possible...I mean, do you think there might be guests who would be uncomfortable about...that she is Algerian?"

"Jane, what the hell are you asking me *that* for? If there is someone who doesn't like her—or who doesn't like *any* of us for that matter, they can get help somewhere else." Lucie gave me a look that signaled I had insulted her, then flounced out into the garden to join the others.

That night, we sat down to the most tender roast chicken imaginable. I can't tell you what Zaza did, but it was some magic with seasoning. And there were tiny Brussels sprouts with some kind of creamy sauce, and new potatoes with fresh parsley. It was intoxicating. Our guests were delighted by the scrumptious dinner, but Lucie and I kept looking at each other with the same thought: it was as though Sophie were back with us.

Françoise didn't come the next morning, and she didn't call.

As expected, our guests each passed their pregnancies during the night, and after breakfast we had the burial ceremony, 'To the Earth.' We reminded them that they had a special bond with each other, and a responsibility to keep the secret of our magical herbs. The guests solemnly agreed. They each chose to become one of the women who could recognize each other by the scar across their palm made by the spade. The three decided to walk back into the village for lunch before their bus, and we bade them a tearful goodbye.

Françoise didn't come later that day, either.

I assured Lucie that Françoise wasn't seriously ill, so she took it upon herself to ignore everything I had said about waiting for the others to agree, and set about teaching Zaza about Our Lady. She shared the history, the story of the T'ana herbs, the secret code of the recipes, and whatever else she decided Zaza needed to hear.

Manon was due back on Saturday. I didn't know whether to smile or cry when Françoise swooped in with Manon early that morning, their arms filled with boxes of fresh eggs, milk and cream, and chocolate croissants.

"Good morning everyone. Look who I found at the bus station," Françoise said in a slightly strained voice. She didn't meet my eyes. I had no idea what would come next.

Lucie said, "Françoise, I hope you are better."

Françoise shot a glance at me and said, "I am fine."

I observed Zaza carefully as Lucie gleefully introduced her. I could only imagine what kind of radar our new friend would have had to develop over the years to sort out friend from foe. Zaza greeted Françoise and Manon graciously and then insisted on making breakfast with the fresh eggs and other ingredients Françoise had brought. Again, she shooed us all out of the kitchen. Manon went to her room to unpack, and Françoise, Lucie, and I set about cleaning and tidying the procedure and counseling rooms from the work of the day before.

Then we all sat down to breakfast. Swiss cheese and mushroom omelets paired beautifully with chocolate croissants and café au lait.

Manon regaled us with funny stories about her daughter, Petite Lucie, who taught in Lyon. Lucie insisted on telling Françoise and Manon about Zaza's training and experience as a nurse, and all the wonderful things about the woman, arguing that she should join us right away.

Manon smiled broadly and said, "That's good enough for me. We can always use another skilled pair of hands and another open heart around here. I'm delighted to welcome you, Zaza."

Zaza was clearly uncomfortable with the accolades. "I don't want you to think you have to say that, simply because Lucie is a good salesman. Let me wash the dishes while you all talk," she said.

"Non, chérie," Françoise said. "Doing the dishes is a job we share. I'll wash, you dry, and you can tell me all about yourself. We'll have our meeting later."

Lucie and Manon set about gathering the linens from the previous guests' rooms to begin the interminable laundry. Françoise filled the sink with hot, soapy water and handed Zaza a dishtowel. I stood just outside the kitchen door listening to their conversation.

"Honestly, I don't know much—really anything—about the Muslim religion," Françoise said tentatively, scrubbing a stubborn spot of egg off a plate.

"Well, I'm not exactly Muslim anymore. I spent the first ten years of my life in that community, but I was just a child. From ages ten to eighteen, I attended a Catholic boarding school—so you and I probably had a similar education," Zaza said, reaching out for the clean plate and drying it carefully. "Then I was enrolled in an internationally run nursing school with girls from all kinds of backgrounds. For almost twenty years, I have helped Brother Timothy care for the people in an Algerian work camp. I have seen what an unwelcomed pregnancy can do to the lives of women—especially very poor women, which is why I want to do this work. My best friends are Brother Timothy and Bernadette—a renegade priest and a former nun—and my dream in life is to live at a convent and provide abortion care. If that is not confusing enough for you, I don't know what is," she said, laughing ruefully. "All my life, I have never quite fit in. I'm hoping this might be the right place for me," Zaza said.

"And a very good place it is," Françoise answered, with a genuine smile in her voice.

"Madame Françoise," Zaza said, cautiously, pausing her drying. "It must be difficult having someone you don't know appear on the doorstep and ask to be taken in. Will you please tell me honestly? Are you all right with me? With my being here?"

I peered around the door, and I saw the furrow in Zaza's brow. Françoise wiped her hands on her apron and took Zaza's hands.

"I am more than all right with it," she said. "I welcome you with open arms."

Utterly relieved, I ceased my eavesdropping.

Later that evening, Françoise and I finally sat down together in the garden. She still didn't look me in the eye.

"Jane, I am so ashamed," she said. "You must think I am terrible."

"I don't know what to think, Françoise. I was so surprised at what you said. But what happened? What changed your mind?"

"When I got back to the farm, I was slamming doors so furiously that Claude was worried, and he followed me inside. I told him that you were about to allow one of 'those' people—a '*pied noir*'—into the cloister, and he stopped me from talking. He put his hand over my mouth! He was trembling. I have never seen him so angry. Then he told me a story he had never shared before. You know, he doesn't talk about his time in that German camp, and I have never pressed him. But he told me that two Algerian men saved his life. He had been tortured, and the men tore pieces of fabric from their own garments to bind his wounds and shared their meager food with him. He was crying the whole time he told me this. In all our years together, the only other time I saw Claude cry was when Anne-Marie and Thomas adopted Henri. My dear husband reminded me that good people and bad people come in every color, shape, and size. He shamed me, and I needed to be shamed. I realized that I have never known anyone who was different from me, but my ignorance does not excuse my incivility. These past two days I have searched my soul to find the Françoise whom you blessed all those years ago. I think I have reclaimed her. Can you forgive me? Can you give me another chance?"

I took her in my arms—this woman who had been such a huge part of my life. "Of course," I said. "I forgive you for being human."

She pulled back slightly and looked at me with fear in her eyes and asked, "What did Lucie say about it?"

"Oh, Françoise, I just couldn't tell her. I made up that you weren't feeling well," I answered, releasing her and shrugging my shoulders.

"*Grâce à Dieu!*" Françoise said, obviously relieved. "But I suppose I must tell her about this. I don't want a secret between us."

Before we all went to bed, I could tell that Françoise and Lucie had talked because they came out of the library with their arms around each other and their eyes red. In the morning, the four of us finally sat down and agreed that we wanted Zaza to stay. She was ecstatic.

I knew that there might be patients who had the same prejudice as Françoise, but I decided that Lucie's approach was best. If there was someone who didn't like Zaza, or any of the rest of us, they could get help somewhere else.

At first, I worried there wouldn't be enough for Zaza to do. Then I saw her restore Sophie's gardens from the disarray they had fallen into when she started to get sick. Then I watched the grace with which she welcomed guests and took them to their rooms. Then I noticed that with a few words or a touch, she could make even the most skittish woman feel comfortable. Then I noticed her healing touch when a woman was in tears. Then I noticed her flair for choosing the right colors for decorating the table. And then there was the cooking. I need say nothing more about the cooking. She had an international palate, and we ate French food, Italian food, Greek food, and traditional Algerian food like couscous, and a delicious breakfast called chakchouka, made with eggs, sauteed onions, and tomatoes. She frequently honored our guests by cooking from recipes they had brought us as part of our secret code of patient records. I gained back all the weight I had lost after Sophie died.

In short order, we all agreed that Zaza had found her rightful place in the world.

CHAPTER 43

A TOWN CALLED MIRACLE

Our Lady, 1979

One morning, Françoise asked to walk with me in the garden.

"You don't need me here anymore," she said. "Lucie, Zaza, and Manon do all the work, and they do it so well. Henri is grown and out on his own, so he doesn't need me. But my cousin's great-granddaughter just had her third baby, and she does need me. You know I love my family's traditional town of Alençon. It is time for me to go."

She was right that there were more than enough hands to do the work, but I wanted to be sure she wasn't feeling pushed out.

"Françoise, I can't imagine Our Lady without you. In so many ways you are the heart of this place. Is this about Zaza? Is there some trouble I don't know about?"

"Thank you for saying that. I feel it, too. It's not about Zaza. She is a dear and I'm glad she is here. It's just time for me to go. It's time for a new generation to create magic here."

So, in June, Françoise and Claude packed up and moved, leaving the dairy farm to Anne-Marie and Thomas.

We spent a quiet summer. There were fewer nights when I cried myself to sleep. It was impossible that Sophie had died two years before. In August, late in those long end-of-summer evenings, I could hear the three of them—Lucie, Zaza, and Manon—sitting in the garden or in the kitchen, laughing over a glass of wine—grape juice for Zaza—talking about the events of the day, debating the best way to care for a particular guest. I heard echoes of years of intimate conversations between Françoise, Sophie, and me.

That rush of memories made me realize it was also time for me to go.

I didn't have any idea where in the world I was supposed to be. I didn't want to live in Japan, California—or Connecticut, for that matter, though I did plan to visit my mother. It seemed like the next chapter of my life should be played out on a new stage.

I kept all our old National Geographic Magazines on a long shelf and pulled random volumes when I wanted something to read with my breakfast coffee. One morning, I came upon an old article that piqued my interest for the first time in what seemed like forever.

"Look at this," I said, putting a 1971 magazine on the table in front of Lucie. "This is where I want to live."

"You want to move to New Guinea?" she asked, looking at the cover.

"No, silly. Look inside—where I turned down the page."

She flipped through the magazine until she came to the article about a wilderness area in New Mexico.

"Just read it," I said. "This is a place with beauty and history—a place where people love the land and where the spiritual tradition matches everything I have dreamed of—everything I learned in Japan, and France, all the things Socorro taught us about the T'ana, the things I learned in California. All the things Sophie loved. This place—this New Mexico—is where I belong, Lucie. I can feel it. I saved you once—this time you can save me. I'm asking for your blessing to let me go."

It is not easy to leave a place you have loved and lived in for more than a quarter of a century. Of course, Our Lady would continue, so I didn't need to move furniture and linens and all the things that come with closing a home. It wasn't too painful to leave behind the art and memorabilia that Sophie and I had collected, but there was one thing that threatened to break my heart. Every time I was in the garden, I wept to think of leaving behind the roses that Sophie had tended so lovingly. It seemed like a terrible act of disloyalty.

One time, while I was crying, I felt Zaza's gentle hand on my shoulder.

"Jane, I know these were Sophie's roses. I promise to take good care of them."

"I know you will. It's just—she loved these roses so much. We scattered her ashes here. How can I can bear to leave them behind?"

"Maybe you don't have to. I can help you dig one out and we'll wrap the root ball so you can take it with you."

"Is that possible?" I asked, wiping my face.

"Based on the climate of your new home, it should be. We'll prune it back and wrap the roots in fabric, and I'll tell you how to take care of it until you can plant it. I think it will work."

I wrapped my arms around her and said, "Thank you, Zaza. You have just put my heart at rest."

And then I was finally ready to go.

But life and death have a way of intruding on even the best-laid plans. A phone call meant that New Mexico had to wait. My mother died suddenly from a brain aneurysm. My cousins told me she just crumpled onto the floor in mid-sentence. Of course, it should have come as no surprise. After all, she was ninety-five. Even though Mother and I were often far apart geographically, we still wrote to each other almost every week. But I couldn't forgive myself for not making the time to visit her. I somehow imagined that she would always be there. Her death, coming so soon after Sophie's, stopped me in my tracks.

Françoise, Lucie, and I agreed that there was no point in them traveling to the States for the service. As much as they loved my mother, they wouldn't have known any of her friends. So I bade them all farewell, kissed the dog, and flew to New York by myself. I thought that at the age of sixty-five, it was time I learned how to be alone.

Mom's Unitarian church community gave her a lovely send-off. Her friends put out the word that I didn't want any casseroles—I could swear there were still some from father's funeral in my mother's freezer! My cousins wanted to move back to their own home, so I was left alone staying in my old bedroom.

I loved New England at that time of year—the days still temperate—the evenings cool, the trees taking on the colors of fire. It took me weeks to sort things out at my parents' house. I cried every morning, sold some things, and gave many things away. Amazingly, the house went under contract quickly. With the sale of the house and the funds my mother left me, for the first time I had some real money of my own.

In the process of sorting through years of memories and all the stuff of my parents' lives, I contacted a realtor in New Mexico. She agreed to mail me information about properties that fit my description—*isolated*—an old, sprawling abandoned school, church, or other religious compound. On the day of the closing of my parents' house, I received an envelope full of musty, faded photocopies describing an old monastery in a place called Milagro, New Mexico, a couple of hours outside of Santa Fe. The printouts were in black and white, and from the note the realtor included, I could tell she hadn't thought much of the place. But I was thrilled. An entire page explained that the compound was once an active monastery, abandoned because of proximity to toxic tailings from a nearby mine. According to the enclosed affidavit from the United States Bureau of Environmental Protection, the mine was cleaned out and no longer considered dangerous. But no one wanted to take a chance, so the property was for sale for almost nothing. I don't believe in signs, but when you need a miracle in your life, and a property becomes available in a town whose name translates to 'Miracle,' it doesn't take much to be convinced you need to reach for the gold ring. I know, *A Town Called Miracle* sounds like the name of a Hallmark movie. As I planned my trip, I remembered exploring the cloisters with Lucie when she was just a child, and wondered if she would meet me in New Mexico to see the property.

Could I turn history upside down?

CHAPTER 44

IT WAS THE ONE

1979-2016

Lucie left Our Lady in Manon and Zaza's capable hands. She and I met at the small airport in Albuquerque. We found a hotel in a part of the city called Old Town. Our room was huge with rough-hewn wooden beds, wide plank hardwood floors, and Navajo rugs. The district was the perfect introduction to New Mexico. We ate tamales at a restaurant with a backdrop of lively mariachi music, and burritos from a street vendor. We bought turquoise bracelets and wide-brimmed hats from Navajo merchants sitting on rugs in the plaza. At a centuries-old chapel off the square, we lit candles and prayed for abortion to remain legal.

"Maybe I should stay here with you," Lucie said, laughing, as she wiped the fragrant honey that dripped onto her chin from a warm sopaipilla.

"Maybe," I answered hopefully, although I knew her heart was at Our Lady.

The next morning, the realtor met us outside our hotel and drove two hours on the highway past Santa Fe, going north toward Taos. She had insisted on showing me several properties she considered more suitable than the monastery, so we made a day of it. We looked at a great big house with a barn in Española, another house and a church in a town called Dixon, and finally, the monastery in Milagro.

I had been polite and inspected the other properties, but the more I thought about the monastery, the more I was sure it was the one. As we drove down the long driveway, I was astonished to see huge wrought-iron gates set into the thick adobe walls in front. Lucie and I gave each other a look that meant nothing to the realtor. We beamed as we got out of the car.

The realtor fumbled with the large key ring.

I reached out and said, "Allow me."

Lucie stood behind me with her hands on my shoulders as I inserted the huge key, which turned with a creak. Lucie pushed one side of the gate open, and I pushed the other. Then we got back into the car and drove to the front of the main building. To my delight, it had a circular driveway. It was perfect. The landscaping had gone wild, with unfamiliar trees and plants, including some cactus. I could already picture Sophie's white roses in bloom.

I finalized the purchase of the property, and Lucie flew back. Though the building needed a lot of work, it had running water and electricity, so I moved in right away.

Zaza mailed the rosebush to me in an old trombone case Manon found in a pawnshop. I followed her instructions about preparing the soil, and how much sun and water the roses would need. It was an unusually warm fall, and the bare rose sprouted tiny leaves within a few weeks of being planted in its new home. That seemed like a wonderful sign. I mulched it heavily to protect it from the coming winter weather.

The renovation of the monastery was a huge undertaking. I asked Françoise's husband, Claude, to fly to the States to help oversee the work because it was so similar to what he had done at Our Lady. One significant difference was that, instead of stone, the buildings were made of adobe, which needed to be shored up and rebuilt in many places. We had to create an entirely new wiring system, but fortunately, the well was still in good condition. I rescued two dogs—or, you know how it is, they rescued me. Gracie, named for the first dog at Our Lady, was a darling black-and-white pooch. Luna was a Miniature Australian Shepherd—tri-colored and all fluffy and prancy. In those first very dark New Mexico nights when I struggled with loneliness and despair, the dogs became my reason for living. They hiked with me every day and curled up with me in front of the fire on the cold nights. It took a while for me to meet people and create a new community of women who wanted to don the habit and create a Special Retreat, so for a while the dogs were my only companions. It was the perfect way to heal.

Abortion was legal in America, so you might think I should have started a clinic—that there was no reason for me to take the risk of providing abortions illegally—or at least extra-legally. Our *Corazon de Gracia* abortions required at least an overnight stay, while a clinic abortion took just five minutes for the medical procedure—a few hours total in a clinic. But I wanted to provide care the way I was used to doing it—in a convent. Just as in France, I wanted to combine abortion care with all we had learned about ministering to women emotionally and spiritually. I trusted there would be women who yearned for the deep resolution and emotional transformation that came with our work. And those were the women who found us. I was still working on a plan to protect us from legal interference when one of my volunteers who lived in Santa Fe brought news.

"The clinic in Albuquerque has a new doctor."

"Oh?"

"This one is a woman."

"Wonderful. That will be a welcome change."

"Her name is Dr. Marston. I wish we could tell her about our services for women who need extra care."

"Dr. *Marston*?"

"Yes. Addison Marston."

Just hearing her name brought back a memory of the shame I felt after I kissed Addie Marston all those years ago at the hot springs. How much I hurt Sophie. Yet that terrible mistake got me into therapy and made my relationship with Sophie stronger. One more complicated chapter in a complicated life.

And so it came to be that Addie and I mended our fences and forged a truce. She agreed to be our medical director. A few times a year she drove her Bronco two hours from Albuquerque to Milagro to sign the documents that kept us legal. We'd sit in front of the fire or in the backyard and sip scotch. Sometimes we'd talk about old times. Sometimes we were just quiet. Addie shared the news that Betty had died suddenly from an aneurysm in 1975. She was sixty-nine. The two women I had loved in my life were both gone.

In the late 1980s, I got a rare transatlantic phone call from Lucie in France. A phone call usually meant either good news or bad news.

"Jane, I am so excited," she began.

"Good afternoon to you, too!" I teased. "What is it?"

"I didn't want to mention this until I was sure it was going to happen. An article I wrote has been accepted by my favorite psychology journal," she said.

She had published before—usually essays in medical journals that were a bit esoteric for me—but I was always glad when she had success.

"How wonderful. What makes this one so special?"

"It is about the split women—the ones who are so deeply ambivalent about abortion. The ones who had such a bad time after their abortions that Sophie talked about all those years ago."

"I didn't realize you had still been following up with them. It was so frustrating for her," I said, remembering the hours Sophie spent poring over the records of our guests.

"It has been frustrating for me, too. You remember I started to work with some of those women when I came back to France? Lately I am seeing these women in a whole new way. Have you heard of WEBA?"

"No. Is it a labor union?" I asked, laughing.

"Jane—I can't believe you haven't read about it. It is part of the American anti-abortion movement and stands for Women Exploited by Abortion."

"I do my best to ignore all of that. It is so hateful," I said wearily.

"I know you do, but you'll ignore this at your peril. Some of the women who are suffering after their abortions are testifying at public meetings that they were misled and mistreated by abortion providers who tricked them into having abortions. The women feel like victims, so they need to find someone to blame. The anti-abortion people are thrilled to showcase them, and are arguing that abortion has caused their depression, alcoholism, drug addiction, or whatever their woes, so it is a perfect fit," Lucie said.

"That is very sad. I remember how hard Sophie tried to figure out how to help those women. But surely it is obvious to everyone that they are very troubled about their choice and, as you say, looking for someone else to blame."

"Apparently, it is not obvious. Some of these women have had more than one abortion, and they still insist that their abortions were the clinic's fault."

"What are your people...our people...saying?"

"That is one of the problems. These patients are sort of disaster for the pro-choice movement. We need everything to be simple, and everyone to be fine. Our side says that either the women were already mentally disturbed before they had an abortion, or that there are so few of them that it doesn't matter."

"But surely they see how much pain these women are in? Didn't you and Sophie always say they were in hell?" I insisted.

"It is likely that the abortion clinics aren't even aware they are seeing them. Remember how Sophie said that the women who blamed Our Lady for their misery didn't even contact us to tell us they were in distress? I think it is the same there. When they are leaving the clinic, these 'split' women seem happy and grateful—just like the 99% of patients who are emotionally okay after their abortions. It is only afterward that they go into that emotional hell. I'm guessing that, to the abortion providers, these WEBAs seem like a political fabrication," Lucie said.

"But they are not!" I said.

"I have worked with enough of them to be well aware this is real. But I know why WEBAs make people angry. These women can't stand to be accountable for the choices they made. Their false accusations threaten legal abortion for other women. It's a very difficult situation. My article is titled, 'Women Split in Two: Emotional Distress and Depression Before and After Childbirth and Abortion.' My research suggests that women who have an emotionally hard time before and after childbirth share many of the characteristics of women who have an emotionally hard time before and after abortion. I guess that is not surprising, but this research seems to be connecting two aspects of women's lives that are characterized by shame, and it brings two parts of *my* life experience together in ways I never expected. The longer I work with these women, the more these parts of my life make sense to me."

"That's extraordinary, Lucie," I said. "Does it mean you've discovered the counseling approach that you need to help these women come to some sort of peace?"

"I'm afraid I still have as many questions as answers. It appears that some of these women grow up being one kind of person for their mother—usually traditional, feminine, and obedient, and another kind of person for their father—smart, independent, resourceful. When they are called upon to make a major life decision, they are paralyzed—stuck between two very different ways of being. If they can, they defer the decision to someone else. But whether or not to have a baby is a decision only they can make. No matter what they do, it feels as though they are betraying half of themselves. I have had some success using Gestalt therapy, where the woman talks with both parts of herself. I feel certain that when abortion clinics have better tools to identify these women ahead of time, they will at least be able to prepare them for the rocky road that lies ahead," Lucie answered. "And when more people see this phenomenon, they will surely find the best way to provide care. We need a larger sample to study. I am hoping this article will catch the attention of some other researchers who can help me delve into this more deeply."

"What a wonderful idea. I can't wait to read your article," I said. "Will you send it to me?"

"Of course. And, Jane, I am going to dedicate it to Sophie. It is her work that even made me aware of this and helped me start to make sense of it all."

"Thank you, my dear. She would have loved to think that there could someday be an answer to this dilemma. And she would have loved to know that you have found some healing in this work." Even hearing Sophie's name still sparked a deep sadness in me, but I was starting to mend, so hearing her name also made me smile.

CHAPTER 45

THE MORAL PROPERTY OF WOMEN

Milagro, New Mexico

In 1980, I was thrilled when Bernadette, Manon, and Zaza decided to move to the U.S. to run the convent in New Mexico. Although I retired from the day-to-day, they still involved me in discussions about major policies.

Petite Lucie, now a doctor, married Françoise's nephew, Henri Duchamps, also a doctor. Along with Brigitte's niece, Lydia, they took the reins in France. Many things are the same as they have always been at Our Lady, though they have modernized a bit. When women wish to take on a mark, they get a slender red tattoo across their palm. Bernadette has become quite proficient with ink. I don't know if Françoise would like that better than a scar or not.

We recently had a guest at the New Mexico convent who surprised us all. Luther was a transgender man. When he lost his insurance, he couldn't afford testosterone, so he began to ovulate again. After nearly two months of wondering what was wrong with him, he was horrified to realize that he had become pregnant. He was a bit overwhelmed by the situation, but completely confident in his decision. We used our usual protocols, and the abortion was successful. He left us with a tattoo on his palm and a year's supply of testosterone patches. So, unintentional pregnancy and abortion are not only challenges for people who identify themselves as women.

In case you thought *Corazon de Gracia* was so much imaginary fairy dust, in 1987 a French pharmaceutical company produced a medication called RU 486, which came close to the wonders of the T'ana's herbal remedy. Lucie called from France to tell me about it.

"Jane, they did it. They invented a medicine that works like *Corazon*!" she exclaimed.

"Socorro has succeeded in synthesizing it?"

"No. A French doctor has invented it. I'm not sure exactly how it works, but they are calling it 'the abortion pill.' This will change everything!"

The company, Roussel Uclaf (hence the RU), discovered the formula for a drug that stops the body's absorption of progesterone, thus killing the pregnancy. When the anti-abortion movement threatened to boycott Roussel Uclaf, the company counter-threatened to take the drug off the market. The brave French Minister of Health, Claude Evin, prevented them from doing that, calling the drug 'the moral property of women.'

At Our Lady, we still use *Corazon de Gracia*.

One of the beastly things about living to be as old as I am now is that almost everyone I love has already died. My parents, of course. Levy died in Paris in 1980, his wife and her sons by his side. Brigitte and Matthieu died together in a boating accident the same year. In 2002, Françoise died of a heart attack. She was eighty-two years old. Claude was already gone a few years before her. I know that Lucie had wonderful memorials for all of them until it was her time in 2013. Abbie attended her 'Celebration of Life.'

When I learned Lucie had died, I had to make a decision. Was there any purpose in *feeling* the amount of grief appropriate for such a great loss? Or might I rely on that old standby of hiding the experience in the drawer and locking it? Her death just didn't seem fair. I had already gone through a funeral for Lucie once, albeit in a nightmare. I was arguably too old to fly—and why would I travel all the way to France to say goodbye to someone who was still so very present in my heart?

I didn't go, but I made an agreement with myself. I asked Abbie to read some of the stories about Lucie aloud. And we wept together. And we laughed together. And we celebrated her. I wish I had been able to do that when Sophie died—let the others in. After all, it was their grief too.

CHAPTER 46

YOU CAN SKIP THIS CHAPTER

USA, circa 1978

The anti-abortion movement picked up steam in the late 1970s at just about the time I moved to New Mexico. I was aware the battle was raging, but most of the time, I was mercifully isolated from it in my tiny village. New Mexico, like France, is largely Catholic, but there is a kind of laissez-faire when it comes to interfering in other people's lives. My presence in the village was greeted with some suspicion, but not hostility. The cloister was so far out of town that I rarely came into contact with people, and they didn't make any trouble for us. But because we had Addie as a medical director, Zaza, Bernadette, Manon, and I didn't have to worry about staying under the radar. That was a different experience for me.

The people who provided abortion care in the rest of the country weren't so lucky. The movement to make abortion and birth control illegal caused great damage and distress to women and abortion providers over these many years, but I am unwilling to give them more than a mention here. They don't understand abortion because they don't understand or care about women. Or children, for that matter. They refuse to support any of the obvious social initiatives that would make abortion less needed — the basic social safety nets that make it possible for women to raise children in health and safety, including the availability of dependable birth control, sex education, healthcare, childcare, safe housing, good education, fair wages, and reduction of violence against women. They think that if they put up enough roadblocks or murder enough doctors, women won't want abortions. The whole thing is about power and control.

George Tiller, one of the doctors who was first injured and later murdered by anti-abortion zealots, had many wise things to say, including this: "Abortion is not a cerebral or reproductive issue. Abortion is a matter of the heart: for until one understands the heart of a woman, nothing else about abortion makes any sense at all."

I couldn't have said it better.

I was going to ask Abbie to go back through my journals and letters, and collect data about the number of bombings and acid attacks, clinic invasions, and doctors and others murdered, and share all that with you. But I have decided not to. The antis have their own agenda that has no place in these memoirs and has nothing to do with our sacred work.

CHAPTER 47

FAREWELL

Dear Reader (as my sweet Abigail is so fond of calling you),

These memoirs are almost complete. I find myself wondering if I have stayed alive just long enough to get to the end. Right now, I am alone in my room, dictating this into my ancient tape recorder. I remember the day I purchased it. The technology seemed amazing—that this little box is capable of holding so much.

You have heard this story before, but I don't share it often and I don't like to remember it. I'd like to put it somewhere else, the way Dumbledore fed his most burdensome thoughts into the Pensieve in the Harry Potter books. Oh, don't be surprised. I am ancient, and I can hardly see anymore, but I have kept up. I can't tell you how many Audible books I have consumed. I even know about *The Hunger Games*! The Harry Potter books filled me with both wonder and hope. The evil was all too familiar—the world has seen it many times under different guises and in different shapes, forms, and languages. The hope that goodness and light are being re-invented as often as evil and dark has kept me afloat in these troubled times. (Are there times that weren't troubled?) But I digress.

I saw many things in Paris during the Nazi Occupation that I have tried not to remember. They are, of course, seared into that oddly shaped part of my brain whose name I can't recall. This neural lockbox is too small to withstand the horrors we humans store in it. That may be why they leak out in nightmares and the ghosts of memories that haunt us. I have built a tall emotional hedge around many of the most difficult things. It is territory I don't intentionally visit. I've told you about the old bookseller my little girls and I watched being marched away in Paris. But I haven't suggested the cruelty and violence that surely came afterward for him, or the torture that almost certainly preceded the death of my dear Aunt Mathilde.

In those days in Paris, we all learned to see—and not see. Helplessness in the face of atrocity can drive you mad. And every day, negotiating the most mundane of life's comings and goings was like walking through a minefield.

But I'm not going to tell you any stories about babies, or blood, or bayonets wielded by cold-blooded Nazi soldiers. I'm not going to convey the unspeakable agony of the shrieks of mothers who have been forcibly separated from their children. I am not going to attempt to describe the unimaginable horror of genocide. I am not going to tell you about what hunger looks like from the outside, or feels like from the inside. The story I am going to tell you again is of a day in Occupied Paris—just a normal day in a world that had lost its mind. I have shared this story in the first volume of these memoirs, but it is never far from my awareness.

I was walking with a five-year-old as fast as it is possible to walk with a five-year-old. Her name was Naomi. She was big for her age—and she refused to be carried, which was a relief because she was quite heavy. She had thick black hair and pink cheeks that a grandmother should have been pinching enthusiastically. In retribution for some act of the Resistance, her parents had been executed with a dozen other innocent people in the town square. A neighbor hid Naomi and sent word to Mathilde.

I had never been sent to rescue a child so young. The older girls understood about taking on a new identity, but I had no idea how to convey the idea to a little one. I tried to make it a game of 'let's pretend.'

"Do you know how to make-believe?" I asked her.

She looked up at me with her lower lip trembling. "You mean like if I act like a kitty and go meow, meow?" she asked.

"Just like that!" I answered, wondering how she would possibly comprehend the importance of this particular game. "Today, we are going to pretend that your name is Catherine Bernard. Can you remember that?"

She looked doubtful.

"Try to say it. Who are you today?"

She glowered. "I want my momma."

"Of course you do, darling. But right now she wants you to play this little game of make-believe with me."

"She does?"

"Yes—she does."

We practiced her new name a few times, but the neighbors were anxious for us to leave their house, so too little had to suffice.

We scurried along, Naomi talking non-stop. Five is old enough to ask incessant questions in a loud voice, but not old enough to understand the need to be quiet.

"Where did those soldiers take my momma and poppa and Mrs. Goldberg and Mr. Stein?"

"I don't know where, sweetheart. But right now we must be quiet and hurry to the school where we can be safe," I whispered. "There are other little girls there who can be your friends."

"But why are we going away from my house? If we go away, how will Poppa find me?"

"Shh. We must hurry!"

"But…"

I stopped abruptly and knelt down so that my face was even with hers. I put on my most serious grown-up expression. "Child, we must hurry, and you *must* be quiet," I hissed.

As I stood up, I saw them. Three Nazi soldiers with rifles slung over their shoulders. They were crossing the road toward us. I can still see them so clearly. In my memory, they approached in slow motion. The first was tall and distinguished-looking. The second one seemed to have a permanent scowl. And the third one—why, he was no more than a boy. *Please,* I said, to whom I cannot say, *please let this be all right.*

Just before they reached us, I bent down again and said to Naomi urgently, "Remember, in this game you are called Catherine." Then I pushed her behind me and stood up as tall as I could.

"Good afternoon, Sister," the tall one said, in surprisingly good French. "Your papers, please."

That wasn't a problem. I was one of the few people who *had* a legitimate passport and visa—and Mathilde had given me fake papers for the little one. I removed our documents from a pocket within my robes, as I had done dozens of times. I tried to stay calm, but the second soldier had a leering expression that made my hands shake. The tall one examined our papers carefully. The one who was ogling me as if he had never seen a woman before stepped behind me, trapping us.

"These appear to be in order. But an American? What are you doing so far from home, Sister?" he asked unctuously.

"I am here on a mission to teach children," I said, my voice quavering in spite of my best efforts. "We are on our way back to the school."

I was shocked that the soldier behind me said, "Damned Roman Catholics think they are better than all of us," and spat on the ground. I only understood a little German, but I understood that.

I never corrected the people who thought I was a nun. I guess I believed it gave me some sort of protection or authority. His acrimony disabused me of my naivete.

"No, Officer," I said breathlessly, turning my head to look at him. "I don't think I am better than anyone. Please, just let us go to the school," I begged, speaking as calmly as I could manage. It was never easy to guess what tone to take with them. Defiance usually led to violence, and I had to protect the child at all costs.

"And who are you, little girl?" The tall soldier was bending down to talk to Naomi. His French was good enough that I feared she would understand him.

She looked up at me uncertainly, and I nodded at her. "I am Caffin. I live in Paris. I am this many," she answered, holding up her pudgy fingers. I believe I had stopped breathing entirely by then. I was sure the fictional Catherine Bernard would not survive another question.

I tried to enfold Naomi inside my robes, as if I could make her disappear entirely. "I have money—just to pay for your inconvenience," I said, putting my hand back into my pocket.

The tall one stood up and looked at me in a way that made my stomach drop. He said, "We have no interest in your money. But we are far from home and lonely. And you are pretty enough. You understand? We would love to get to know you better this fine morning. Kurt. Tend to the brat. We have business with our dear American sister."

The boy took Naomi by the hand and glanced at me with a look that I could only interpret as an apology.

There was not a soul on the street to cry out to. Resisting would not save Naomi. Left by herself, the child was doomed. So I did the only thing I could—I followed the two of them around the corner into the alley behind us.

I don't want to tell the rest of this. You can imagine it, but please don't let it be seared into your memory as it is seared into mine. You can picture the alley where they took me. I thank whatever God there may be that they didn't force the child to watch. I had never been with a man before, but that was incidental. The alley—the stone building—my face pushed against the wall as one of the soldiers held me. My robes bunched up—my underwear torn away. My forehead bruised and skinned against the stone. My tears—whether tears for myself or for relief that mine might be the only blood spilled, I'm not sure. When they had each had a turn and left me in a heap, they began arguing.

"What about the brat?"

"What about her?"

They laughed and ordered the one named Kurt to bring the child to me. I clung to her, faint with relief, as they marched away without a backward glance.

I held on to Naomi so tightly that she tried to squirm away.

"Are you all right, Mam'selle?" she asked sweetly.

I wanted to scream. I wanted to cry. I wanted to die. I wanted to disappear off the face of the earth. But here was this child whose life was somehow, by some miracle, saved. I found my voice. "Of course, chérie. I just tripped and fell," I said, trying to catch my breath. "I'll be up in a minute, and we'll be on our way. I just need to sit here for a little while."

I was numb. I was more lost than I had ever been. I didn't know how to find myself again, so I relied on what had always helped me.

"Why don't you come down right here beside me and I'll tell you a story. I'm afraid it is a sad one."

"I don't like sad stories," she said.

"I don't either. But this is one you have to hear." There was a painful throbbing where I had been violated, and the unpleasant sticky wetness that the soldiers left trickling down my legs, but I ignored the sensations as much as I could. I was still shaking too hard to stand up. I pulled Naomi down and close to me and began a story that I had to tell to many little girls.

"Once upon a time in a kingdom not so very far away, the king and his soldiers acted like mean little boys and they wanted more land and riches for themselves. They were so mean that they decided to steal their neighbors' lands. They marched across the border with their big guns and the neighbors were so frightened that they gave the king whatever he wanted."

"I don't like this story," Naomi said in a small voice.

"I don't like it either, my darling. But I am afraid you must hear it. I am afraid we must both hear it." Naomi snuggled under one of my bruised arms. I winced, but held her close. I continued.

"The mean king and his mean soldiers saw how easy it was to steal land. As long as they were willing to scare people and even kill them, they could get anything they wanted. Before long, they had stolen land from neighbors on all sides. They had hurt many people, and everyone was frightened. They were richer and more cruel than ever before. One day, the king decided that of all his neighbors, there were some he hated more than the others. These were the Jewish people—like you, Naomi, and like my dear Dr. Levy."

Naomi had burrowed her head even deeper into my shoulder, and I know she was only partly listening.

"I don't like doctors," came a tiny voice.

I continued. "The king said he would not rest until the Jews were removed from all of his vast territories. He sent soldiers to all the places the Jewish people lived, and took them all far away."

"Like he took my mamma and poppa?" Naomi whispered.

"Yes, my darling, just like that. But your neighbors hid you so the mean soldiers wouldn't take you, too. And now we will go to the special school and soon I hope we will find a new home for you."

"I don't want a new home. I want my mamma and poppa," she whimpered.

"I know. I know." I held her even tighter as she cried.

"What is the end of the story?"

"For you, the end of the story is a wonderful new family who loves you and who lives in a country where the mean soldiers do not come."

"And for my mamma and poppa?"

"For them…" I hesitated. I had more answers for a twelve-year-old—this child was so young. I decided truth was more merciful than hope.

"For them, my sweet one, there is a beautiful heaven."

She pulled her head away from my shoulder and looked at me. "Where my Bubbie is?" she asked.

"Yes, that's right." I smiled at her, and she gave me the tiniest smile back.

We sat there until I thought I could walk. The tearing between my legs was painful, but I managed to hobble along, Naomi telling me all about her beloved Bubbie.

I am no hero, lest you are thinking that. I bartered the little I had in order to save Naomi's life and my own. In my mind, I made a good bargain. When Mathilde asked about my bruises, I attributed them to clumsiness. With the chaos we faced every day, there was honestly no one looking very hard, even my devoted Aunt Mathilde. The last thing anyone needed was someone else to console. So I took care of myself, longing for my father to whisper in my ear the Gaelic endearment he saved for special times—*mo chuisle*—my pulse. But longing made me feel more alone. How does one attend to individual victims when humanity and even civilization itself are under attack?

The truth is that it was *my own* abortion—the brief physical and emotional encounter I had with an untenable life, the gentle and loving removal of that life that Levy managed in spite of his tears, the secret I added to my already long list of secrets, the shame that I had somehow allowed this to happen to me, the cellular understanding of my impotence in the face of male violence—it was all these things that shaped my life.

I was changed. There grew within me a fury I had never known before. It fueled my already existing desire—my unquenchable thirst—for justice and fairness and kindness. On the nights I was too afraid to step out of the school with girls who needed to be taken to the safe house, from there to get a boat, and from there another boat, I summoned the fury like some kind of obedient electric charge, and I could do whatever I had to. In the mornings when we had bad news and grieved the disappearance of yet another trusted ally, the fury dried my tears before they were shed. When we found a chance to get Lucie out of Paris, it was that fury that let me stand, unblinking, behind Levy, as he produced our counterfeit documents. And it was that fury that propelled me to provide care that women need, in sanctuaries that they deserve. I earned those scars that Sophie gave me so reluctantly and lovingly all those years ago. The gift to me—the blessing next to the wound—is the white-hot anger that has lasted all these years, a renewable energy source like the sun.

Are you uncomfortable when I tell you about my anger—the anger that is not attractive in a woman? I'll just say that if more women were furious, we would have a better world. A better world if women stepped up and took charge. If women acted on their convictions—without permission. Without authority. Without apology. It would be a world that values people for who they are, not for how much money they make. Or how much power they have over others. A world in which human beings take responsibility for our impact on the planet. Where businesses and towns and cities and nations don't have to become constantly larger. Where we care for each other, and welcome new lives when we choose to bring them into the world. It's those thoughts that sustain me now. There are millions of people all over the world who will not settle for having someone else's moral and political rules govern their lives. Millions who care so much about women and children that they will demand that motherhood must be freely chosen. They are rising with energy and vision far beyond mine. Can you feel their power? It is just beneath the surface, and it will break through one day soon.

I suspect that when the time comes for me to go, as it surely will soon, the fury that has fueled me for so long will allow me to welcome death, to merge myself with all the energies of this amazing and terrible world. I have no regrets about my work. I don't feel any sense of guilt about breaking men's laws. But I do have one apology to make. I must admit that I failed despite everything I did and believed. The transformation I dreamed of and yearned for did not occur. Medical care of all kinds, including abortion care, is still given without regard to our emotional and spiritual needs. The new world I envisioned for women and children and all living things and the very planet that is our mother—has not come to be. And for that, I am deeply, deeply sorry.

As I touch the thin scar on my palm, I hear the voice of the T'ana wise woman—*As long as you have this scar, you will honor the life returned to the One. Each time you see the scar, you will remember your love and courage and goodness. When the scar has faded, you will turn your face toward the future, but this nascent life will always look down upon you and protect you.*

As I contemplate that scar, just a few of the names etched onto my heart appear: Jeanette, Lana, and Kikuyo. Catalina, Manon, and Charlotte. Aiki, Lucy, Rose, Lana, Stacy, Lili, and Coco. Edna, Ricki, and Gertrude. Françoise and Lucie. Mimi. And me. All we wanted, all any of us wanted and deserved, was the freedom and authority to have ownership over our own lives. We understood our choices and were willing to take whatever joy and sorrow came with them. We laid claim to our own lives with a furious love. Some people have said that abortion is a tragedy, but I know it is a grace.

Like so many of the women I cared for, our world is at a crossroads. I have had my opportunity to learn what I would risk for justice.

It is your turn now.

Jane Smith
Our Lady of Perpetual Grace, Milagro, New Mexico, 2016

AUTHOR'S NOTE

Like Jane and Abbie, I started to write these books in 2016, anticipating the inauguration of the first woman president, Hillary Clinton. For years, Republican state legislatures passed insane rules and regulations designed to make it impossible for clinics to provide abortions. I wanted to write stories about providing abortion care as I hoped it would be—the way it *should* be done—without politically motivated restrictions, and with care for the emotional and spiritual wholeness of the patient.

By the time I was ready to publish, the Supreme Court had overturned Roe v. Wade. There has never been a more important time to share our stories about abortion.

Without Apology is a work of fiction based on real events in real life. However, some of the story comes from my imagination.

- Dr. Nick's invention of a suction device for abortion comes many years earlier than Lorraine Rothman's 1970s invention of the Del-Em, a DYI mechanism for menstrual extraction made with a glass jar, tubing, and a stopper. During the 1970s, the vacuum aspiration machine developed by Dr. Harvey Karman and Dr. P.G. Sathe became the tool used by clinicians all over the world.
- A lecture by Carl Djerassi in Dallas in the 1980s gave me the idea that the United States Navy had an obligation to provide abortions in Japan after the war as part of its guardianship of that country, as I depicted. I can't find any evidence that it actually happened.
- As far as I am aware, the concept of helping a woman *connect her head and her heart* to find resolution about her pregnancy choice began in the 1980s at the clinic I ran in Dallas. I have brought that work into the present with my website, beforeandafterabortion.com.
- Although there are more than 50 indigenous peoples in Peru, none is called the T'ana, and the medicines attributed to the T'ana in this work are fictional. However, medication abortion, now called mifepristone, is real. Over 30% of abortions in the U.S. are accomplished with medication.
- Abortion has long been the safest outpatient procedure done in the United States. Prior to the overturn of Roe v. Wade in 2022, 90% of abortions were done within the first twelve weeks of pregnancy. Most women who choose abortion prefer to do it as early as possible. It is deeply ironic that the cruel and arbitrary legal, financial, political, and bureaucratic obstacles erected by the anti-abortion movement—the

new laws in more than half our states—make abortion care almost impossible to access for many women. This inevitably leads to women getting care later in pregnancy than if they had been able to get pills by mail, telemedicine, or access a clinician in their own communities. This increases both the cost and the risk.

- To my knowledge, there are no convents providing abortion care, although they are sorely needed.

- As far as I am aware, there was no abortion collective in Detroit in the 1960s—however, there was a collective in Chicago between 1969 and 1973 called "Jane" that was reportedly responsible for providing nearly 11,000 safe abortions.

- A word about language. In our modern world, people may identify as male or female, non-binary, trans, gender-neutral, or whatever works for them. People who do not identify themselves as women may need abortions. I am using the word 'women' because the unique historical experience of women is central to my stories.

- The women Sophie worries about who are so deeply ambivalent about their choices are modeled on clients I have come to call *Women Split in Two*. While these women may represent as much as 1-2% of abortion patients, they are invisible to clinics because they rarely contact their medical practitioners to share their deep distress after their abortions. They are well known in the political movement for the claim that abortion caused a panoply of negative aftereffects ranging from alcoholism and drug addiction to suicidal ideation, hence abortion should be banned. In my nearly fifty years' experience as an abortion counselor, I have seen that women who have abortions without being emotionally resolved about their choice may have a very, very hard time. However, the problem is not the abortion, just as damage from a peanut allergy is created by the allergy, not the peanut. At issue is the history, beliefs, and emotional disposition of the woman. Because this phenomenon is largely invisible, it has not been researched. I hope someday a neutral scientist will do research to learn how to support women who insist they want an abortion, while exhibiting beliefs and behaviors antithetical to a positive outcome after an abortion. Rather than treating women with compassion, this phenomenon has been weaponized against abortion access. There is more about this on my website, https://beforeandafterabortion.com.

Where are we now?

How can you help? At this writing, abortion is practically unavailable in half the states in this country. While the majority of the public now supports legal abortion, well-funded anti-abortion forces are hard at work with propaganda spreading lies and half-truths designed to sow doubt. **Make no mistake, their final goal is to pass legislation criminalizing all abortion and birth control. They want to establish a Christian nation that has never existed except in their imaginations. Men's and women's roles will be firmly and legally proscribed. Women will stay at home and have babies. Men will go to work. And somehow, everyone will be white. If this reminds you of the _Kinder, Küche, Kirche_ (Children, Kitchen, Church) slogan of the Third Reich, you are dead on. It is time to take these people seriously. They have told us their plans. We can no longer pretend we don't know. Be furious! Speak out! Don't apologize for demanding justice and democracy!**

If you or someone you love needs an abortion, IneedanA.com is an excellent resource. Jessica Valenti's extraordinary _Abortion Every Day_ on Substack will keep you apprised of the constant assault on women and abortion care. If you want to donate or volunteer, Google _abortion advocacy and activism_ to find a list of groups that need your time and money. Make sure you are registered and vote, especially in the states where an abortion referendum is on the ballot.

It can be hard to raise a controversial subject, but you can talk with your friends by saying, "I don't know where you are with the issue of abortion, but I believe strongly that parenthood should be a personal and not a government decision." You will find that most people agree with that. If we don't find the courage to risk and fight for our rights, we can't be surprised when someone more committed than we are erases them.

Over the past decades, I have specialized in working with women who were having a difficult time deciding what to do, or were troubled by their choice of abortion. I have written these books for you, too. If you are one of those people, please go to my website, beforeandafterabortion.com.

I have written this trilogy to share some of the stories I experienced in my work, and to leave the legacy of the importance of emotional and spiritual resolution in everything we do. If the books in this trilogy meant something to you, please write a review on Amazon and tell your friends and post about them on social media.

Most books from an independent publisher only reach about 200 people—roughly the friends and family universe of the author. Since Roe, more than 70,000,000 abortions have been provided. I know there are many people who would like to know Jane and the stories of her life. Please help me reach them.

DISCUSSION QUESTIONS

1) Jane and Sophie have known Henri since he was born. As a youngster, the little boy spent lots of time with them. He was hugged and cuddled by many of the women who came to the convent for an abortion. He is naturally curious about the women. What do you think about their initial explanations to him of their work? How would you explain abortion to a child?

2) As Henri gets older, he understands abortion the way the Catholic Church teaches about it, and he is horrified and refuses to come to the convent or even talk with Jane and Sophie. They mourn his absence, but don't try to convince him to see abortion the way they do. How would you handle a situation like this?

3) Brigitte was orphaned and raised in the Catholic Church. She was taught the anti-Semitic views that many French people had. When she learns that her family was Jewish and converted to Catholicism to protect themselves, she looks at many things, including abortion, from a different perspective. Have you ever known someone who had a complete change of heart and mind about an important issue? Have you ever made such a change?

4) Do you think it was worth it to teach Mme. Trédivic, the illegal abortionist, to provide safer care if she didn't want to listen to women's hearts?

5) What do you think made Jane risk her relationship with Sophie by kissing Addie?

6) How would you describe the approach the T'ana women took to abortion care?

7) What do you think about the scarring the T'ana women did on patients? What do you think was the purpose of the scarring? Would you want a scar in this situation? What was Françoise afraid of?

8) Were you familiar with the history of legal abortion in England, France, and the U.S. as it unfolds here? Had you heard of the speak-out in Greenwich Village that Lucie attends? Are you familiar with the Jane collective that performed thousands of illegal abortions in

Chicago which was the inspiration for the group in Detroit in *Without Apology*? How did reading about this history make you feel?

9) How did you feel about Lucie leaving her young daughter (*almost* thirteen) to move back to France?

10) Jane faces one failure after another in her mission to convince abortion providers that attending to women's hearts and spirits is an essential part of care. How would you have gone about it?

11) How did you feel about Françoise's prejudice against Algerians? Were you aware that Algeria was a French colony in the 1920s?

12) Many women in American society have learned to apologize just for taking up space on the planet. It's not a defect, it is a coping mechanism. Notice how often you say, "I'm sorry." How often do men say it? Could it be that it is not only your right, but your responsibility to take up space? To share your wisdom and experience?

    Not apologizing for your existence doesn't mean becoming insensitive or inconsiderate. If you make a mistake, could you say, "I made a mistake?" or "I wish I had done that differently?" How would "I'm sorry" feel if you reserved it for times you actually needed to ask for forgiveness?

13) What was your response to Jane's only apology?

ACKNOWLEDGMENTS

Much gratitude goes to my partner Shelley Oram, herself a writer to envy, who read, re-read, and skillfully edited the manuscript in the midst of her own brutal course of chemotherapy. As always, she gave me good advice that I usually took, and for years, has been my champion.

My beloved developmental editor, Diane Zinna, author of *The All-Night Sun*, also read and gave exceptional feedback in the midst of illness. It was Diane's early comment that spurred me on. "I don't think you know how good your book is." Every writer deserves to be read as closely and generously as Diane has read my work.

In 2016, Shelley and I traveled to Peru and met a wonderful guide, Adriana Socorro Cucho. It was Adriana who inspired me to invent the indigenous T'ana healers. Thank you, Adriana, for reading these chapters, encouraging me, and lending me your beautiful name for Lucie's dear friend.

Milles baisers to my trusty writing group, Annie Lewis and Phyllis Leavitt, who provide constant and unwavering love, advice, and support.

My love to all the staff of the Routh Street Women's Clinic in Dallas, where I did my best, made so many mistakes, learned so much, and invested my heart.

Thanks to November Gang members, who taught me so much and helped me hone my skills in our constant pursuit of ideas to improve abortion care.

Deep gratitude to my beta readers! Annie Baker, Terry Salas Merritt, and Arlena Ryan. I hope the finished product will live up to their enthusiastic and loving support. And special thanks to my ideal reader, and ideal person, Karen Thurston. Your enthusiasm, love, and encouragement from the very first pages you read so long ago have been like wind carrying the kite of this project.

My longtime writing teacher, Anya Achtenberg, was the person who broke it to me that my original book was too long to publish, so, bingo, I had a trilogy! Her encouragement and insightful feedback are central to my writing journey. My Anya classmates over the years from all your various locales and time zones have helped me make *Without Permission, Without Authority,* and *Without Apology* into books I am proud of.

Jennifer Leigh Selig, Empress Publications, has been a skillful midwife to the birth of these books into the world. I am grateful for her experience and guidance.

Thanks to artist and designer extraordinaire, Sarah Hewitt, for her support and help with finding the cover designer Lee Avison, and with making labels, bookmarks, and business cards. Sarah's support in the midst of my chemotherapy helped me believe there would be another side.

Thanks to Lee Avison, ABCD Book Cover Art, Design & Marketing Support, creator of my first cover, for *Without Permission*, and for the lovely image and design expertise for *Without Apology*.

Edgard Rivera at the StepBridge studio in Santa Fe helped me create the audiobooks I wanted to offer right from the start.

I am forever grateful for the many sources of encouragement and guidance about how to publish in the independent space.

My heart holds memories of the thousands of women who have trusted me with their most personal and intimate stories over the past half-century. I hope the work to meet your emotional and spiritual needs made a difference in your lives. I carry so many of your stories in my heart. I have recounted some of them, in disguise, in these books. I hope you will see yourselves in some of them. For those who carry unresolved feelings about abortion, I have written these books for you. Here I offer a roadmap to forgive yourself, heal, and reclaim the knowledge of your own goodness.

Although Jane shares her heartfelt apology that her work has not transformed the world and the way abortion care is delivered, in these books she has left a blueprint. It is not just abortion that involves a patient's heart and soul—it is nearly everything we call healthcare. Western Medicine can be proud of its astonishing scientific advances, but it should be ashamed that so many deep elements critical to a person's well-being are intentionally overlooked. In the best of abortion clinics, there is a marriage of soul and science. It is time to demand that for all our care.

ABOUT THE AUTHOR

Charlotte Taft has worked in abortion care for more than half a century. Though most women do well with the experience of abortion, there are some who struggle. Charlotte developed tools to identify and assist the women who need deeper emotional exploration to experience peace and confidence with whatever decision they make.

After earning a bachelor's degree from Brown University and a master's degree in feminist studies from Goddard College, Charlotte served as the director of an abortion clinic in Dallas, Texas, for seventeen years. During this time, she worked with her staff to pioneer Head and Heart Counseling, a unique style of abortion counseling tailored to meet the emotional and spiritual needs of each patient.

In Dallas, Charlotte served as the media's go-to person on the topic of abortion. Charlotte was interviewed by national publications such as *The New York Times*, as well as appearing on dozens of local and national television programs, including *The Today Show*. Her non-fiction publications are available at Rewire.com.

Charlotte is featured on the 2020 FX documentary *AKA Jane Roe*.

With her partner Shelley Oram, Charlotte created *Imagine* to provide experiential workshops and retreats to deepen abortion providers' understandings of ourselves and our work. Charlotte served as the director of the national non-profit organization, Abortion Care Network, for six years, where she was at the helm of supporting independent abortion providers and fostering open conversations around abortion.

Today, Charlotte lives in rural New Mexico with Shelley, her partner since 1988. Both are breast cancer survivors, and, so far, survivors of the Trump apocalypse. Charlotte continues to work with women who need help looking deeper in order to make a decision and resolve difficult feelings after an abortion. Her website beforeandafterabortion.com offers insightful videos designed to further assist women in finding peace before and after an abortion. Visit her author website, charlottetaft.com, to learn more about *Without Permission, Without Authority,* and *Without Apology.*